Praise for Leslie O'Kane
and her Molly Masters mysteries

"Endearing characters, touching family and friend relationships, and a feisty heroine."
—DIANE MOTT DAVIDSON

"O'Kane delivers a satisfying whodunit."
—*San Francisco Chronicle*

"Molly Masters is a sleuth with an irrepressible sense of humor and a deft artist's pen."
—CAROLYN G. HART

"O'Kane is certainly on her way to making her Molly Masters series the *I Love Lucy* of amateur sleuths."
—*Ft. Lauderdale Sun-Sentinel*

By Leslie O'Kane

*Published by The Ballantine Publishing Group

GIVE
THE DOG
A BONE

Leslie O'Kane

FAWCETT BOOKS • NEW YORK

A Fawcett Book
Published by The Ballantine Publishing Group
Copyright © 2002 by Leslie O'Kane

All rights reserved under International and Pan-American Copyright Conventions. Published in the United States by The Ballantine Publishing Group, a division of Random House, Inc., New York, and simultaneously in Canada by Random House of Canada Limited, Toronto.

Fawcett is a registered trademark and the Fawcett colophon is a trademark of Random House, Inc.

ISBN 0-7394-2513-7

Manufactured in the United States of America

To Christine Jorgensen,
a wonderful writer and friend

The author wishes to thank the members of her critique groups for their wise suggestions, encouragement, and friendship lo these many years; Maggie Mason for sharing her enthusiasm for goldens; and Edie Claire for answering bizarre questions with such patience and clarity.

Chapter 1

This was astonishing. According to the figures on my computer screen, my finances were in the black for the first time since I'd opened my dog-psychology business four months ago.

"Yes!" I pumped my fists, then pushed off against my desk to whirl my chair in a circle across the linoleum floor. Too energized to stay seated, I rose and dashed to my glass door, weighing the notion of rushing outside to do my Happy Dance on the sidewalk. Boulder being the Exercise Capital of the World, chances were that I would accidentally trip a jogger or collide head-on with a skateboarder or roller-blader.

From this angle up the concrete stairwell, I could view the sharp, angular peaks of the Flatirons. Above this small section of the Rockies, the azure sky was cloudless. I smiled at the glorious sight, aware that this sunny weather was unlikely to last through the day. Storm clouds would brew by late afternoon. Thunderphobic dogs would quake and eventually go wild with fear, and my phone would ring with new clients needing my services.

Maybe I could even afford to take Russell, my office-mate and boyfriend—although he was thirty-three and I was thirty-two so the "boy" designation was a misnomer—for a celebratory lunch. I returned to my chair and scooted back to the computer screen to recheck my finances and calendar. Financially I could swing it, provided we went to a fast-food restaurant and split the fries and cola. Schedule-wise, however, my day was booked solid from ten-thirty on.

From somewhere just beyond my open windows, a man shouted, "Maggie! You come back here this minute!"

I turned. The man was standing directly in front of my window, the limitations of its view such that I could see only his brown pants from the knee down. Those pants, too short to be fashionable, revealed a pair of mismatched socks—one blue and one green—and Hush Puppy suede shoes. I could not see Maggie's shoes.

"Come here, Maggie! Get your furry little butt over here!"

That order got me out of my chair. Immediately deducing that "Maggie" was an off-leash dog, I shuddered at the thought of the busy intersection nearby. With a handler this inept at verbally controlling his dog, Maggie could run into traffic.

"Hey, get back here!" the man cried.

Just as I reached the door, a large, young-looking golden retriever came galloping down my concrete office stairs, too fast for me to swing the glass door out of her path.

"Maggie, sit!" I automatically shouted, but it was too late. She clunked her head hard against the glass. The impact staggered her. She sat down and looked at me, wearing a dog's typical oops–silly me bearing: head slightly lowered on her shoulders, the tip of her tongue showing as she panted.

The moment I pulled the door partway open to check on her, Maggie barged inside my office. By then the man with poor dog-handling skills and mismatched socks had reached the steps. While I attempted to hold the door for him, Maggie jumped up on me, her weight pushing me back from the door.

Being only five-feet tall, I'm often outsized by my canine clients, so I usually arm myself with a noisemaker to distract ill-mannered dogs. Having been caught unprepared this time, I crossed my arms and rotated so that the dog was facing my back, while I said sternly, "Maggie, down!"

Meanwhile, the large man, trying to enter, shoved the door into his dog and me, just when Maggie had dropped down on all fours. She was shoved into the back of my knees, and I was sent sprawling.

"Oh, man! Are yous all right?" he asked as I got up and turned to face him, trying hard not to greet the question with obscenities. By no means was this the first time I'd been knocked flat by a dog, but it *was* the first time a dog had served as the owner's battering ram.

Although he'd gotten down on his knees to examine Maggie's eyes and head, I assumed that he had meant the "yous" as plural for his dog and me, so I answered, "I'm fine."

Still focusing exclusively on the dog as he ran his palm gently over the top of her head, he said, "I meant Maggie. Can't believe how hard she bashed her head just now. She didn't see the glass." He got to his feet and looked at me. "You know, you should put up a decal at a dog's eye level. A cat sticker, or something."

"I'll take that under advisement." Though tact has never been my strong suit, this was a response I'd taught myself to use whenever a client—or, in this case, a prospective one—gave me really stupid advice.

Maggie's owner was nearly six-feet tall and broadly built. His midsection resembled a pickle barrel and stretched his teal knit shirt to its maximum. A white undershirt showed beneath the collared shirt's v-neck opening. He seemed to be in his late fifties or so and was completely bald. He chuckled. "You better be Allie Babcock, or I got myself a whole lot of explaining to do."

"I'm *Allida* Babcock," I said pointedly, not appreciating having my nickname used by someone I'd only just met. Especially not by someone who'd advised me to put a cat decal on my glass while *he* recklessly allowed his dog to run off leash. "And you are?"

"Kenneth R. Culberson. The 'R' don't stand for nothing; I just wanted a middle initial. You can call me Ken. You want I should call you Allie or Miss Babcock?"

"Allida, actually."

In a clear case of canine curiosity, Maggie trotted over to me and attempted to get far too personal with her sniffing. I warded her off with my knee.

Her owner put his hands on his hips and glared at his dog. "For cryin' out loud, Maggie! Watch your manners! You don't even know this . . . this—" He paused long enough to peer into my face, and then, as if this double check had verified his suspicions, said, "—woman. Apologize to her this instant!"

Maggie jumped up on him instead of doing whatever it was he'd expected her to do—slap a paw on her forehead, perhaps, and exclaim: "Wherever are my manners!" in the King's English. Shoving his dog aside, he then stomped his foot and wagged his finger at her. "You're really testing my patience today, young lady."

Maggie did not cower or show any signs that she'd ever been struck by her owner. She merely began to enthusiastically sniff the floor to trace the scents of previous clients. My impression so far was that this was a healthy adolescent dog that happened to be in the care of someone who didn't have the first clue how to train and communicate with her.

"Are you interested in hiring me as a therapist for Maggie?"

"Thought I already did that. Di'n't you get my e-mail, asking for this appointment?"

"E-mail?" I repeated, then suddenly realized that I should have made more creative use of my computer time this morning. "Oh, no, I didn't. I only recently went online, and I really don't check it often enough to set appointments that way."

"Good thing you was here, then," Ken said, grinning

affably. "That's got to be another good sign. See, I visited your Web site, and I knew right—"

He broke off when I whipped my head around, having caught sight of Russell Greene swinging open the door, his gaze focused on the magazine he carried. He has an intense fear of dogs. Nevertheless, we share this main entrance to our two-room offices; but when he sees or knows that I'll be with a large canine, he rounds the building to use the back entrance, which circumvents my office.

"No, Russ," I cried. "Go—"

It was too late. As he stepped inside, Maggie raced over and jumped up on him.

Russell shouted, "Yeiaa!" The dog knocked him sideways and pinned him against the wall in the blink of an eye.

"Turn around, Russell," I said, sweeping up my noise-maker from my desk drawer.

He did so just as I pressed a button that emits a loud, shrill noise. Maggie promptly dropped down on all fours and looked around, trying to find the source of the noise.

In a classic demonstration of poor dog-handling, Ken rushed over and threw his arms around Maggie to pat her chest. No doubt he thought this was calming her down, but to a dog's way of thinking he was rewarding her bad behavior.

The color had risen in Russell's handsome face. Though six inches taller than I, he too was easily dwarfed by a large dog, making his fear all the more acute.

"I'm sorry, Russ," I murmured. My own cheeks warmed with empathy on his behalf.

Ken stood up. I expected him to apologize to Russ for his dog's bad manners, but instead he asked, "Why do you guys do that? Turn around like that when Maggie jumps up on you?"

"A dog that jumps up only has an interest in the person's face," I answered quickly, realizing that Russell needed a moment to collect himself. He really hated having his phobia revealed to strangers, who couldn't begin to know that his earliest memory was of his brother being attacked by a German shepherd. "The dog wants to sniff your breath, which lets the dog pick up on all kinds of clues about you. Plus, sticking his face in yours gets the dog the attention that he craves. He has no interest in the back of your head."

As I'd hoped, my mini aren't-I-dog-wise lecture had done its trick. Russell had brushed himself off, regained his natural color, and now stepped forward with a proffered hand toward Ken Culberson. I blocked the dog's path to the men, then gave a rudimentary introduction while the two of them shook hands. Russell had rolled up his magazine tightly in his left hand and was keeping an eye on the golden retriever. Though too kindhearted and sensitive to strike a dog, especially in my presence, he would not hesitate to swing at the air between to prevent her from getting too close. I doubted that such a gesture would sit well with Ken. Just in case, I petted Maggie to distract her while Russell excused himself and entered his office.

Ken plopped down in a wooden chair against the wall, and Maggie immediately leapt into his lap. I winced, mentally estimating their considerable combined weight, and listened for telltale creaking noises to indicate the chair legs were on the verge of collapse. Though his face was momentarily blocked by his dog, Ken said pleasantly, "Nice guy."

"Yes, he is." I sat down in my desk chair and, though the answer was already obvious, asked, "What can I do for you, Mr. Culberson?" While I spoke, the dog spread herself across his lap, giving me full view of her owner's round, guileless face.

"Ken," he corrected. "Well, Allie, I got me an unusual problem. You see—" He broke off as Maggie sat up again in his lap and blocked our view. "Settle down there, Maggie!" We waited, and she finally dropped her chin down to rest on Ken's knees. "Maggie here is my late ex-wife. Or, rather, I should say she's—" he gestured in the air "—whatchacallit. Channeling her spirit."

My *own* spirits instantly sank while my heartbeat increased. Apparently Ken Culberson was not treating Maggie like a fellow human merely out of ignorance, but because he was delusional. I said calmly, "You think your dog is channeling your late ex-wife?"

"No, no. I don't *think* so. I know so."

I forced a smile. The city of Boulder was renowned for its tolerance of all kinds of belief systems and lifestyles, which extended to its canine population. Dog Rolfing and other varieties of massage were big business here. At the Humane Society, dog owners were now called dog *guardians.* The actions of FIDOS—Friends Interested in Dogs in Open Space—routinely made headlines. Suggestions, however, from potential clients that their dog possessed some person's spirit typically came from starry- or droopy-eyed individuals in their twenties.

"Mr. Culberson, I've got to warn you that I'm just a dog therapist. In other words, I don't do exorcisms on dogs, though I'm sure you—"

He held up his palms and cut me off. "I knew you wouldn't believe me. No one ever does. That's all right. I got proof."

With considerable effort, he reached back and wriggled around on his chair while Maggie kept herself balanced on his lap. He finally retrieved his wallet from his pants pocket and removed a Polaroid photo, which he held up to show me.

Curious, I rose and took the photograph from him to get a better view. It appeared to be a snapshot of a cluster of kibble on tan-colored carpeting. I looked at him, awaiting an explanation.

Ken widened his eyes and said solemnly, "Believe it or not, Maggie did that, all on her own. I di'n't move a single piece of dog chow."

"I don't understand, Mr. Culberson."

"You don't?" he asked. " 'Scuse me for a moment," he said to his dog and gently lowered her to the floor. He got up, saying to me, "Can't you see it says, 'You,' with an—"

He pulled the photo out of my hand as he spoke, then flipped it around and returned it to me. "No wonder. You was looking at it upside down. See the letter *u* and the exclamation point?"

"It does look like the letter *u*," I agreed as I examined the photo a second time, "but that strikes me as nothing more than an interesting coincidence."

He shook his head, his jowls moving like gelatin with the motion. "See, that's what Mary, my ex, was always calling me . . . one of the reasons I left her. 'Hey, *you*, take the garbage out. When *you* coming home?' And like that. Never 'Ken' or 'Honey,' just 'you.' Meanwhile, right after Mary died, Maggie starts carrying her dog food toward me, piece by piece, and lays it down at my feet, just like you seen here."

"Were you sitting at the dinner table at the time? Dogs who've been treated as human members of the family often get into the habit of bringing their chow out where their owners eat. That's not at all unusual and, by the way, can be easily corrected. All you have to do is patiently tell her no and move the food back to her bowl."

"You're missing the point, Allie. Ever since she started channeling my ex, Maggie don't like to be treated like a dog."

"Of course she doesn't. Given an opportunity to, for example, eat filet mignon while seated on a cushy couch, what dog would opt for a bowl of kibble on a tile floor?" I returned the picture to him, while he was pulling out a second one. "Has she spelled anything else since then?" Such as: *My owner is not at all well*, I thought, but keeping my expression placid.

"Course not. She won't eat dog food now. It's pretty hard to spell with a pork chop."

I laughed in spite of myself, though all I could think was: *This guy needs a therapist for himself, not for his dog.* I glanced at the second photograph, which showed a slightly thinner and decidedly hairier Ken Culberson beside a petite, frumpy-looking, red-haired woman. She would have been attractive, if not for her frown.

"See?" Ken said. "Can't you see the physical similarities? The hair color? The sad brown eyes?" He gestured at Maggie, who was trotting back and forth between the door and Ken, trying to signal that she was ready to leave. "Plus the two of 'em liked all the same foods."

"Feeding a dog table food exclusively is not good for her. It wreaks havoc with the dog's digestive system and can lead to tooth decay and an imbalance in protein intake. That, in turn, can cause the very overexuberance which we're now witnessing in your dog."

"But she *thinks* she's a person. So I got to feed her people food. You wouldn't feed hay or birdseed to a *woman* who thought she was a *dog,* now would you?"

"No, but I also wouldn't feed her dog chow." Though it's possible I'd put the person's meal in a bowl on the floor, I added to myself. I held up my palms, suspecting that I was about to have to ask this man to leave. "Mr. Culberson—"

"Ken," he corrected again as he reclaimed his seat. This time his oversized lapdog seemed content to sit by the door. "You gotta know two things here before I can hire you. One is, money's no object. If you got the time to work eight-hour days, seven days a week for the next month, even if I got to double your salary to get you to do it, I'm ready and willin'."

The kah-ching! sound of a cash register resounded in my brain. An instant later, my common sense returned. "We can't even begin to discuss salary and schedules at this point. First, we need to see if we can agree on what I can and cannot do for you and your dog. What *I* do is work with the owner to resolve a dog's behavior problems; however, it wouldn't be at all difficult for you to locate a psychic, or whatever you think you need, if you want to exorcise your ex-wife's spirit from Maggie."

"Already tried that. Went to see some lady named Theodora. Di'n't do no good. She claimed she just needed a few more sessions. Thing is, though, Maggie was always exac'ly the same." He rolled his eyes. "I hate to be so s'eptical, but I gotta wonder. Theodora might've been more a rip-off artist than a psychic."

"Maybe you can find a better one, then. But, Ken, I simply can't accept any job in which I'm being less than up front and honest. So I have to tell you *up front* that I don't believe your dog is possessed, just untrained and spoiled."

He looked at his dog, currently rolling on the small welcome mat in the doorway, delighting in some scent that she found there. I hoped that Ken was considering how unlikely it was that his late ex-wife would have done such a thing, but he said, "Well, I can 'preciate your opinion, even if it's wrong. See, the thing about Maggie is she's drivin' everyone nuts in the neighborhood. She chases cats up trees every chance she gets. Brings home bones 'n' stuff that doesn't belong to her. Barks at everyone who tries to set foot on the property 'n' chases them off." He winked at me, adding, "And before you ask, yes, Mary used to do all that, too."

Understandable that she'd been his *ex*-wife, then. "Maggie needs some serious training. But neither I nor any trainer or dog behaviorist can bring about any substantive improvement in Maggie's behavior without your assistance. That's only going to work if you'll stop . . . thinking of her as your ex-wife and start treating her like a dog."

I heard Russell's muffled chuckle through his door. My cheeks warmed a little at the possibility of his overhearing. If so, he must be getting quite a kick out of my exercise in futility here.

Ken put his hands on his hips and shook his head as he looked at his dog. "Mary's not going to like this."

"I'm sure she won't. But *Maggie* will appreciate it. You see, Ken, dogs are pack animals. They don't mind taking their rightful place behind the leader of their pack—their owners. But if the owner isn't willing to take on the leadership role, it's the dog's nature to assume control. Maggie needs you to be the leader, Ken, or sooner or later she's going to get hit by a car, or hauled off by animal control."

He sighed and nodded.

"It's difficult to let go of someone we once loved," I hesitated, wondering if this applied to Ken despite his divorce, but went on, "even if she *was* your ex-wife. I don't mean to be judgmental or to overstep my bounds, but maybe you should talk to a counselor. Boulder has more therapists per capita than any other city on the planet, and it wouldn't be difficult for you to locate someone competent."

"Already seein' someone," Ken said sadly. "A psychologist. He's got an office just a little ways from here."

"I'm glad to hear that."

Ken put his hands on his knees and leaned forward for emphasis. "See, Allie, the thing is, your Web site said that you could not only handle most behavior problems in canines, but also teach owners how to communicate with their dogs."

"That's true. I can teach you how to communicate according to a dog's perception of the world."

He leaned back in his chair and dragged a now trembling hand over his bald pate. "I need to do that. I need to tell Mary how sorry I am that I killed her."

Chapter 2

Any hope of this being a fruitful venture completely deserted me. Though I tried to sound relaxed, my voice came out in something of a squeak as I asked, "You killed your ex-wife?"

The sparkle had left his eyes, his round face now crestfallen. His lip trembled slightly as he nodded and took in a deep breath. "I sure di'n't mean to. Still can't figure out how it happened."

"You mean it was an accident?" I asked hopefully.

Ken sank back against his chair, and Maggie hopped onto his lap again. "I dunno. I can't remember a thing about it."

So he'd blocked the woman's death from his consciousness. Nonplussed, I eventually murmured, "I see," though I didn't *see* at all.

Ken began to cry. He held Maggie upright in his lap, using her large head to shield my view of his face. For the sake of Ken's pride, I grabbed a pen and notepad to make myself appear too busy to have noticed his tears. I drew a large, sharp hook and told myself that my doodle could serve as a reminder for future business dealings: whenever someone offered to double my usual fee, there was bound to be a catch the size of a meat hook.

After a few moments, Ken dried his tears with the back of his hand, then allowed Maggie to settle across his lap. He cleared his throat and, with eyes averted, said, "See, Allie, I dreamt I was driving the car that hit her. Only, it was too vivid for a dream. And they never did find the car from the hit-and-run . . . so I must've been drivin' some stranger's car. 'Cuz at night, Maggie keeps telling me that that's exactly what happened. Even though I thought I was someplace else at the time."

"Maggie talks to you at night?"

"Mm-hmm."

I rubbed my forehead. Ken was just not stable enough for me either to accept money from him or to work with him one-on-one. "This isn't going to work, Ken. I'm very sorry. I can't give you the kind of assistance with your dog that you're seeking. When I say that I help people learn how to communicate with their dogs, what I—"

Ken had immediately begun shaking his head and now got to his feet, ignoring Maggie as she was unceremoniously dumped on the floor. "You can't just turn me away like this, Allie."

He stepped forward. Although he towered over me, his demeanor was sorrowful and not at all intimidating. I merely looked up at him in silence.

"You're my last chance. If you don't help me, I'm gonna lose my dog. They'll take her away from me. You gots to help me. I already told my neighbors I hired you. That's the only reason they said they'd hold off on callin' a dogcatcher."

He dropped to his knees and embraced his dog, who started licking his face. Regardless of how distorted this man's sense of reality might be, there was not a doubt in my mind that the loss of his dog would devastate him.

Ken turned his pleading eyes toward me, as did his dog an instant later. "Just come over to my house once. That's all I ask, Allie. Work with me 'n' Maggie just one time. Then, if'n you still think it's hopeless, you can quit. But it might be enough to at least show my neighbors I'm trying."

For me to consent went against my brain, but to decline went against my heart. It was obvious to me which organ would win this battle, but it was imperative to at least ensure that I would be reasonably safe alone with him and Maggie in his home.

"Ken, I can't talk to you while you're on your knees like this. Have a seat and fill me in a little on this psychologist you're seeing."

"What do you want to know?" He adjusted his position so that he sat cross-legged on the floor. Maggie promptly spread out beside him, resting her head in his lap.

Despite his large frame, I now had such a firm perception of his childlike emotional maturity that I did what I do when I'm working with kids and their dogs—lower myself to their eye level. I sat down on the floor. "Do you mind telling me his name? And would you object to my asking him specific questions about you and your background?"

"No, I don't mind at all. It's a good idea. Might let you discover I ain't half as crazy as you think I am. It's Dr. Thames. Terry Thames. Like I said, his office is nearby, on Walnut."

"Okay. I'll talk to him. You'll have to tell him yourself that you're giving him permission to answer my questions."

He nodded emphatically. "I'll do that right away."

"Also, it might be helpful for me to learn more about what happened to your late ex-wife. What was Mary's full name?"

At my mention of the name "Mary," Maggie promptly sat up and looked at me. That was odd, but Ken probably called her that so often that she thought of it as a second name, similar to how some dogs are told "no" so frequently that they think the word is an extension of their names.

"Mary Martin," Ken answered simply.

"Wasn't . . . that the name of the original actress from *Peter Pan*?"

"Different Mary Martin." He studied my features, then chuckled. "You really *do* think I'm nuts, huh? You were scared I thought I used to be married to Peter Pan!" He let out a loud guffaw.

His thinking of himself as having been married to the actress who played Peter Pan didn't seem nearly as out-

landish as believing that his possessed dog had told him
that he'd killed her. But maybe that was just me.

Ken went on, "She took my last name, and she never
stopped using it. Even after our divorce. So her full name
was Mary Martin Culberson."

"All right, Ken. I'll talk to Terry Thames and, depending on what he says, I'll get back to you about a trial session." He nodded and I continued, "You've told Dr.
Thames about hearing Maggie talk, haven't you?"

Ken grimaced and adjusted his position so that he was
slightly farther away from me on the floor. "Uh, Allie,
Maggie doesn't talk. She's a dog."

"Yes, I realize that, but you said a couple of minutes
ago that Maggie told you that you killed her. Killed your
ex-wife, rather."

He furrowed his brow, letting this sink in for a moment.
Then he got to his feet. "I meant in my dreams. Maggie
talks to me in my dreams. Like I said, I ain't all that crazy."
He bent down and held out a beefy hand to me, which I accepted. He pulled me to my feet with such ease that I felt
like the warm-up weight in a clean-and-jerk competition.

"I'm glad to hear that," I replied honestly. "It was nice
meeting you, Ken. And you, too, Maggie. Let me just get
your address and phone number before you go. I'll let you
know later today what I decide."

He reached into his back pocket and handed me a
piece of paper on which his name, address, and number
had already been scribbled. "Good luck callin'. Only got
one line and it's hooked to my modem, so it's hard to get
through. You'd be better off just coming straight over
there. Like it says on the paper, I'm in unit thirteen."

"Unit thirteen?" I repeated. "Are you in a trailer park?"

"Yep. But don't let appearances deceive you. I got loads of
money. Jus' don't like to spend it on furnishings and junk like
that. Can you come this evening? Say around six, maybe?"

"I really can't commit until I've had a chance to speak
to Dr. Thames."

As if he hadn't heard me, he grinned and said, "Good. I'll see you then." He bent down slightly. "Come on, Maggie. We better get going."

To my surprise, he whipped out a green service-dog vest that had been tucked into the back of his pants. He fastened the vest around Maggie's neck and shoulders.

"Maggie has a service-dog designation?"

"Yep, from my doctor. It's all official and everything." He met my eyes. "See, Allie, I don't function so good when we're apart."

In certain settings, without Maggie nearby, he probably had panic attacks, which is a medical condition that warrants the service-dog designation. Nevertheless, this dog was surely the worst-trained "service dog" in existence.

Ken returned his attention to Maggie, who must have known what was coming next, for she was trying to keep away from her owner. "Come on, Maggie. I'm gonna have to put a collar and leash on you. You know they won't let us on the bus otherwise."

"You didn't drive here?" I asked, thinking that if he didn't drive at all, he couldn't have been the driver of a hit-and-run accident.

"Stopped driving after . . . you know. After I runned Mary down."

"Oh. Sure," I mumbled, embarrassed that I hadn't figured this out myself.

In a Houdini-like move, he pulled out a collar and leash that he had fastened through his belt loops. At the sight of the collar and leash, Maggie crouched slightly. From this position she could spring in any given direction. She backed as far away from Ken as my small office allowed. Ken clicked his tongue and glanced at me. "She hates this, lemme tell you."

"That doesn't surprise me," I said, merely observing as Ken cornered his wriggling dog and fastened the collar around her neck. "This is one of the first things we're going to have to change, though. Maggie needs to get used to wearing a collar and tags. Even when she's inside your house."

"Really?"

I nodded.

"Hoo, boy. That's not gonna go over big. Whatever you say, though." He grinned, gave me a wink, then opened the door. Maggie raced ahead and, despite Ken's bulk, half pulled him up the stairs.

The moment Ken was out of sight, I tapped on Russell's door and swung it open. He was poring over some schematics he'd spread across the oval-shaped coffee table in front of his couch.

"Hi, Russ. I just wanted to apologize for your greeting today."

He gave me a big smile that made me feel wonderful. "That's okay. Though I'd much rather it had been you jumping up on me instead of one of your clients."

"I'll remember that. But it's generally a good idea for the therapist to be better behaved than the patients. They think of me as their role model, you know."

"Darn!" Russell said, snapping his fingers in mock disappointment. He then paused and added, "Um, be sure to tell me in advance when that dog's going to be here. I have a hunch she's going to be a major project for you."

"I haven't actually agreed to take Maggie on yet. Eighty percent of my work is with the owner, not the dog, and I'm not sure Ken is up to the task. He's convinced his dog is channeling his late ex-wife."

Russell merely nodded, verifying my suspicion that he'd overheard. I had a lot of work to do and turned my thoughts toward that. Thinking out loud, I murmured, "I'm going to call the newspaper. See if anyone there can tell me anything about his ex's death."

"Sounds uplifting." In an unconscious gesture, he smoothed his dark mustache as he got to his feet. "Allie, I'm going to have to go to Palo Alto for a week or two. Part of this project I've taken on."

"When are you leaving?"

"Tomorrow. I just found out myself this morning." He walked up to me and asked gently, "Can we have dinner tonight?"

"Sure. I'd love to. It might have to be late, though. If I do take Maggie on, I'll have to go over to Ken's home at six, and it'll be a lengthy session. I could meet you at a restaurant at eight-thirty."

"I was thinking maybe dinner at my place." The way he asked—his voice suggestive and his eyes searching mine—made me suspect he was intending for this to be more than just a meal.

To my disappointment, my fight-or-flight instincts immediately kicked in and I heard myself reply, "As long as it's just dinner we're talking about here."

Russell's face fell. "Think about it, Allie." He reached out and caressed my cheek. Though his touch felt wonderful, it was unlikely to change my mind. I'd only been physically intimate with one man in my life, and that had led to the worst possible heartbreak—the week before our wedding, he ran off with my bridesmaid. The prospect of risking that kind of pain again was much more frightening to me than that of being trapped in a room full of rabid dogs.

Russ continued, "I know you're scared to move our relationship to the next level, but *I'm* scared of losing you." He let those words sink in for a moment, then forced a smile. "Why don't you bring one of your dogs over tonight? That way we'll both be phobic. And afterwards, I'll be gone for a whole week . . . no awkward moments the next day."

"It's not just fear that's stopping me, Russell." Unable to meet his eyes, I dropped my vision. "However much we might care for each other, I'm not sure that we're truly right for each other."

Russell wasn't moving a muscle. I finally looked up and saw the pain written there. I felt a pang in my own heart, but knew that I had to be honest.

"I'm sorry, Russell. I know we've been dating for almost

four months now, and you've been so understanding and wonderful. But I can't give you a 'yes, for now.' It has to either be a 'yes, forever,' or my answer has got to be 'no.' "

The muscles in Russell's jaw were working, but his expression bore no malice. "All right. At least this way, if you ever do say yes, I'll know how much that means to you." He kept his voice even, but his words were clipped. He sat back down on his couch and returned his attention to his diagrams. "By the way, our decision to sleep together would be every bit as significant to me as it would be to you."

I felt awful now but was determined not to be distracted from my job. Shutting the door between us, I went back to my desk, called *The Daily Camera*, and asked for their librarian. When she was on the line, I explained that I was a "therapist" in Boulder and that I needed to know about the death of a woman named Mary Martin Culberson, a Boulder resident whose death occurred within the last two years.

She was unable to locate any information in their database, and so I called the coroner's office in Boulder. They also had no record of Mary's death, either under *Martin* or *Culberson*. Most likely, this only meant that Mary had not died in Boulder County and that no one had sent an obituary notice to the *Camera*. It also meant that I would probably go to my appointment with Ken and Maggie not knowing as much as I wished I did. Unless Terry Thames knew about Ken's ex-wife's death and was willing to share that information with me, that is.

Dr. Thames's number was listed in the yellow pages. I called and a man with a deep, pleasant voice answered.

"Hi, this is Allida Babcock. May I speak to Terry Thames, please?"

"Allida. Yes, hello. I just now got off the phone with Mr. Culberson. He said you'd be calling." He sounded less than thrilled.

"I'm wondering if we could get together briefly today to—"

"I'm afraid I'm booked from ten A.M. on. How would tomorrow work for you?"

"Ken is hoping to have me start working with his dog today." I glanced at my watch. Nine-forty. "Are you available right now?"

"No, I have phone calls to return." He paused. "I could try to squeeze you in afterwards and before my first appointment, but we'd only have a minute or two."

"Even a minute would be great. Thank you. I'll be right over."

"See you then," he said and hung up.

With our offices only five blocks apart and downtown parking a rare commodity, I rushed out and headed down the hill on Broadway on foot. I soon reached Dr. Thames's office, one corner of a small wooden structure on west Walnut. The entire south side of the block was occupied by a red-brick office complex, but the north side featured a series of old, small houses like this one, which had been converted into businesses. With the mountains serving as a dramatic backdrop and with their well-maintained gardens and lawns, these erstwhile homes in the middle of the business district were picturesque—provided one ignored their surrounding superstructures and the ever-present traffic.

I entered his small but pleasant waiting room. The plush, pale blue carpeting probably had a nice, soothing effect on his clients, but would only have revealed the shedding of *my* clients. The room was deserted, and I listened for a moment for the sounds of activity from the inner office. Hearing none, I tapped lightly on the door.

"Just a minute," came his deep voice.

A moment later, a tall, attractive, white-haired, fiftyish man opened the door. He wore typical business attire for Boulder—dark blue trousers and a pale blue collared sports shirt. Though his expression was inscrutable, his voice was nice enough as he said, "Hello. Allida?" He held out his hand, and I shook it.

"Yes, hi. Do you have some time to speak with me?"

"I suppose so. I've got all of five minutes till my first patient arrives." Though this unenthusiastic response seemed to be aimed at eliciting an acknowledgment about how good it was of him to work me into his schedule, I felt I'd already done this over the phone.

He led the way into his inner office—also small, with a little writing desk in one corner and four maroon uphol-stered chairs forming a square. Two walls were lined with bookcases jammed with books and, on the lower shelves, well-used toys. He sat down in one of the four chairs and gestured for me to take the seat across from his. I sat down, and he regarded me for a moment.

"Well, Allida, I guess you and I are colleagues. You call yourself a dog *psychologist,* right?"

Though his voice was not blatantly snide, the implied snub was unmistakable and made me bristle. "You can think of me as a dog trainer who specializes in behavior problems, if you find that less offensive."

He smirked a little. "I don't mean to marginalize your profession. I've known Ken Culberson for quite some time now and have his best interests at heart. That's not always the case with the people he chooses to bring into his life."

"I'm sure that's true. He mentioned the psychic he hired."

"Perfect example. I want to prevent Ken from barking up yet another wrong tree." He smiled at his quasi pun. I kept my expression blank, and he continued, "Several months ago, I referred him to a social worker to help him with basic living skills, such as, I presume, how to be more discerning in his business dealings. Since I'm so pressed for time, you might want to talk with her instead." He rose as he spoke and went to his desk. "Rachel Taylor. She works for a private agency that provides care for adults with a wide range of needs and dependencies." He fetched a business card and handed it to me. He remained stand-ing, as if our discussion was over.

Pocketing the business card, I said, "I can understand your concern, but it's a bit off-putting to be compared to some rip-off artist who passed herself off as a psychic. I intend to help Ken learn that his dog is just that—a dog—and teach him how to be a better owner."

"That sounds reasonable." He sat down again, but glanced at his watch on its black leather band.

"I just have a few questions. How long has Mr. Culberson been under your care?"

"I'd rather not answer that specifically. Let's just say, long enough now for me to know him quite well."

"Is he dangerous?"

"Not in my opinion, no."

"So I take it that he didn't have anything to do with his wife's death?"

Dr. Thames hesitated, then, as if weighing each word, answered slowly, "He did not kill his ex-wife, no."

"In your opinion, would my convincing him that his dog does not possess his ex-wife's soul be harmful to his mental stability?"

He stared past my shoulder at the door, then raked a hand through his white hair and leaned forward to meet my eyes. "That's the million-dollar question. You see, Allida, I'm trying to rid him of that delusion myself. It would be far better for Ken if you would wait a couple of months before you embark on any of this."

"Under normal circumstances, that would be fine with me. The problem is that Mr. Culberson is under the impression that Animal Control could take the dog away from him soon. And he exerts so little control over Maggie that that's possible, especially if she were to bite someone."

He snorted. "*Maggie* struck you as a possible *biter*?"

"*Any* dog can bite, especially a totally untrained one." I was tempted to hammer my point home by informing him that goldens had the highest incident rate of bitings. I also knew, though, that that was a deceptive statistic, caused by the breed's popularity.

He lifted a shoulder, his focus locked on mine. "You asked my opinion, and that's it. We're at cross purposes.

My concern is for my client, Ken. Apparently yours is for the dog."

"No, I'm saying that the two are inexorably linked. That Ken would be very damaged were his dog to be removed from his care."

Again, he leaned forward. "Allida, I want to get Ken to a sounder place mentally. He's at a critical juncture of his therapy. I don't want you or anyone else getting involved and undermining my work with my patient."

"Have you already expressed these concerns to Ken?"

"Yes, but he still wants to work with you. Against my advice."

I rose, frustrated and annoyed. "Then we *are* at cross purposes, aren't we? When I work with my clients, I see my role as twofold. I work to establish a healthy, mutually beneficial relationship between the dog and the owner. For that to happen, I need the owner's cooperation and trust, which I try to earn. Frankly, I'm surprised that you seem so ready to dismiss the therapeutic benefit that a beloved animal can give to its owner."

He got to his feet as well and stepped forward. Though he maintained a pleasant tone, he said, "Allida, you are not qualified to discuss what is or is not 'therapeutic.' "

The remark galled me. I studied his face, but saw no registry of emotion whatsoever. I turned toward the door. "I'd better go before your patient arrives."

He clapped his hand on my shoulder. I whirled around and glared at him. He said evenly, "You want to work with Ken's dog, fine. Maggie's so untrained she's miserable to be around, yet he won't go anywhere without her. That's one of the issues we're working to resolve. But let me warn you. If you take advantage of my patient's financial situation or do anything that's injurious to his precarious mental health, I'll slap a malpractice lawsuit on you faster than you can say 'Chihuahua.' You got that?"

Chapter 3

Too late, various comebacks to Terry Thames's verbal challenge ran through my brain as I made the short hike back to my office. Forcing myself to look at the situation from his perspective, I could understand his attitude. It irked me, though, to be presumed guilty until proven innocent. He was the one whose therapy had thus far failed to convince his patient that his dog was not his late ex-wife. Which one of us needed to validate his or her credentials?

He'd said that Ken was not dangerous, though he'd qualified the statement with "in my opinion . . ." Not exactly a ringing endorsement, but sometimes it's appropriate to keep one's expectations low when entering into a new relationship. I decided that I would indeed add Ken and Maggie to my list of clients, on a trial basis. I never could resist a good challenge; at five-feet tall, I'd been the starting point guard on my college team.

My first appointment of the day was with a rambunctious one-year-old Jack Russell terrier. The adorable Eddie on *Frazier* was no doubt partly responsible for the growing popularity of this breed during the last decade. Jack Russells' intelligence and energy, when combined with lack of diligent training, made for exasperated owners.

My session with Eddie's untrained alter ego proved to be a piece of cake compared to my next appointment with a beautiful buff-colored Akita mix, easily twice my size. The owner was a young woman who'd gotten the dog when he was a cute twenty-pound puppy. Now she was considering putting him up for adoption, unless a few hours under my tutelage could undo a year-and-a-half's worth of her neglect. As I left, she said with a sigh, "If only you had a magic wand." I managed to resist replying, "If I did, I'd bop you on the head with it." I tend to be more patient with dogs than with their owners.

I grabbed lunch on the run, then drove to another appointment. Rapidly overtaking the sky, huge gray clouds now loomed over the mountains. The impending storm couldn't be better timed. My next client was a seven-year-old yellow Labrador named Sunshine who, ironically enough, was afraid of thunder. Devil's Thumb, the pricey neighborhood in the foothills where this Labrador lived, tended to get the brunt of the storm fronts. On two different occasions, Sunshine had injured herself badly when she jumped outside through closed windows in her crazed attempts to "escape" from the storm.

To date, the desensitization program we were using had met with only partial success. I'd given Sunshine's owners an audio tape of thunderstorms, which they were playing at increasing volumes, counterconditioning Sunshine by offering her treats when the taped noises began. We actually needed a good month or two without full exposure to a storm for the treatment to work, but we didn't have that luxury. Today I'd come armed with phosphorus pellets, a homeopathic cure, which worked wonders on some dogs.

A thunderstorm began within minutes of my arrival. Sunshine went berserk—to use a less-than-technical term—and her owners opted for the pellets. I showed them how to drop the pellets into the back of Sunshine's throat and told them to "wear gloves when handling the phosphorus" and to "exhibit confidence throughout," albeit that was easier said than done. Sunshine was still drooling and an emotional wreck after the first dose, but calmed down after the second.

Afterward, as I pushed out the door, her owners thanked me profusely. I tempered their enthusiasm with warnings about relapses and a rehash of instructions for how they could handle this on their own next time.

My day raced along, and at six P.M., I pulled into Ken's trailer park. Maggie ran up to my car before I was in sight of unit thirteen. Aware that some hot rod could zoom around the corner at any moment, I hit the brakes and opened my door, intending to get out and coax her into the back seat. Before I could even get my seatbelt unfastened, she leapt onto my lap, squeezing her large, furry body between me and the steering wheel.

"Maggie, back seat!" I said, wasting valuable air to do so. I tried in vain to push her off me, but there was no room for me to maneuver.

The dog gave me a wet lick on the face, which, with my arms pinned, I was helpless to prevent. Then she turned to face forward and look through the windshield, honking my horn in the process.

My cheeks grew warm. This was not one of my finer moments of canine management. The very last thing I wanted now was to attract attention; *I* sure as heck wouldn't hire me, were I a mere witness to my current predicament.

I sucked in enough air to say sternly, "Maggie, down!"

No reaction.

I bounced in my seat as much as I could and ran through any other command she might know. "Off! Move! Down! Go away!"

Nothing.

"Don't you know even one command?" I whined, which only inspired her to turn around again and pant into my face.

In a move born from utter frustration, I tried to make myself sound more like her owner and cried, "Mary! Get the hell off me!"

Still no reaction. With effort, I managed to reach around her and shut off the engine. I considered my limited options. My car door was open, so I might be able to slither out from under Maggie head first onto the street.

Either that or I could whistle as loud as possible right in her ear, which would be unpleasant for us both—for the dog's sensitive eardrums and for me as she scrambled to get away from the sound.

From somewhere near the car, a person groaned. A moment later, I recognized Ken's voice as he said, "Ya see that, Allie? This is the other reason I gave up my car. Mary here always insisted on driving."

He leaned toward me and tried to grab his dog, which would have been much easier had he put her collar on her as I'd instructed him to do earlier. "Come on, Mar—Maggie. Get out of there. Give the poor dog gal a break."

It wasn't bad enough that I was pinned into my car? Now I was being called a "dog gal"?

"Hey!" he cried, beaming at me. "I just realized something. If you worked with cats instead of dogs, your nickname could be Allie Cat. Like an alley cat. Get it?"

I had no response to the remark. After a minute or two of tugging and cajoling, Maggie hopped down onto the sidewalk. Finally free, I rocketed out of my car to stand beside the two of them. I brushed paw prints off my now mottled khakis.

Ken was still wearing his too-short brown slacks and his teal shirt with the undershirt showing. His bald head was dappled with beads of perspiration. "Sorry 'bout the mud. You was headin' over to see me, right?"

Short on patience, I growled, "Listen to me, once and for all. This—" I gestured with an open palm at the golden "—is not your ex-wife. This is a dog. And, frankly, even if she *does* possess your ex-wife's soul, I don't care; she's in a dog's body now. You cannot, repeat *cannot*, treat Maggie like a person. She can't roam the streets of your trailer park unleashed. It is too dangerous. Sooner or later she will get hit by a car, or she'll bowl over some little toddler who'll get badly hurt, thanks to you."

I paused to take a breath and let my words sink in. Ken's affable expression was unchanged, so I continued. "She has to be taught simple, doglike commands, such as: Sit. Stay. Lie down. Come. And that all-important 'off.' Now if, for any reason, you can't accept what I'm saying, I will help you find a trainer you can relate to better." I combed my fingers through the bangs of my sandy-colored hair and said evenly, "Am I making myself clear?"

He raised his eyebrows. "Yes, ma'am. Yous any good at your job?"

I glanced at my car and said, "Not counting the past five minutes or so, yes, I am."

"Then what would I want to hire someone else for?" He waggled his thumb. "You can't go 'n' leave your car in the middle of the road like that. Follow me to my place." Just then, Maggie started galloping down the sidewalk. "Better yet, just follow my dog." He gave me a sheepish grin, then pivoted and lumbered down the sidewalk in the same direction as Maggie.

I got into my car, repeating the phrase "job security" to myself as I followed them. Moments later, I arrived at unit thirteen, and Ken let me inside his home.

His living space was just as cluttered and disorganized as I'd imagined it would be. The furnishings in the living room were hidden behind numerous stacks of newspapers. He led me to the kitchen, which had been essentially converted into a workshop. Electronic parts and gadgets covered nearly every flat surface, including the top of his computer.

"Sorry 'bout the mess," he said, pulling out what appeared to be the only chair in his home that wasn't buried under newspapers or tiny gadgets laid out on paper towels. "Not much reason to clean up the place. Maggie here never seems to mind."

"Did Mary used to object?" I couldn't help but ask.

"Nope. Not so long as I di'n't mess with her stuff or her personal space. Mary was really into marking territory. Just does it in different ways nowadays."

At that, I made a mental note to myself to keep the conversation off Mary. Hanging on the wall was what

looked to be a patent, now so yellowed with time that it
was illegible. "Are you an inventor?" I asked.

"Used to be. Way back, I used to repair TVs and would
tinker around with the rejects and odd parts. Wound up in-
venting a type of circuitry that made for the faster, denser
screen sweeps 'n' clearer picture we got nowadays. You know
how folks are about their TVs. Can't live without 'em. Made
me a rich man. But you know the inventor I admire?" Without awaiting my reply, he went on, "The guy who figured out
to put the magnet on the electric can opener so's the lid won't
fall into the soup." He tapped his index finger against his
bald temple. "That's what I call good thinking."

"Yes, now that you mention it, the magnet was a nice
touch."

Ken, noticing that I was still standing, rose and cleared
off a second seat at the table by dumping its contents onto
the floor. Then we both sat down. He grinned, took a deep
breath, and placed his hands on his knees. "So, Allie.
Where do we start?"

With his perfect segue, I pulled from my pockets the two
devices that I'd found the most beneficial in my years of
training countless dogs. Showing him the first device, I explained, "This is a clicker. As you can see, it's just a little
rectangular plastic device with a metal piece inside that
makes a clicking sound when you push it with your thumb.
You use it to signal when the dog is doing what you want
her to do."

Ken said, "Cool!" and took it from me, clicking it wildly
till it sounded as if he were giving rapid-fire Morse code.

I held up the second object. "This is a type of collar that
lets you control the dog's head position during leash training, which you're going to be doing a lot of. I also have a
third tool, which you heard me use on Maggie back at my
office. It's a noisemaker for startling the dog when she's
misbehaving. Used correctly, it can get quick results."

I showed him how to fasten the Gentle Leader collar—
by offering a treat that coaxed Maggie to stick her muzzle

through the loop, and then fastening the clip behind her ears. "She's probably going to try to rub this off on the carpet," I warned.

Maggie, however, had other ideas. She shook her head a couple of times, pawed at the strap across her muzzle once, then took off at a dead run. I'd never seen a dog actually try to outrun a collar like this, so the reaction caught me by surprise. She barrelled straight toward— and then through—the screen door.

"Maggie, come," I automatically called after her, in yet another waste of my vocal chords.

"Oh, crap," Ken said. "She knocked down the door again."

With Ken lumbering behind me, I raced through the door and into Ken's backyard after the dog. She had built up a full head of steam and was soon out of sight. A sturdy-looking, square-jawed woman watched us from her position on a small lawn adjacent to Ken's.

"Maggie," I cried again, clapping my hands. It was no use. I turned to Ken. "Do you have any idea where she might be going?"

He shook his head and shrugged for emphasis. "Could be anyplace, really, though she'll prob'ly stick to the trailer park. We better split up. She was headin' due west, so I'll go northwest, you go southwest."

"I've got a spare leash in my pocket. Do you have hers with you?"

"I'll go get it," he said and pivoted on his heel to return to his trailer.

I glanced at the square-jawed woman. She was staring at me so blatantly that I decided I might as well acknowledge her presence and walk up to her.

"Hi. Did you happen to see which way Ken's golden—"

She shook her head and gestured for me to keep quiet. In a hushed voice, she asked, "You got a death wish or something, lady?"

"Pardon?" She didn't answer at first, so I added, "I'm just here to work with Ken's dog."

She pointed with her impressive chin in Ken's direction, who had just disappeared inside his home. "You're not safe with that maniac. Believe me. I know. These walls are thin. I've lived here as long as they did."

"*They?* Meaning Ken and Maggie?"

"Not hardly. I mean him and Mary. Back when she was still alive." The woman brushed her unkempt black hair away from her eyes, staggering slightly in the process as if she were intoxicated. She looked past my shoulder and I followed her gaze.

Ken had emerged from his trailer and lifted the leash to show me. He waved at the woman beside me and called pleasantly, "Hello, Ruby."

She lifted her chin and waved, but her expression bore no warmth.

He called to me, "I'm headin' out now. To look for Maggie."

We watched as Ken started to head northwest in search of his dog. Under her breath, Ruby asked me, "You ever see any pictures of her? Of Mary?"

"Yes, why?"

" 'Cept for your hair and face, you're a dead ringer for her. And I might just mean that exactly." She let out a laugh that was halfway between a guffaw and a cackle, while I mused that a lot of us were "dead ringers," except for our hair and faces. "He's got a thing for small women. A dangerous thing. He killed her, you know. Ran her down with his car."

The woman was probably drunk, and I had a dog to find, yet she'd scared me enough for me to ask, "Do you know that for a fact? Did you tell the police?"

She scoffed and, again, tossed her hair back from her face. "As if they'd want to know. Police don't listen to people like me, to trailer trash. And they don't care about the deaths of people like us, neither."

"How long ago did Mary die?"

"He kill't her 'bout a year 'n' a half ago. Just a few months after, he brought home Maggie as a tiny pup. As if he could just replace her with a dog."

"They were divorced before the accident. Right?"

"Oh, sure. They got divorced two years ago—nearly a half year before he kill't her. But she was still over here all the time, arguing with Ken, till her so-called accident."

Our conversation had roused the attention of a second neighbor who'd been sitting on her front stoop. She rose and ambled toward us and said, "Lady, don't you listen to Ruby. That man wouldn't hurt a fly." As if to augment her point, she suddenly smacked her hands together and killed some insect that had been circling her.

Wiping her hands on the thin cotton fabric of her faded housedress, she stopped right beside me, then narrowed her eyes at me. I had to resist the temptation to step back. She was a large, unattractive woman in her sixties, with short gray hair and pockmarked skin. I couldn't tell if she was Hispanic, African-American, or a well-tanned Caucasian. She studied me through her thick spectacles, which had blue plastic frames. "Who's this you talking to, Ruby?"

Ruby turned and started walking southwest, toward the portion of the trailer park that Ken had assigned to me. "Ah, she's that dog lady Ken told us he was gonna hire. Now she needs us to help her find Ken's dog."

Actually, I didn't especially want their help, but for Ken's sake, didn't want to be rude. These women were probably the neighbors who'd threatened to call a "dog-catcher." I smiled a little, thinking that at least I'd matured from a "dog gal" into a "dog lady." Maybe I should put that on my business card—Allida Babcock: Dog Lady.

That thought reminded me that I'd yet to introduce myself. "My name's Allida Babcock."

We walked in silence for a moment, the women not introducing themselves despite my giving them my name. After a while, Ruby once again pointed with her impressive chin, this time at me. "She's the one my vet told Ken not to see."

"Some veterinarian advised Ken *not* to hire me?" I asked. My ego got the better of me and I cried, "I have an excellent working relationship with a good number of veterinarians in Boulder."

"Not according to Dr. Palmer you don't. I been going to her for several years. Rather, my dog has. She knows everything. And she says you're no good."

Unable to dismiss such a challenge to my abilities, I said with unmasked irritation, "I've never heard of Dr. Palmer. So I'd be rather surprised if she's at all familiar with *my* work."

The large woman who'd joined us gave me a jab on the shoulder, which was probably meant to be friendly, but actually hurt quite a bit. "Oh, don't you worry about it, Allie. Palmer's another of those cute little women Ken's drawn to. Like you. He probably took one look at her and signed Maggie up without even checking to see if the woman went to vet school."

Feeling more than a little edgy at this point, I said to her, "You know my name, but I don't know yours."

"Yolanda Clay," she said, extending her hand. I automatically shook her hand, but regretted it. She had a bone-crushing grip. And I couldn't help but recall that she'd squashed an insect with those same hands just a short time ago.

Resisting the urge to wipe my palm on my khakis, I turned my attention to Ruby. "And this Dr. Palmer is Maggie's vet, too?"

"Yep. Her office is right across Violet," she said, naming the street that formed the southern border of the trailer park. "A lot of us take our animals there, because it's so close by. Plus, like I said, she knows everything there is to know about dogs."

"I wonder if she knows where Maggie is," I grumbled, deeply resentful of this Dr. Palmer. Apparently the feeling was mutual, though I truly was without a clue as to why or how this could be the case.

Ruby started chortling. "Locating that dumb mutt don't take no genius, hey Yolanda?" She pointed ahead with her chin. Maggie was trotting down the street toward us, proudly carrying what appeared to be a bone.

"Thanks for helping me find her," I said, not meaning it.

Ruby patted me on the shoulder. "Don't mention it. But if you want to keep yourself alive, remember what I told you."

I nodded.

"Ruby! What do you keep saying those kind of things for? You know well as I do that Ken's harmless!"

The two women turned around and wandered off side-by-side, bickering about Ken. As they rounded the corner, Ruby was claiming Ken had "a violent temper and done Mary in," but Yolanda kept punctuating the air with cries of "Nonsense!" and "Bull crap!"

I shifted my attention to the dog. She stopped when I was too close for comfort, no doubt having recognized me as the person who'd put the collar on her. She lowered her head, ears back, her tail wagging slightly. I stopped as well. It is not a good idea to approach a strange dog that's carrying a bone. The dog often assumes the person is going to try for the bone and is quite willing to defend it.

"Maggie, come," I said, slapping my thigh.

Maggie dashed past me, swinging a wide arc around me. She was still wearing her Gentle Leader collar, at least.

I turned and followed.

"Hey!" came a cry from the other side of the street. It was Ken. He waved at me and picked up his pace in my direction. Meanwhile, Maggie split the distance between us and headed toward Ken's trailer in a direct line across people's yards. I waited. Ken joined me and said, "We don't need to chase her no more. She's just heading back to the house."

I fell into stride alongside him. Though he was already winded, he seemed to take one step for my two with his long legs.

Maggie had the pink nose of a digger, and we found her burying her newfound treasure near one corner of

Ken's trailer. Ken immediately went toward her, leash at the ready. "You embarrassed me, Maggie. You made this nice gal search the neighborhood for you."

I walked over to them as he snapped on the leash. She shook her head and pawed at the unfamiliar collar, but my attention was soon focused on the dug-up portion of the lawn. Unlike most dogs, Maggie hadn't been scattering her bones in various locations, but had been stockpiling them in this one spot.

I knelt down for a closer look; my heart instantly began pounding.

"Mr. Culberson, did Maggie bring all these bones here herself?"

"Course. You di'n't think I brought 'em here, did ya?" He let out a guffaw. "She's got quite a collection going, don't she?"

"Where is she getting them?"

He shrugged. "She keeps diggin' 'em up from someplace. Don't rightly know where. Someone's lawn, I guess. Or maybe the playground."

A partially hidden pair of bones had caught my eye. It looked for all the world as though this were an ulna and radius—from a human forearm.

Chapter 4

I studied Ken's broad face. His expression betrayed no trace of apprehension at my seeing the bones that Maggie had collected. He reminded me of a Saint Bernard—large, loyal, steady, and slow-witted in some areas. If these bones were from a human skeleton, I simply could not believe that Ken was aware of it.

I peered behind me to see if Yolanda or Ruby was watching us, but spotted neither of them. Ruby's warnings about Ken had unnerved me. I hoped that these bones had nothing to do with Mary's death—and with the coroner's lack of records. "Um, Ken? Could you tell me more about how Mary died?"

With his dog's leash firmly in hand, he took a seat on the edge of the cinderblock steps to his front door. As before with this topic, he instantly looked ill at ease and ran his palm over his scalp. "Not much to tell, really. Whatcha wanna know?"

"You said she was struck and killed by a car. Is that right?"

He nodded. "Down in Broomfield." Worry lines now creased his forehead. He sighed. "Don't know what she was doing there. Prob'ly shopping, knowing Mary."

"So she'd been a Boulder resident at the time?" I asked, wondering if so, why the person I'd spoken to at the *Daily Camera* had been unable to locate an article about the woman's death. Broomfield was only a fifteen-minute drive from south Boulder, and a hit-and-run would normally be reported in the local section.

"Yep. For the last fifteen years, even. She bought her own house after we split up, but used to come over all the time, even so. Di'n't live all that far away. Up in North Boulder. One a them fancy developments out there." He gestured vaguely to the east.

Though Ken was still holding onto her leash, it was long enough to allow Maggie access to her stash of bones. She had rotated to face away from Ken and was now kicking dirt back onto the bones. Little clumps of the hard, dry soil were spraying up and hitting Ken on the legs, but he remained oblivious.

"Was she buried here in Boulder?" I asked, wondering how long it would take for him to get the connection between Maggie's stash and my asking all of these questions about his late ex-wife.

He shook his head, his lips set in a frown. "Baltimore. They held the services there for her 'n' everything. Guess her folks came out 'n' got her, uh, body."

I nodded. If there was a tactful way to ask him whether or not he was certain that Mary's remains had indeed been sent to Baltimore, I didn't know what that was. If Ken was telling me the truth, however, which he certainly appeared to be, there was no chance that these were Mary's bones.

Satisfied with the amount of dirt she'd kicked onto her stash, Maggie trotted up the steps to sit beside Ken. As she did so, Ken suddenly exclaimed, "Dang it all!"

"What's the matter?"

He held his legs out straight. "Look. I got mismatched socks on again." He shook his head and turned toward his dog. "Can't you do a better job picking out my socks, Maggie? You want me to go around lookin' like a fool?"

"Research has shown that dogs are color blind."

He got up and dusted himself off. "Yeah, yeah. So was Mary, but she used to pick 'em out for me by pattern.

Shoulda known better than to keep lettin' her bring me my socks."

Maggie let out a noise that sounded eerily like a chortle. Just as I glanced at her, the dog winked. I quickly looked away. This had been too long of a day. I was starting to anthropomorphize, too.

"Ken, I'm going to have to borrow your phone. We've got to get the police out here to look at these bones of Maggie's."

He searched my features. I'd caught his full attention. "Why?" With jaw agape, he looked at the loose soil where the bones were still only partially hidden, then back at me. "You don't think they're Mary's, do you?"

"No," I met his eyes, which were now full of fear. "These can't be Mary's because, as you just told me, she died in a car accident some twenty miles from here, and her remains are in Baltimore."

"Yeah, but you wouldn't want the police to look at some ol' soup bones she dug outta someone's garbage. You're saying they got to be human bones, right?"

"I think so, but it's not all that easy to—"

"Oh, jeez! Who else's bones *could* they be? Maybe that's why Maggie's been possessed by Mary in the first place. Maybe Mary's ghost is haunting . . ." He let his voice fade, but grimaced as if sickened by the possibilities he was considering. "I don't know anyone else who died in the last couple years."

"These bones could have been buried for twenty or thirty years, for all we know. And I'm not certain that they're human. They just don't look like . . . your average T-bones to me."

Ken pressed the heels of both hands against his temples. "This is my fault. I shoulda looked at 'em. Always figured it was Maggie's property and she wasn't hurting nobody. I mean, it's not like the neighbors caught her diggin' in their yards again."

My stomach lurched at a thought that occurred to me.

Could Maggie have dug up some kook's murder victim who'd been buried in a backyard? In any case, I reminded myself, these bones were a matter for the authorities, not for me.

We went into his trailer, and I placed a call to the police, using their nonemergency number. I explained that, while I was uncertain, the bones that I'd seen looked like a human's ulna and radius. Ken paced beside me the entire time, forced to step over various objects in his path, but unable to sit still.

To my annoyance, I was put on hold and then the female dispatcher came back on the line to ask if I was certain that the bones looked like that of a human's forearm. I repeated that, no, I was not certain. She told me that a patrol officer would be there shortly, then she asked me to stay and watch over the "remains" until they could arrive. I agreed to do so and hung up the phone.

Ken immediately stopped pacing and looked at me expectantly. Frustrated, I glanced at my watch. I'd wasted nearly an hour already and had made zero progress with Maggie.

This was stupid of me. I hadn't gotten a good enough look at any of the bones to say for certain that they were human. It was far more likely that Maggie had happened onto some large, buried pet from years past. Now Ken was badly upset, I would be late getting to Russell's, and I would make local police lore as a "Dog Lady" who couldn't distinguish a human bone from an animal bone.

I touched Ken's arm and said quietly, "We have to wait here for the police."

"Are they gonna arrest me?"

"Of course not," I immediately answered.

"Good. 'Cause I don't know what I'd do with Maggie while I'm in jail. They prob'ly won't let me keep her in my cell with me. And anyways, I won't *let* her go with me. Ain't her fault, what happened to Mary."

"Ken, we may as well make use of my time. Maggie needs to work on her leash training, for one thing."

As if he hadn't heard me, Ken went over to a tall stack of newspapers and rummaged through them until he reached a spot in the middle where rectangles had been carefully cut away from each paper. He pulled out an old shoe box. "Okay, Allie. Do me a favor. Keep track of your hours, so's I won't have to." He popped the lid off the box, which was filled with hundred-dollar bills. He counted out ten and held them out to me. "This should last for a while, right?"

"You're giving me a thousand-dollar cash advance?"

He shrugged. "Don't have a checking account, so I can't give you a check."

This was so utterly bizarre. Here I was in a run-down trailer, a pile of bones in the yard, and a box of money hidden inside one of the many stacks of newspapers. For all I knew, Ken could be a forger, or even a bank robber turned murderer. Maybe a shift in my career focus to let me become "Allie Cat Babcock" wasn't such a bad idea after all.

I eyed the other numerous stacks of papers, wondering if they also housed shoe boxes full of cash. "You . . . don't have all of your money here in the trailer with you, do you?"

"Course not. Rachel wouldn't let me do that."

The name was familiar and, thinking back to my appointment with Ken's psychologist, I asked, "Rachel Taylor?"

He nodded. "She's my social worker. She keeps people out of homes . . . like where adults gots to go when they can't take care of themselves no more. She gives me all kinds of advice on how to do stuff." He shrugged. "See, at first, when Mary divorced me, I di'n't do so good, so Dr. Thames thought Rachel would be good for me to talk with. And she is. She's great. She said I need to keep my money in a bank, 'cuz there could be a fire or somethin'. I got it all in a savings account at the credit union." He patted his box as he returned it to its hiding place. "This is just my petty cash."

"Aren't you afraid it'll get stolen?"

He spread his arms to indicate our shabby surroundings. "This don't exac'ly look like a place where there's a batcha money hidden, does it?"

"No, but . . . what about supposed friends? Or neighbors? People who know about your box of money?"

"Nobody knows. 'Cept Mary, here." He patted his dog on the head. "And Rachel. But she don't know where I keep it hidden. Only you know that."

"You and I just met today. How do you know *I'm* trustworthy?"

He patted his dog again. "Maggie likes you. She don't take to bad people." He rubbed his palms, grinned, and said, "So let's get goin' on this leash training. Okey doke?"

I pocketed the money, despite my concerns. The police would be here soon. If, despite my instincts to the contrary, Ken proved to have gotten his money from some illicit means, I could turn over the money to the police as evidence. Otherwise, I could do as he asked—keep a running tally of my hours and expenses. In the meantime, I might as well try to give him his money's worth.

The police dispatcher had asked me to keep an eye on the bones, and I decided I could best do that by staying in their vicinity. "Why don't you keep her leash on her, and let's go outside?"

"Sure. Just mind your step, gettin' around the screen." Ken had leaned the sliding door, still off its tracks, into the opening. I moved the door aside, then waited while Ken pulled Maggie through. She strained against the leash with all four paws spread.

On the bright side, Maggie had kept on the collar I'd brought for her. If nothing else, her getting used to wearing that was a step in the right direction. With profuse apologies, Ken eventually moved her past me, and I balanced the screen in the doorway again.

For the next several minutes, I showed Ken how to use the clicker in conjunction with tidbits. "The neat thing about using the clicker is that the dog thinks she's training *you* to click it and give her a treat. That way, you get Maggie's full attention and enthusiasm."

Like many woefully undertrained dogs, Maggie made great initial strides by virtue of finding something to challenge her and to encourage her owner to reward her. The concept of heeling, though, was completely foreign to Maggie. Ken soon grew frustrated at trying to turn and block her path when she attempted to lead. He looked at me in exasperation. "You sure all this leash stuff is necessary?"

"Yes. You're strong enough to maintain a good grip on her, but what happens if someone else needs to take her for a walk? Or what if her clasp breaks, and she decides to run into traffic? Think of it from her perspective. All of her life, she's been taught to believe that it was her duty to lead the way."

"Yeah, but Mary got mad when . . ." He sighed and swiped some dots of perspiration off his forehead. "Mind takin' over for a minute? I gotta go get a drink of water."

He handed me the leash, and Maggie instantly turned and tried to back away in an effort to free herself. I slapped my thigh, then clicked my tongue and gave her a treat. A strange hissing noise broke my concentration, and I looked around. It seemed to come from the direction of Ruby's trailer.

I heard a definite "Psst" this time and led Maggie in that direction to investigate. The beckoning sounds were coming from Ruby's yard.

I did a double take when I spotted the top of Ruby's head. She was kneeling behind a shrub. "Are you talking to me?" I asked.

"Yeah, Allie," she said in a partial whisper. "Don't tell Ken, but I need you to take a quick look at my dog."

Though I kept her on a short leash, Maggie bowled her way through the shrub and promptly started licking Ruby's face. She cursed and swatted at the dog. I pulled Maggie away and got her to sit, then asked, "Why can't I tell Ken?"

"He won't like me hornin' in on his appointment with you."

"I'm in the middle of my work now, but I'll come over

afterwards. That would be the black Lab mix you mentioned earlier?"

She rose and nodded, her black hair now every which way. "He seems to be having a hard time standing up."

"Does he have physical problems? Hip dysplasia?"

"No, but I think—" She broke off and cursed under her breath. "Here comes Ken again." She shaped her hands like a megaphone and called to Ken, "I jus' need to borrow your dog lady for a minute, Ken. I'll get her right back to you."

Ken waved pleasantly and said, "No problem, Ruby. How's T-Rex? Haven't seen him around the last couple days."

"Fine. He's just sleepin'," she called back, then said under her breath to me, "He's been sleeping all day now."

"For twenty-four hours? Without waking?" My sense of alarm was rising. With the downward spiral my day was taking, the horrid possibility of my discovering a dead dog seemed to be a logical progression. Without hesitation, I handed her the leash and said, "Here. Give Maggie back to Ken."

"It ain't like he stopped breathing!" she said as I rushed past her and into her trailer.

A medium-large black dog was lying on his side on a small throw rug just inside the living room, which, I noticed, was almost as messy as Ken's. I knelt beside the dog and placed the back of my hand near his nostrils. I could detect his warm breath on my skin, and his rib cage was moving up and down in regular, peaceful intervals.

Because this was a totally unfamiliar dog, I backed away; the expression "Let sleeping dogs lie" doesn't come from nothing. "T-Rex! Good dog," I called, trying to rouse him, to no avail.

Ruby came in, letting the screen door bang behind her. T-Rex opened his eyes for just a moment. Ruby clicked her tongue. "He just kind of picks his head up every now and then."

There was no telltale whitening of the fur around his muzzle. "This looks like a fairly young dog. How old is he?"

"He's six. Used to have so damned much energy that I couldn't even control him. That's when I started to see Dr. Palmer."

"Uh, oh. You've been giving him a prescription tranquilizer, haven't you?"

"Yeah, but Dr. Palmer said—"

I gritted my teeth. I needed to set aside the question, for now, of why the dog had apparently been sedated just because he was energetic, for God's sake. "Your dog is overmedicated. Let me see your prescription bottle." I made a quick calculation. T-Rex weighed about sixty pounds, and he was acting as though he'd been given at least fifty milligrams of acepromazine.

Ruby retrieved a nearly empty bottle of pills, saying, "See? I'm s'posed to give him two of these a day."

I glanced at the label. "These aren't tranquilizers, they're Clomicalm, an antidepressant. Does T-Rex have a second prescription for acepromazine?" She was looking at me with such a blank expression on her face that I snapped, "A second bottle of pills. Just for when you're taking him to the vet or someplace he's afraid to go."

"Oh." Her cheeks turned red, betraying the fact that the implications of my question had dawned on her. She shrugged and said, "Yeah, but I . . . didn't give him that. I gave him two of . . . whatever you just said it was." She pointed at the bottle in my hand.

"Could I see the other prescription, too, please?"

She brought me that bottle. I sighed with relief to see that these were also 25 mg tablets. The 50 mg dose he'd obviously been given by mistake was not going to kill him. I looked again at the Clomicalm label. She was only supposed to give him one pill a day, not two.

I handed her back both bottles. Trying to be tactful, I said, "I don't have my reading glasses on. Could you tell me what the labels say, please?"

She scoffed and put a hand on her hip. " 'Scuse me?"

"I'm trying to find out what's going on with your dog so that I can help him. I need to know how much medication you've been giving T-Rex and when."

"I . . . do exactly what it says there on the labels. Maybe you should leave if you can't help T-Rex anyways."

"So you give him two pills of the tan-colored tablets with a morning treat every day?" I said, testing.

"Right."

"That would mean T-Rex is receiving twice his prescribed medication."

She furrowed her brow. "I jus' meant that's what I gave him this morning. 'Cuz giving him just one hasn't made much difference." She looked down at T-Rex. "You think my dog is gonna be all right?"

"I hope so. We have to watch for respiratory failure. But he seems to be breathing fine."

She nodded and sighed in relief.

"I am not a veterinarian, Ruby, and can't give medical prescriptions, but my advice would be to stop all medications to T-Rex immediately."

"But then he'll be . . . acting as out of control as that damned Maggie!"

"In my opinion, it's very likely that he simply needs to be better trained. At this stage in my career, I can't volunteer my services free of charge, but the Humane Society has obedience classes that are reasonably priced, and maybe they'll provide scholarships, if money is an issue."

"Ain't it always?" she snarled.

I felt a bit trapped, wanting to do something to help T-Rex but knowing that his drug-ingestation was best left for a skilled veterinarian to handle. "Please take your dog to a vet."

She set her sturdy chin and glared at me.

"I'll be right next door if T-Rex's symptoms change," I murmured.

She nodded, but continued to glare at me.

Now that I'd ascertained T-Rex was not in immediate danger, I became aware of relentless barking from Maggie and saw the cause as soon as I left Ruby's. A policeman, a tall man with a long, sharp nose, had finally arrived next door. Beside the officer, Ken stood anxiously shifting his weight from one foot to the other. Meanwhile, Maggie was trying once again to break free of her leash, in Ken's grasp. Either Ken or the officer had used a spade to remove a portion of the dirt covering the bones, and the officer was staring down at them with interest.

He nodded when I approached. "Evenin'. You must be the person who called this in, right?"

"Yes, and I—" I broke off when I spotted what appeared to be the skeletal remains of a hand. I'd been on the verge of apologizing for bringing him out here, most likely for nothing, but that was no longer necessary. I quickly looked away, feeling slightly nauseated.

"I swear, Allie," Ken said, "I never noticed that hand in there. It's Mary's. I just know it."

"Mary?" the officer gently prompted.

"My ex-wife. Mary Martin Culberson. She died four months ago."

Now I was beginning to have some real doubts about Ken. "Your next door neighbor, Ruby, told me she was killed a year and a half ago. Was she mistaken?"

He shook his head. "That's just when the accident took place. Mary was in a coma for over a year."

"And you think these are her remains?" the officer asked. "Is her grave nearby?"

"No," Ken said. "Baltimore."

The officer glanced at me, then back at Ken and said, "I'm going to have to call in some cri— some investigators. They'll probably need to take these bones to the lab . . . run some tests on them." He pointed at Maggie, still barking incessantly. "Put your dog inside, sir, so we can talk more easily."

"Can't I keep her with me, so long as she's on her leash?"

Her barking had long since surpassed my tolerance level. I clapped my hands twice to distract Maggie. Before she could resume barking, I said, "Good dog," and gave her a tidbit. "Officer, this is a service dog, believe it or not, and the man needs her to be with him whenever possible." Maggie stared at my pocket for more treats.

"How long will she stay quiet for?" Ken asked.

"A couple of seconds, or as long as you'll give her treats in exchange for—"

Maggie started barking again.

"—not barking."

Ken dragged his hand over his bald pate. "It's okay. I'll just lock her in the bedroom and shut the window. Much as she hates that."

Once Ken and Maggie were inside the trailer, the officer indicated Ken with a motion of his eyes and asked me quietly, "Do you and this man know each other well?"

"We just met today, when he hired me to work with his dog. He seems to be delusional about his late wife's death. Ex-wife's death, rather. His therapist told me that he didn't kill the woman, however."

"What's his therapist's name?"

"Terry Thames, a psychologist. He has an office downtown."

Ken returned, looking very agitated at the sound of Maggie's muffled yet frantic barks from inside his home. The policeman gestured at the bones. "Anyone touch these?"

"No, sir," Ken responded, squaring his shoulders to take on the bearing of an army private to his captain. "Just Maggie."

"Can I speak to her?"

"You just had me put her in the house!"

"Maggie's the dog," I said, suppressing nervous laughter.

"Did the dog dig them up from your property here?"

"No, sir. She keeps finding them someplace and haul-
ing 'em home."

"It's important that we find out where that is."

"She had a bone with her when she was coming from
that direction," I said, pointing toward the road south of
the trailer park.

"There's some heavy equipment out that way, near the
road. Right in front of the clubhouse," Ken said. "I think
they been laying pipes down for some new homes."

"When did she first start collecting these?" the officer
asked, indicating the bones with a slight motion of his head.

Ken shrugged. "A week . . . or two or three ago, I
guess. And I just . . . never looked at them. It was Allie
here who said they might be human."

The officer asked Ken to show him where his phone
was and asked me to remain outside. I sat down on the
step and waited. Several minutes elapsed, and I suspected
that the officer was questioning Ken. A second patrol car
pulled up, and the first officer emerged from Ken's trailer
to speak with him.

By now both Ruby, her square jaw set in a frown, and
Yolanda, peering out from her thick lenses, were standing
by the side of the road. "What's going on?" Ruby called.

"Nothing to worry about, ma'am," the first officer
called back.

After some discussion, the newly arrived officer asked
Ken to show him where this "heavy equipment" was located,
and the two of them headed out, Maggie once again barking
vociferously from inside the trailer. Meanwhile, the first officer asked me to sit in his patrol car with him "for some privacy," and to tell him what I knew about Ken Culberson.

I recounted my initial meeting with Ken as best I
could, my conversation with Terry Thames, and how
Maggie had run off and then returned with the suspicious
bone. I deliberately, however, left out my conversation
with Ruby regarding her suspicions about Ken.

Ken was wide-eyed and sweating profusely by the time

he and the officer returned to his property. Having seen
them coming down the street, the first policeman and I
got out of the car. Ken brushed right past us and said, "I
gotta go tell Maggie I'm back."

"We'll come with you," said the officer who'd accompanied him to the construction site. While Ken led the
way into his home, the officer said quietly to the other,
"Something's not right. There's another bone there, but it
hasn't got a speck of dirt on it. It's just lying out in plain
sight, no footprints or marks anywhere near. Looks like
someone tossed it there."

Ken had already closed himself in the back room with
Maggie. The first officer called, "You all right in there,
Mr. Culberson?" His hand was resting on the holster of
his gun as he asked.

Ken, Maggie in tow, emerged. "I'm fine, but I gotta ask
you to witness some paperwork for me."

" 'Scuse me?"

"Made some changes to my will, and I need someone
to witness me signing 'em, just in case I'm . . . tied up for
a while."

Changes to his will?

The policemen looked at each other. "I . . . guess so,"
one replied.

Maggie, meanwhile, had resumed barking at the two officers. Over the noise, I asked, "Ken, you're not feeling . . .
in fear for your life for any reason, are you?"

"Naw, I been needin' to take care a this for a while now,
'n' don't get many visitors for official witnesses." He
looked at Maggie, once again his eyes reminding me for
all the world of a sad Saint Bernard's. "Allie, can you try
'n' do something to help calm her down?"

"Sure thing." I clapped my hands and called, "Maggie,
come." Not wanting to face Ruby and Yolanda outside, I
took Maggie into the kitchen and worked with the clicker.
Remarkably, really, she instantly became so engaged in the
game of getting treats for tricks that she ignored her owner

and the two officers in the other room. But my thoughts were only partially occupied with the dog; I was more concerned with Ken. I suspected that he was scared he was not only about to be arrested, but that he would be incarcerated for a long time. Surely, though, he had nothing to do with the bones in his yard, and the police would let him go.

Maggie began barking again when the doorbell rang. I tightly gripped her leash, and we joined the others in the living room. Ken opened the front door, where another policeman stood. This officer, a slightly pudgy man, nodded in greeting to his fellow officers, then focused his gaze on Ken and said sternly, "Ken Culberson?"

"Yes."

"Would you come with me, please?"

"Am I under arrest?"

"No, sir. We'd just like to ask you some questions at the station house. We've got an open case of grave desecration that we're hoping you can help us resolve."

Ken straightened his shoulders and said indignantly, "I'd never let my dog desecrate on somebody's grave!"

All three police officers tried to cover their laughter. "No, Ken, he's talking about grave robbing," I explained. "You're thinking of something slightly different."

"Grave robbing?" Ken repeated. He returned his attention to the policemen, who had quickly regained their composure, and said, "But Mary ain't got a gravestone, so how was Maggie 'n' me s'posed to know we was robbin' her grave?"

I winced. Predictably, the officers exchanged glances. The last to arrive placed his hand on Ken's shoulder and said, "How 'bout telling me all about that on our way to the police station?"

Ken grabbed his head, his eyes white with fear. He nodded. "Allie? You'll see to it that my Maggie is taken care of while I'm gone, won't you?"

"Of course I will." I grabbed a pen, scribbled my number on a corner of the top sheet of newspaper in the nearest stack, tore around my writing, and handed the fragment of paper to Ken. "Here's my home phone number. But, Ken, get yourself a lawyer before you say another word."

He shut his mouth, gave me a single nod, then went out the door. Predictably, Maggie tried to bolt out the door with him and nearly succeeded in pulling me along. As the last officer started to shut the door behind him, I asked, "How long do you think this will take?"

He shrugged. "Now that a *lawyer*'s going to be involved, I wouldn't hold your breath." He looked back at me, his surly demeanor softening a bit. "Best case, a couple of hours."

"And worst case?"

"That's going to depend on what he has to say."

Chapter 5

The moment the officer pulled Ken's front door shut, Maggie scurried up the stacks of newspapers in front of the window. Hoping it would help her to feel at least slightly more in control, I released my grip on her leash. As the car bearing her owner drove from sight, Maggie let out a great howl that had some ten different tonal pitches within one long exhale of canine despair. The effect was halfway between a ghostly wail and the greatly amplified rumblings of an empty stomach.

She raced to the kitchen to see if the back door was open, which I'd already slid shut. I followed her and took a seat at the table to demonstrate that I wasn't on the verge of leaving her completely alone. After pacing and whining at the glass door, Maggie rushed to my seat at the kitchen table and tried to jump into my lap, which I prevented; cuddling her would only reinforce her behavior. When I bent down to pet her, she pulled away. She was so desperate to convince me to follow her to the door that she put too much body English into her turn and fell into a scrambling somersault.

"Oh, my goodness," I cried. "You poor thing. It must be so frightening to be separated from your owner for the first time. I'm so sorry, Maggie." It struck me a moment later that I was doing exactly what I'd admonished Ken for doing earlier—treating her as though she were human—but then I decided that nowhere in the Great Book of Dog Psychologists was it written that we can't talk to our patients. This was especially true when there were no witnesses.

"Come, Maggie," I said, rising and heading toward the living room. She was about to go there anyway, but this way I could reward her for responding to my command. She trotted toward me, but she appeared to not even see me. "Good dog!" I got on my knees and tried to throw an arm around her neck to stroke her, but she pulled away too fast.

She darted between me and the wooden front door, panting and letting out audible whines of increasing frequency and intensity. After three or four round trips, she made a hell-bent dash for freedom. She barrelled head first into the door, letting out a little whimper of pain after the thud of her impact. Stunned, she sat down.

While Maggie was still seated and doing nothing destructive, I operated my clicker. The dog showed no recognition of the sound whatsoever.

"Maggie! Treat!" Still nothing. She raced past me toward the back door. I lunged for her leash. She dodged past, leaving me calling helplessly and stupidly, "Maggie gets a treat!" I winced when the thud of dog-head-on-sturdy-glass resounded an instant later. *That* wasn't what I'd had in mind, either.

Maggie had a full-throttle case of barrier anxiety. "Damn it! I should have seen this coming!" I chastised myself.

Hearing a man's voice outside, I looked up and saw a couple of men wearing dark blue wind breakers that sported some official police emblem. The sound of Maggie bashing against the sliding glass door had caused them to rush to the doorway. These must be the crime-scene investigators that the police officer had said would be arriving.

Maggie began trying to claw her way through the glass at them. The two men stared at her. I managed to grab her leash. She jumped against the door, still clawing at the glass with her front paws.

"I could use some help in here!" I called to the officers

as I pulled Maggie back onto all fours. She jerked madly, trying to whip her head from side to side while pulling back, but I got both hands on the leash and held tight.

"What do you want us to do?" one of the men said to me through the glass.

"Door's unlocked," I said. In a hand-over-hand operation, I worked my way up the leash in an attempt to get more immediate control of her.

Behind me, they slid the door open. That opportunity to escape and chase after her owner gave Maggie renewed energy. She was tugging and rearing with the force of a bucking bronco.

"Is he gonna bite?" the other man asked.

"Not while I've got her on such a short leash," I said, having worked my way down the leash so that I was holding on right underneath her chin.

"That dog's going to hurt himself, crashing into things like that," his companion remarked as he shut the door behind him.

Still holding onto Maggie's collar for all I was worth, I fought the temptation to scream at him: Does the word "duh" mean anything to you?

"What can we do?" the first man asked.

I had to get my keys out of my front pants pocket and wasn't willing to let one of these men do the honors. "Steady her for a moment." He wrapped his arms around her, and I braced myself as I released my left hand. Sensing the loosening on her leash, Maggie pulled harder.

"Yow!" She nearly yanked my right arm out of the socket. I got my keys out and tossed them on the floor in the direction of the officers. "The red Subaru out front," I said, restoring my two-handed grip on the dog's leash. "Behind the back seat. There's a dog seatbelt. Looks like a small harness. Bring that."

He dashed out, the remaining investigator now shaking his head and chuckling. "I'd help you, if there was more room to grab her. I mean, you must weigh all of, what, eighty pounds dripping wet?"

"With any luck, you'll never find out," I growled at him. "Sit!" I shouted at Maggie just as she seemed to be doing so anyway, really only in an effort to try a new way to break free from me, but this was the opening I needed to reassure her. She sat down, and in a high-pitched voice full of feigned enthusiasm, I clicked my tongue and said, "Good dog! That is such a good dog!"

Maggie had made a tactical mistake. She'd managed to back herself into a corner. It was only going to be a matter of time till she figured out that she could barrel into me just like she had the door, only with better results.

"Can you please take her leash from me for a minute?"

He hesitated a moment, but then said, "Sure," grabbed the leash firmly, and I let go. My fingers felt as though they'd been turned into painful arthritic claws. Maggie strained against the leash, but knew she was no match for this much stronger male person now holding her.

The other investigator returned with the dog seat belt, and I snapped it around Maggie's shoulders and asked the officers if they'd keep a hold on her leash until we got her into the back seat of my car.

"You're going to put this dog into a *car*?"

"She'll be fine. She'll think I'm taking her to her owner. And she'll be belted in the back seat where she can't get into trouble."

We made our way outside. As I'd predicted, far from resisting, Maggie tried to outrace us to the car. I had the harness buckled into the seatbelt before she knew what hit her. Now, though, she tried to get free from that, but the belt held her in a less-than-upright position, so she couldn't get her limbs fully extended to put much force into anything.

I allowed myself a brief sigh of relief, but knew that my work was far from over. "Lie down." She almost was in a fully prone position, but the key was to give the command first so that I could praise her. The instant her belly was fully on the back seat, I said, "Good dog, Maggie," and stroked her. She needed desperately to be soothed, but doing so in advance of her reaction to the command only rewarded and encouraged her wild behavior.

The men were watching her with expressions of disgust on their faces. "Are you going to be all right with that dog?" one asked.

Holding up one finger, but still keeping my vision focused solely on Maggie, I said, "Lie down. Such a good dog. Hand me the pen and pad in the glove box. Please." I dashed off a note to Ken indicating that Maggie was fine—which was reasonably accurate—and that I was taking her home with me, so he should call me there. Then I asked the investigators, "Could one of you please go back inside, stick this on the table, and lock the door behind you?"

"Sure thing," one of them replied. I thanked him and started the engine, though the question *Now what?* was foremost on my mind. Maggie would only develop barrier anxiety again, once inside my home with no sign of Ken.

"You need some of T-Rex's Clomicalm, don't you, Maggie?" I glanced at Ruby's trailer, but was not about to give Maggie another dog's medication.

I drove off, deciding to keep taking left turns to buy me some time until I could devise a plan. Just about the second revolution around the trailer park, I gasped at a realization that hit me like the proverbial ton of bricks: My dinner with Russell!

Maggie was letting out frantic little whines with her every pant. "Oh, Maggie. You know what? If I had even an ounce of sanity, I'd be making love for the first time in *years* right now with a wonderful man who loves me. But, no, I'm driving in circles with a frantic golden retriever, who's never even been taught her own name. Yes, Maggie. That's right. I'm the one who should be on Prozac. It's we *people* who are the crazy ones. And don't let anyone ever tell you otherwise."

Maggie let out a long, plaintive whine, still struggling to get into the front seat. We were on Violet again. It occurred to me that, somewhere nearby, was Maggie's veterinarian, Dr. Palmer, who, sight unseen, had been bad-mouthing me. It was unlikely that her office was still open at this hour, but it was worth a shot. Maggie truly was in need of narcotics—not as a means to deaden a dog's exuberant temperament as with T-Rex, but to alleviate high-level anxiety, which was the intended purpose of the medicine.

I slowed and scanned both sides of the street. The office must be well hidden. Finally, though, I spotted a sign for an "animal clinic" and headed down the long gravel driveway.

The small, older, two-story white-painted building at the end of the drive was obviously a home that had been converted into a business. From the layout, it was clear that the office was in front. The lights were on upstairs, though not in the office area. I parked, reached back and reassured Maggie for a minute or two, then went to the door. A plaque on the door read: Joanne Palmer, DVM. I pushed a button and a buzzer resounded.

While waiting for Dr. Palmer, I kept an eye on the windows of the car. Maggie whimpered and raised up as much as the seatbelt would allow, no doubt hoping that Ken would be here.

A woman came to the door, keeping a chain in place and opening it only a couple of inches. "Can I help you?" she asked.

I was startled at her appearance, or at least by what little I could view through the crack in the door. She was a petite, strawberry blonde, who bore a slight resemblance to the picture of Mary that Ken had shown me. "Are you Dr. Palmer?"

"Yes."

"I have a badly distressed patient of yours in my car. She's experiencing severe separation anxiety."

"Just a moment." She unfastened the chain and swung the door fully open. The illusion that she looked like

Mary Martin Culberson was lost. Though she had roughly the same short stature and slight frame as Mary, facially they were quite different. This woman had a hawk nose, thinner lips, and a rounder shape to her face. Even though she'd opened the door, she held up her palms and said, "Ma'am, my office is closed. Is this something that can wait till morning?"

"No. I'm sorry. It really can't."

She peered at me, wiped her hands on her jeans, and said, "Let me take a quick look."

We had only taken a couple of steps, when she caught sight of the golden through the window and said, "Maggie? How did you get *her*?" She turned toward me. "Are you a friend of Ken Culberson's or something?"

"Not exactly a friend, no. He hired me to work with Maggie." I said purposefully, "My name's Allida Babcock."

"*You're* Allida Babcock?" she asked in surprise.

"Yes, and I've heard you have a negative opinion about me."

"It's nothing personal. It's that you're purporting to be a dog therapist when you don't have the medical credentials."

"I've made no bones about that." I winced a bit at my inadvertent pun, but went on. "In fact, I've teamed with several of your colleagues to help dogs on Clomicalm make effective use of the drug."

She opened the back door of my Subaru. Maggie struggled to get closer to her. "That's a good doggie, hey sweetie," Dr. Palmer murmured soothingly, scooting onto the seat beside the dog.

Though impressed by her rapport with Maggie, I was now pretty agitated myself. Having a local veterinarian assume that I'd been trying to pass myself off as a veterinarian needed to be resolved; my business depended upon referrals. I leaned inside the car myself and said, "I know *you* prescribe Clomicalm for your patients."

"Of course. I'm sure you're aware that separation anxiety is suffered by as many as ten percent of all dogs. And forty percent of all canine visits to the veterinarian are related to separation anxiety."

"Right, but don't you recommend dog trainers, if not behaviorists, to help the dogs adjust?"

"No. That strikes me as an unnecessary expense to my patients." Still petting Maggie, she gestured with her chin in the direction of the trailer park. "A percentage of my clients can't afford tacked-on services."

"But why *dissuade* your clients from getting professional help in the dog's behavior modification? Without behavior modification, the medicine doesn't work."

"That's *your* opinion."

Through a tight jaw, I replied, "It's an opinion that's been backed up and documented in years of studies at various locations around the world. By the way, another patient of yours could use a thorough check-up soon. T-Rex."

"T-Rex? The Lab mix?"

"Do you have more than one patient by that name?"

"Yes, I do. An iguana, actually."

"Well, *I'm* referring to the dog," I snapped. "He's been overmedicated. He was in a drug-induced stupor this afternoon."

She stopped stroking Maggie and gave me her full attention. "How can that be? I gave his owner the right prescription for that size dog."

"Yes, but I don't think Ruby, his owner, can read. She got acepromazine confused with Clomicalm."

"Oh, Jeez," she muttered under her breath.

Maggie began to wail, having realized that the extra attention from Joanne Palmer was not getting her any nearer to her beloved owner. Joanne got out of the car and brushed past me without a word.

I trotted after her. Over the dog's cries, I said, "I don't want us to be adversaries. I'm hoping we can work together."

She scoffed. "I have some samples inside my office. I'll

give you those, and if Ken finds that she needs more, he can bring her back to get her regular prescription refilled."

"*Re*filled?"

"Yes. Maggie's already on a regular dose of Clomicalm." Dr. Palmer added under her breath, "Though she obviously hasn't had any recently."

"That's odd. Ken didn't mention anything about that to me."

"Probably because he could tell you're irrationally predisposed not to use it."

"That's not true. I haven't said *anything* against the use of Clomicalm, which *combined* with behavior modification, is effective." I fisted my hands and crossed my arms. My professional reputation was on the line here; a Boulder veterinarian bad-mouthing me could put me out of business faster than anything else. "Frankly, *you* seem 'irrationally predisposed' to dismiss me and what I do for a living."

She frowned and searched through a large medicine cabinet, grabbing a small two-pack sample.

I went on, "The only difference between us in our feelings toward Clomicalm is that, as with my own medications, I try to use drugs only when absolutely necessary. I try hard to give behavior modification every reasonable chance to work before resorting to meds."

"Of *course* you do, since you can't prescribe them."

"Even if I could, I'd feel the same way. We don't need to drug out dogs simply because they're pack animals and we're not."

"And yet you came running to me for pills for Maggie," she said in a haughty voice.

"Yes! Like all medications, Clomicalm has its uses. And its limitations. T-Rex is currently suffering from ACP's limitations right now."

She glared at me. "I don't think you and I will ever be able to work together."

I clenched my jaw to prevent myself from spewing venomous remarks that would only make matters worse. And after all, however vehemently I disagreed with her having told dog owners not to hire me sight unseen, I'd come to her for help after hours, and she was obliging me.

She pivoted and strode toward the door. "Where *is* Ken, anyway?"

"At the police station."

She froze, then met my eyes. In the softer tones that she'd so far reserved for Maggie alone, she asked, "Does this have something to do with his ex-wife?"

"Why do you ask?"

"Because he thinks he killed her. It wouldn't surprise me if he did. And frankly, having met the woman and heard a few horror stories, I'm not even sure his actions weren't justified."

Chapter 6

I said nothing, and Dr. Palmer held the door open for me. "Here," she said, as I started to walk past her. She thrust a two-pill sample packet into my hand. She then shut and, with more noise and vehemence than necessary I thought, locked her door behind me.

"Thank you so much," I grumbled—but with a smile. I returned to my car. Maggie was howling at the top of her lungs.

I got a soft dog treat out of a bag in my glove box, then crowded into the back seat with the suffering dog. I squished both pills into the treat and fed this to Maggie. In her current hyperagitated state, this single dosage was unlikely to have a major effect. At this point, however, every little bit helped.

What to do now? I was already almost an hour late for my dinner date at Russell's house. The very least that I owed him was a face-to-face apology. A face-to-face-to-furry-howling-face would have to do.

Knowing that the sound of my voice would soothe her some, I thought out loud while heading back down Dr. Palmer's driveway. "Maggie, I sure wish you could tell me what is going on with your owner. Do those bones in your yard really belong to his ex-wife? Did he kill her?" I paused and considered that thought. "That seems so hard to believe. But then, I only met the man this morning. He does seem to be . . . living in his own world, in some ways. Maybe he has a violent temper. Maybe he killed her, but sincerely believes she died from her injuries in a hit-and-run accident. He claimed she'd died a few months ago, and yet your neighbor thought she died a year-and-a-half ago. Could she really have been in a coma for a full year? You'd think something like that would make the newspapers."

Continuing my patter of monologue, which was augmented by the occasional doggie whine emanating from the back seat, I headed toward Russell's. The sun had finally set behind the mountains; this was late June, nearly the longest day of the year. At the moment, that seemed literally true. We drove through downtown Boulder, then southwest into Russell's cul-de-sac, which was nestled into the foothills in the Devil's Thumb area. He lived in a two-story condominium that was unexceptional on the outside but quite nice inside.

This close to the foothills of the Rockies, the townhomes on Russ's side of the cul-de-sac were in a depression and lower than the half-dozen spaces for guest parking. The medication did seem to be calming Maggie down, so maybe this was as good a time as any for me to leave her alone for a few minutes.

"Please, don't have gone all out for dinner, Russell," I murmured as I parked and shut off my engine. If he'd gotten carried away with putting a major meal together, I would only feel even worse about bowing out.

The dog immediately tried to scramble to her feet as I got out of the car. "Maggie, I'll be right back. Be a good doggie and get some sleep."

She started barking, and I left the window open a crack, calculating that I could run down the steps to Russell's, apologize, say good-bye to him, then return to the car before she could go too crazy.

With the sound of Maggie's frantic, but somewhat muffled barks trailing after me, I raced down the long flight of flagstone steps, reached Russell's door, and rang the bell. The sounds of classical music and some wonderful dinner scents—bearing no resemblance to fast-food takeout—greeted me as he swung open the door. The place bore the unmistakable ambience of muted and flickering candles. He gave me a big smile and said, "Hi, come on in."

Wallowing in my own guilt, I stayed put on the welcome mat. Russell looked especially handsome. He was wearing the indigo shirt that I'd once told him was my favorite. I, on the other hand, had not had the opportunity to change out of my dog-hair-laden khakis and T-shirt.

"Russell, I am so sorry. I'm not only unconscionably late, but I can't stay. I've had to . . . bring my work home with me tonight." I gestured in the direction of the sound of Maggie's cries. "I've got a howling dog in the car."

"Why? What happened?"

"It's Ken Culberson's golden. He's the large, bald man you met at my office. He was taken to the police station for questioning. His dog's been burying human bones in his yard."

Russell's eyes widened. "He has a human skeleton in his yard?"

"No, not . . . the whole skeleton. Just . . . a hand and a few random . . . Anyway, Russ, I'm really sorry, but—"

"Couldn't you put the dog on my patio while we eat?"

"Much as I'd like to, that's never going to work. You remember what she was like at my office. She's large for a female golden, and she's ten times more anxious now than she was then. She's totally inconsolable."

Russell stepped out beside me, pulling his door shut. "Let's give this a try anyway. What's the worst that can happen?" He started up the walkway toward my car.

"I don't know, but I've got a feeling we might find out shortly."

Despite my better judgment, we got Maggie out of the car. Although she insisted on leading the way, Maggie could be handled on leash fairly easily because she was desperately hoping to find Ken at the end of whatever path she might be set upon. I took her around the string of condos to the back, while Russell met us at his gate and let the dog into the small fenced-in patio.

"So far, so good," Russell said, though he was already pale and keeping his distance from Maggie.

"Now comes the hard part, though. I've got to get her leash off and slip in your back door without her."

"You can't just leave the leash dangling?"

"It could get caught on something out here and she could injure herself."

The medication had definitely helped; I managed to get her to lie down for a few seconds, which was long enough for me to get in the condo alone. Naturally, however, she went berserk the moment the door was shut. She barked at us and put her front paws against the sliding glass door. From this angle, she looked almost bearlike.

Watching her, Russell shrank back a little. "Can't you give her some medicine to calm her?"

"Already did. This *is* her calm state."

"Do you think it would be better if I shut the drapes?"

I shook my head. "Odds are that would make her worse."

He forced a wan smile, pulled a chair out from the dining table for me, and said, "Let's eat, then."

Maggie's barks were too annoying even for me to handle. "This just isn't going to work, Russell," I said again with a sigh. "Come to think of it, I'd better call my mom and make sure it's all right for me to bring Maggie home."

"Want me to put your dinner in a doggie bag? Pun intended." Russell wiggled his eyebrows at me playfully, reminding me how much and why I truly liked him.

"I guess," I muttered. "I feel so bad, Russ. You went through all this effort, and here I am, late, and now everything's in shambles."

"It's not your fault." He shifted his vision to Maggie. "There's nobody nearby who could watch the dog for an hour or two?"

"No, but . . . maybe Ken's home by now. In which case, I might be able to salvage things yet."

I called the police station and asked if Ken Culberson could come to the phone. The receptionist or dispatcher—whoever answered the phone—gave me the runaround, making it difficult to tell even if Ken was still there. I called his place and got no answer.

Giving Russell a sad shake of my head to let him know my efforts had failed, I called my mom. After a roommate fiasco a couple of months ago, I had temporarily moved into my mother's house, along with my two dogs—a German shepherd and a cocker spaniel. She'd since acquired a collie, so this would be a fourth dog added to our canine menagerie. Mom didn't sound too thrilled, until I mentioned that it was a golden, which cheered her; she's always loved that breed.

To my surprise, Russell had dished up while I was on the phone as if it were a foregone conclusion that I was staying for dinner, after all. He served rack of lamb, julienne green beans, yams. The moment I sat down, the phone rang. Russell fielded his first noise-complaint call from a neighbor.

This was so unfair to him, I could barely keep up any semblance of pleasant company. We both gulped down his wonderful meal as if participating in a pie-eating contest. When the phone rang for the fourth time, I rose, said, "Everything was delicious, and I hate to eat and run, but I don't have much choice. I've got to get the dog out of here."

Russell got to his feet as well, ignoring the ringing phone as best he could. "Thanks . . . for coming."

I gave him a quick kiss. "Have a good trip to Palo Alto. I'll see you when you get back."

"Okay."

Using the knee-first method honed from years of dog training, I squeezed out the back door and prevented Maggie from entering. As we left the patio, Russell called out, "Good-bye, Allida."

Feeling the weight of both his disappointment and my own, I climbed the steps with Maggie to the parking area. I glanced down and saw Russell still standing at the bottom step, watching. I called back, "Don't give up on the two of us."

"I never will." He turned and went back into his home.

Mom lives in Berthoud, a bedroom and farming community northeast of Boulder, roughly halfway between Boulder and Fort Collins, the next sizable city. Over the past few years, Berthoud had become popular with yuppies. Housing prices had therefore skyrocketed, downtown shops were becoming more upscale, and the "quaint" descriptor had become hackneyed. At this hour, I could normally make the drive in forty-five minutes, but Maggie was still not on her best behavior. Then again, since I'd yet to discover what her "best" behavior might be, maybe this was it.

I tuned the radio to a music station and found that she would sing along, as long as I did, too. We had quite the time of it, singing Paul Simon's "Graceland" together, all of her words being "woooo," which made fine accompanying lyrics.

I'd sung my throat raw by the time we arrived. Because Maggie was on edge and would be catching my dogs unaware, I left my car in the driveway and brought Maggie to the front door instead of parking in the garage as usual. Maggie was so engrossed by the scents of the various dog tracks up my walkway that she even let me lead.

My mom must have heard us coming, for she swung the door open. Her long hair was in its usual braid. Though she's four inches taller than I am, we're frequently told how similar we look, so I like to think of her as being exceptionally attractive. After such a trying day, she was a sight for sore eyes. I said, "Hi, Mom," wanting to hug her.

"What a beautiful dog," she replied, greeting Maggie with the kind of enthusiasm that, every now and then, gives me a pang of jealousy. Rarely do her eyes light up that way at the sight of me, but then there's something to be said for the comfort of familiarity, even if that comes in tandem with some boredom. "Has she eaten dinner yet?"

"I don't know, come to think of it. Certainly wouldn't hurt to feed her something."

My dogs rushed over to greet the dog and then me. If

they were any less well-trained and accustomed to my bringing various animals home, my having her enter on-leash would have been asking for trouble, especially in the off-leash dogs' territory. Sage, Mom's collie, as the newest and least-trained of our canine menagerie, gave Maggie a couple of bear-in-mind-that-you're-on-my-turf barks.

The dogs proved a good distraction for Maggie, and the medication was probably a bigger help than I could measure. A couple of hours after our arrival, we got the dogs settled in and went to bed ourselves. Maggie seemed content to wedge herself between Sage, Mom's collie, and Pavlov, my German shepherd, on their respective makeshift beds in a corner of the kitchen.

The phone rang, awakening me from a deep sleep. In a daze I reached blindly for the phone beside my bed, my stomach already tightening. Calls at this hour were never good news. I muttered a hello.

"Allie? It's Ken. Ken Culberson. Do you still have Maggie with you?"

"Yes. She's . . . fine. She's sleeping. Are you okay?"

"Fine. Yes. Glad to be home. Can you bring me Maggie, right away?"

"Now?" I glanced at the illuminated face of my alarm clock. It was two-twenty in the morning. "You want me to drive into Boulder *now*?"

"If you don't mind."

"I was sleeping, Ken, and I don't want to have to drive to Boulder now. Not unless this absolutely can't wait un-til morning. Can you wait for Maggie till then? Till day-break, at least? Please?"

"I s'pose I can wait. I'm just . . ."

"Maggie's fine. She gets along with my dogs just great. Did everything go all right at the police station? Do they know whose bones those are yet?"

"They think they're from a grave of some person I never heard of, but I'm still thinkin' they're Mary's. Funny

Never mind. You're trying to sleep. Anyways,

thing is . . . an you get Maggie back here?"

how soon ling in the morning. Eight A.M."

"First I'm just . . . surprised this is all right with

"Oean, Maggie."

Mar I implored. I did *so* want to get back to sleep.

I talk to her?"

tated, knowing better than to upset all of the dogs,

was a small price to pay so as to avoid leaving the

t this hour. "Uh, yes. Just a moment." I opened my

Maggie was waiting right on the other side. She rushed

leapt onto my bed—something I don't even allow my

ttle cocker spaniel to do. Feeling like an idiot, I held

. the phone to the dog. "Go ahead, Ken," I called.

"Maggie?" I could hear Ken shout. "That's my girl. You be good for Allie, and I'll see you in the morning, okay?"

The dog, in the meantime, was totally confused at hearing her master's voice on the phone. She barked a little and did a full three-sixty on my bed as she tried to find Ken.

"Allie? Give Maggie a hug for me. I'll leave the door unlocked for you in case I oversleep. All right?"

"Fine. Good night." I hung up. I looked at Maggie, who had already settled onto my bed. I was so tired that I had a fleeting thought of just letting her get away with it, but then scolded myself. Consistency is the key to eliciting desirable behavior in mice, men, and dogs, after all.

"Maggie, down." When she didn't respond, I grabbed her collar, pulled her off the bed using all of my strength, then said, "Good dog." and ushered her out the door, shutting it behind me. She was soon howling, undoubtedly annoying my mother in the other bedroom. I muffled Maggie's cries by sandwiching my head between two pillows and, eventually, fell asleep.

At seven A.M., I tried to get Maggie back into my car. This dog would either be my personal crowning achievement—as far as redefining her behavior patterns—or a glaring failure. She recognized immediately the *harness for* the dog car seat and resisted my attempts to pu *it on her.*

Even with my mother's help, we had a diff. *time.* Eventually, however, we out-persisted the dog, ar *time.* found myself fighting my way through the rem *on* commuter traffic.

The traffic was worse than usual, and it was after e thirty by the time Maggie and I reached Ken's trailer pa The entire park seemed eerily quiet. As I pulled into Ken gravel parking space, I eyed the property of both of hi. neighbors, Ruby and Yolanda, but their places seemed quiet as well.

Maggie meanwhile was straining for all she was worth to get out of her seatbelt and inside her home to see her beloved owner. I decided that there was little risk in her running off, so I broke one of my own cardinal rules and, the moment I'd undone her harness, allowed her to run out without a leash. She was waiting with her front paws up on the door yipping happily to get in before I could climb the steps.

Keeping my eye on Maggie, I gave a quick glance at Maggie's bone stash. The bones were gone, but the police had left the yellow plastic police-scene tape surrounding the area that they'd excavated from Ken's front lawn.

I rang the doorbell, thinking how this was one of the joys of my job. I love to see happy reunions between dogs and owners. Dogs give us what we fully grown humans aren't capable of always giving—unconditional love.

There was no answer, and I tried to waylay the sense of concern that immediately hit me. He had gotten home really late and could be expected to oversleep. Still, between the bell and Maggie's plaintive cries, he would have to be quite a sound sleeper to miss all the racket.

"Maggie, down," I instructed as I tried to pull open the screen door, or that portion of it which wasn't already shredded from Maggie's claws. She obeyed in her eagerness to rush around this door.

The solid wood door was unlocked, as he'd said it would

be. Immediately, I regretted not having said something to him last night. Leaving a door unlocked after all of the bizarre goings on yesterday seemed an unnecessary risk.

Maggie bulled her way through the door, using her muzzle as such an effective wedge that the doorknob was wrenched from my grasp.

"Ken? It's Allida."

No answer.

There was an eerie aura about the place that made my skin prickle. And, if possible, the house was messier today than it had been yesterday.

Maggie raced ahead and into a room down the narrow, dark hallway. There were still no sounds of Ken's rising and greeting his dog.

I waited for a moment, hoping to hear Ken's voice. When no acknowledgment came in answer to Maggie's sharp barks, my angst increased tenfold.

"Ken?"

The household was still silent, save for Maggie's little whines and the beating of my own heart. Something was wrong. He had been so anxious to see Maggie, I couldn't believe he'd simply leave his house before we could arrive.

Much as I didn't want to, I followed Maggie's path down the hall and into the last room on the right.

Maggie had jumped onto the bed where Ken's massive form lay prone, dressed in boxers and an undershirt. The dog was nuzzling Ken's hand desperately, trying to get him to respond.

One look at his face—at his wide-open mouth, the fixed expression of horror on bulging, unseeing eyes, and the blue skin tones—told me that Maggie's efforts were useless.

Ken Culberson was dead.

Chapter 7

I looked away quickly, but knew that the hideous sight had already been emblazoned into my memory. My initial shock gave way to an overwhelming sense of sadness and outrage. Was this natural causes, or had Ken been murdered?

My senses were reeling. Sick and dizzy, I staggered toward the door, but dimly realized that, behind me, Maggie was whining and nuzzling Ken's motionless fingers. I couldn't leave her like this.

"Maggie. Come," I called from just inside the doorway, unable to look. She ignored me. I took a deep breath and walked up to her, but nearly gagged when I stepped on something soft. Luckily, it was just Ken's pillow.

Though my hands were shaking and I was battling nausea, I managed to snap the leash onto Maggie's collar, then pulled her away from Ken's body and into the kitchen. After some searching, I located his phone, dialed 9-1-1 and told the male dispatcher that Ken Culberson, the owner of this trailer, was dead. He asked me a series of questions, which I answered with my thoughts focused on my own question: Why?

A second insidious question popped unbidden into my mind: Had Ken known his life was in imminent danger? His dog was a service dog, as designated by his doctor. I had never even asked what the diagnosis had been; Ken could have had a sleep-apnea disorder to which Maggie was attuned. Maybe my failure to bring her to him when he asked me to had caused his death.

The dispatcher said something about whether or not anyone else was "on the premises."

I felt faint. "I don't . . . I've got to go outside."

"Allida? A patrol car will be there momentarily. Stay on the line and—"

I hung up the phone and stumbled outside, dragging Maggie with me on her leash. I sat down on the cinder-block back steps, trying not to think about the scene in his bedroom. I struggled to keep taking deep breaths, to not lose control.

Maggie, too, was trembling. I was giving her as much room on her leash as possible. She sensed that something was dreadfully wrong with her owner, for she wanted to stay next to me now, rather than with Ken. Letting out one last whimper, she lay down on the step below mine and rested her chin on my feet. Her attitude broke my heart. I cried softly and stroked her fur, saying, "I'm so sorry," over and over again.

"Hey!" a raspy voice cried, "You there!"

I dried my eyes and looked up. Ruby marched toward me, her strong jaw set in a frown. She was wearing a slightly stained peach-colored blouse and shorts.

Trailing behind her, T-Rex struggled to keep up. His head was hanging and his gait implied that he was ready to lie down and sleep the moment his owner stopped tugging on his collar.

At the approach of another dog, Maggie got up intending to investigate. She let out a little whine of protest when she found that her leash was too short and my grip on it was too strong.

Ruby dropped the leash to place her hands on her hips and give me a full body-English glare. "I got a bone to pick with you!" Despite the hour, she seemed drunk; her speech was slurred and her equilibrium slightly off kilter.

Meanwhile, T-Rex yawned and lay down where he stood—on the hardpacked dirt behind my car. Unable to find my voice, I merely met Ruby's eyes and waited for her to release the hounds of her anger upon me.

"You got some nerve! You told that veterinarian that I can't read, didn't you!"

All I wanted to do was make her vaporize—tell her to get the hell away from me, that I couldn't deal with this now.

"Answer me, damn it! You gone deaf?"

"It was in your dog's best interest to let Dr. Palmer know that," I muttered.

"You had no right! I can read just fine! I'll have you know I got myself a high school diploma."

I managed not to retort: Maybe so, but can you *read* it? "Ruby, I meant no harm. Clomicalm and acepromazine are serious drugs that can do more harm than good if administered incorrectly. I was simply concerned that your dog get the correct dosage from this point forward."

"Yeah, well, whatever. You were wrong about him. T-Rex is on just the right amount of medication. Dr. Palmer said so. And my dog's just fine now. See?"

She gestured at her dog, who was now lying on his side, asleep on the hard earth in another dog's territory, which, for a healthy, lucid dog, was unheard of. Ruby was attempting to stare me down, hands on her hips.

"Your dog looks lethargic to me, Ruby."

"Yeah, well—" with a jerk of her elbow she gestured at Maggie "—if that's true, he probably caught it from Maggie."

I said nothing, but made a mental note to lower my vocabulary several grade levels when speaking with Ruby.

At long last, sirens in the distance grew louder, and Ruby seemed to put a couple of things together. Her angry scowl changed into a look of alarm. "Hey! What are you doing here alone? Where's Ken?"

"Still in bed."

As the sirens drew closer, she searched my face, her overplucked eyebrows raised in eager curiosity. "Did something happen? Are the police coming here because of you?"

Before she could repeat the question, two police squad cars and one sheriff's car pulled up, and Maggie stood up and began to bark. This finally roused T-Rex, who rose and joined Maggie in a barking chorus.

"What's wrong? What happened?" Ruby asked while two police officers and a sheriff approached. Her voice was shrill and she jerked her head to look at the officers and then back to me. She looked like a human version of her barking dog.

The officer from the first car asked her, "Do you live here, ma'am?"

"No, that's my place there." She pointed.

"Go home, please, ma'am. We'll come speak to you in a few minutes."

She ignored his request and looked again at me. "Where's Ken, Allie? Is something wrong with him?"

The officer began guiding her to her trailer, saying quietly, "Please, ma'am. We'll be over to speak to you as soon as possible." She continued to protest, but the officer kept cajoling till she finally relented and entered her home.

A second uniformed policeman came up to me in the meantime. "I'm Officer Hobbes. Are you . . ." He paused as he glanced at his notes.

I answered for him, "Allida Babcock. Yes. I placed the call to nine-one-one. He's in there."

"Anyone else on the premises?" a second officer asked from behind him.

"No. Not as far as I know, anyway."

Beside me, Maggie was barking as loud as she could.

"Show us where you found him."

"Wait. Whose dog is that?" one of the policemen asked.

"She belonged to Ken Culberson," I answered, "the man who died."

"We can't let that dog back in the trailer right now."

"Did he live alone?" Officer Hobbes asked me. "Just him and the dog?"

"Yes."

The other officer nodded. "I'll call Animal Control. Is there some place you can put her in the meantime?"

"There's no need to have Animal Control lock her up. I'll take care of her for a couple of days myself."

"I'll take her," a woman called. I turned toward the voice. It was Yolanda Clay. She was wearing the same housedress she had on yesterday. Her pockmarked face bore a scowl and she strode toward me with a no-nonsense march. "The dog can stay with me for a while."

I protested, "But I can't—"

"Would you rather keep her in your car, miss?" the officer suggested.

I felt incapable of making any decisions, so I went with the easiest one and handed the leash to Yolanda. "I'll come get her as soon as I can."

"Did somebody kill Ken last night?" Yolanda asked one of the officers. I saw two officers immediately freeze at the question and exchange glances.

"Did you see or hear anything that makes you think so?" he asked her in reply.

She nodded. "I seen that Rachel Taylor, Ken's social worker, come snooping around here at something like three in the morning."

"Did you see her go into Mr. Culberson's trailer?" the officer asked.

"No. She was just driving past when I saw her, but she's your killer."

"You think that Mr. Culberson was murdered?" he asked.

She narrowed her eyes, looked him up and down, and held up a palm. "Oh, that's right. Could've been natural causes. Even though the whole neighborhood's talking about how y'all hauled him off to jail yesterday. And how a skeleton was dug up in his yard."

"Well, ma'am, we'll have someone come speak to you."

"Uh huh. In other words, get outta the way. Come on, Maggie. Let's go home."

I led the officers inside Ken's home. At the corner of the hallway, I said, "He's in there, on his bed." I looked at the officer who seemed to be assigned to keeping an eye on me. "Can I go sit outside, please?"

"Sure. I need to ask you a few questions. I'll come with you."

The officer opened the front door and we went out to the front steps. "What's your relationship to the deceased? Friend? Neighbor?"

"I'm his dog's . . . therapist."

He grinned, then seemed to immediately realize that this wasn't an appropriate response and nodded somberly, making yet another notation. I carefully told the officer my story—how I'd come to be here in the first place and discovered Ken's body. Afterward, I explained, "Supposedly, Ken was wealthy. He paid me a thousand-dollar advance out of a shoe box hidden in a stack of newspapers. The second one to the right of the front door in the living room. You'd better see if it's still there."

"We'll . . . do that."

I turned back toward Officer Hobbes and asked, "I'd like to go check on Maggie for a minute."

"Maggie?"

"The dog. Ken's dog."

"All right. Afterwards, can I give you a ride to the police station? We'd like to ask you some questions, take your statement. Just a formality."

"Sure," I replied as if I weren't frightened to the core. It was obvious to me that, if Ken's death was not by natural causes, the police were prepared to make me a prime suspect.

Officer Hobbes and I sat in an unexceptional room at the Boulder Police Department. Our conversation had been interrupted several times, when he'd had notes handed to him and sometimes excused himself from the room entirely. So far, I had explained yet again about my phone call from Ken at two-twenty A.M. and how I'd arrived at around eight thirty-five. I had seen enough cop shows to expect that his kindness to me so far was an act, intended to convince me that he and I were confidants. As such, it seemed to me that it was his turn to answer a question or two. "How did Ken die? Was he murdered?" I finally asked.

"The autopsy results will tell us that, but in the meantime we're considering this a suspicious death." He glanced at the papers in front of him. "I see that you're the one who called yesterday about the bones in Mr. Culberson's yard."

"Yes. There were a pair of bones that looked like those from a human's forearm, and apparently I was correct."

He nodded and said nothing, as if expecting me to go on, but I had nothing more to say on the subject.

"You saw the dog carrying this bone after she'd run away from you?" he prompted.

"That's right. I'd put a collar on her, the same one she's wearing now, and she ran right through the screen door, which I hadn't anticipated. When she returned, she was carrying a bone."

"Had you known about her collection of bones prior to that?"

"No."

"Not even that she had a likelihood to pick up a bone, if she found one?"

A *likelihood?* I mentally repeated. "Well, most dogs will pick up a bone they find, unless they've been specifically trained not to."

Hobbes leaned back in his chair. "As a dog expert, maybe you can help me figure out something. If I were to, say, toss a bone into a park where there are a number of dogs off-leash, I could be fairly certain a dog would discover it?"

"Of course."

"Right away, would you say?"

"Yes," I answered with a shrug that showed my impatience. "Isn't this common knowledge? That dogs collect bones?"

"I suppose it is. So then, going back to my example of tossing a bone into a public area, wouldn't it be hard for me to ensure that one specific dog got hold of a particular bone I wanted him to have?"

"Yes. Unless you tossed it to that specific dog. Or that dog was the only one around when you tossed it into the public area."

"I see." He nodded as if what I'd said had been enlightening.

I furrowed my brow, wondering where all this was going.

"Ever heard of—" he paused and consulted his notes "—acepromazine?"

I stiffened. "ACP. Yes, it's commonly known as 'doggie downers.' It's usually prescribed for particularly stressful situations, such as when a dog's going on a trip in an airplane. Ken's neighbor, Ruby Clay, had an ACP prescription for her dog. Why?"

"Ever carry them on you, for use with your dog clients?"

I was fully alert now and my thoughts were racing. Why would he be asking me about this? Could Ken have been drugged into a stupor? "Never. Nor do I prescribe them. I can't. I don't have a veterinary license."

The officer looked again at his notes and nodded, scratching his cheek. "Did you recently crush a tablet in Mr. Culberson's kitchen while you were working with his dog? Or suggest that he do so?"

"No. And I can't ever picture Ken giving a soporific drug to his dog. I didn't know him for very long, just since yesterday in fact—the one day—but I do know how he treated Maggie, and I don't believe he would sedate her under any circumstances."

The officer had shed his casual act and was now staring at me intently.

I continued, "As I'm sure you know, acepromazine would make a person, as well as a dog, drowsy." And would have rendered poor Ken, that bear of a man, much easier to suffocate, I thought. I fought back a shiver of revulsion at the memory of stepping on the pillow on his floor. Was that the murder weapon?

Officer Hobbes stared at me for what seemed like several minutes, but was probably only a few seconds. I also knew that ACP had been used in suicides, but I was not about to bring up that possibility, because I was absolutely certain that Ken did not commit suicide. Officer Hobbes asked, "What are you planning on doing with his dog?"

"I haven't had the time to think about that yet."

"Want us to call Animal Control? They'll keep her at the Humane Society till you decide."

"I don't think that'll be necessary. I can always keep her at my house for a while. Have you contacted any of Ken's relatives yet? I've got to see if there's anyone who he might want to have take Maggie."

He gave me what looked to be a haughty smirk. "Guess that's your responsibility."

"Pardon?"

"Mr. Culberson did tell you, didn't he, about the codicil in his will?"

"Codicil?" I repeated.

"Yeah. He had a couple of my fellow officers witness the thing last night."

"I remember him doing that, but I never saw it myself. And Ken didn't tell me anything about his will."

"The dog gets all of Mr. Culberson's money. Last night, he appointed you as her temporary guardian. You're to find her a permanent home with someone who knows her, and if you can't, you're to adopt her yourself."

I scoffed in utter disbelief. "What? Is this some kind of a test?"

"No. We've got the will in evidence already, but I assure you, that's what it says."

"Oh, God." I dropped my face in my hands, stunned at the implications of what this meant. I'd only just met Ken and Maggie yesterday. How could I possibly choose among his circle of loved ones who should have his dog?

"It's not like we could be talking about a lot of money," Officer Hobbes went on. "I mean, that trailer must be worth all of, what, ten thousand? Maybe less."

Judging by what Ken had told me, he also had an enormous bank account. With an officer acting as if he suspected me, however, this wasn't a great time to reveal that piece of information, which they could—and no doubt soon would—easily discover on their own. I sat up straight again. I knew I was innocent, damn it all. "Did they find the shoe box during their search?"

"Sorry?"

"He had a large amount of money in a shoebox. I told one of your fellow officers about it when we were at Ken's home."

That hideous scene in Ken's bedroom popped unbidden into my consciousness. There was an empty shoe box in the corner of his room. Was this the same one that had been filled with cash yesterday?

"Roughly how much money would you say you saw in that box?"

I tried to make a mental image of those stacks of hundred dollar bills. "I have no idea. It was all in hundreds, or at least, the bills that I saw on top were. How many bills could you stack into a large shoe box? A few hundred? So maybe thirty thousand dollars. I don't know."

"It didn't strike you as odd that a man in a rundown trailer would have thirty thousand dollars in cash lying around?"

"Of course it did. He told me he was well-off but didn't care where he lived. That he'd made a batch of money on an invention of his."

Again, the officer stared at me. Things looked horrid for me. I'd found the body. I was temporary guardian of Ken's inheriting dog. A drug used to sedate dogs was apparently used in the crime, and I was a "dog expert." *Shit!*

I checked my watch. "I have an appointment with a client in about twenty minutes. Can I go?"

He leaned back in his chair while studying my face. "If you want to go, by all means." He gestured at the door. "We'll probably have a few more questions for you soon, but we know where to find you."

My head spun at the thought of poor Ken, dying before his time, and how I could possibly get Maggie to readjust to the loss of an owner she'd bonded with so completely, let alone make it clear to the police that I was innocent. But I was determined to behave like the competent adult I knew I was. Okay, *tried* to be. Regardless, dogs in both my professional and personal life were depending on me.

I returned to the trailer park to collect Maggie, who was definitely delighted to see me. I attributed her enthusiastic response to her association of me with her owner. She was still hoping that I'd bring her back home, and that this time Ken would be his normal self. Yolanda greeted me with a host of questions about what had happened to Ken and what I'd learned from the police, although there was now no shortage of police officers in the neighborhood. Vowing to keep to myself any mention of crushed ACP in Ken's kitchen, I answered, "They haven't even told me if they consider his death a murder."

She made a dismissive noise and said, "Course they do. They ain't *that* stupid."

"True, but the police tend to ask questions, not to answer them."

She pursed her lips and nodded solemnly. "We all need to watch our backsides."

No kidding, I thought. I wasn't about to discuss how I'd been appointed to select the guardian of Ken's now wealthy dog, and instead thanked her and told her I was in a hurry while pushing out the door.

Maggie was getting better at accepting her banishment to the back seat. When we arrived at my client's house, I opened the four windows for Maggie and parked in the shade. I had no choice but to leave her there for an hour while I worked with a rather surly standard poodle named Redux.

Because Redux's owner, a shy, elderly widower, had decided not to take charge of his pack, Redux had decided to stake out his territory by urinating on his master's bed. "Master" was not pleased. This quickly escalated into Redux's determining when he could and could not be petted, and he had snarled and snapped at one of the grandkids when visiting for a weekend last month.

I explained things from his canine's point of view and lectured the man on how important it was, for both his and the dog's perspective, to establish that he—not his dog— was lord of his domain. He listened patiently, then said, "I kind of already realize it's important. It's pretty important to me not to have my bed peed upon." I chastised myself for stating the obvious, then spent the rest of our session giving practical advice on how to set things right.

To my happy surprise, Russell's car was in his parking space when I completed my house calls and returned to the office. Maybe he'd had a change of plans and didn't need to go out of town after all. I rushed to park beside his avocado green Volvo, unfastened Maggie's belt, grabbed hold of her leash, and raced down the steps, halfway pulled by Maggie.

Hoping to avoid a repeat of our first meeting in which she'd clunked her head on the glass, the moment she reached the bottom step I said, "Maggie, heel," then gave the leash a tug.

Maggie promptly stopped and waited for me. "Good dog! There's hope for you yet."

My heart was racing as I silently pleaded with the universe to make it true that Russell wasn't leaving town after all. I wrapped Maggie's leash around a desk leg, gave Russ's office door a rap, then opened it. He was seated at his desk. "Russell, hi. I thought your flight left at the crack of dawn this morning."

He rose. "It did, but I got a later flight." He glanced at his watch as he rose from his chair. "Really have to go now, though."

"Did you forget something?"

"Yes."

He gave me such a passionate kiss that my knees almost buckled.

"I forgot to kiss you good-bye," he said.

I searched his eyes, now unable to stand the thought of having him leave. So what if we lacked interests in common? We could discover some as we went along. "Do you really *have* to go on this trip?"

He nodded. "If I want my business to stay afloat, I sure do." He picked up his carry-on suitcase and handed me his key chain. "My spare keys, in case you need them for any reason. I'll call you tomorrow or Thursday. All right?"

"Yes. Please. Do."

He grinned at me, then pushed out the door. I watched him leave, then dropped into the nearest chair. Why was my heart on this constant yo-yo with Russell? "Who am I kidding?" I muttered to myself. I knew the reason for my indecision; I just didn't want to admit to the after-effect of all those late-night talks years ago. My ex-fiance and I used to chat about our future home on its large chunk of land where we'd live happily ever after with a half-dozen dogs. Though I'd long since given up the man, I'd clung with both fists to the dream—to someday owning the homestead and the dogs. Russell, with his fear of dogs, would never fit into that picture. How was I to choose between love and the lifestyle I've always wanted?

After giving myself a moment to collect myself, I returned to my desk and freed Maggie from her leash. My schedule had been jumbled, thanks to the dreadful events of the morning. It was going to take some juggling to get things straightened out.

Checking a small appointment book in my purse, I noted with relief that I hadn't missed any appointments yet. My mornings tended to be much lighter than my late afternoons and evenings. That's because dogs primarily misbehave when their owners are out of the house, so my work often revolves around clients' work schedules.

My office door squeaked behind me, and as I turned, Maggie launched into attack-dog mode. Her hackles were raised and she pulled so hard on her leash that she managed to move my desk slightly.

"Maggie, sit," I said. The key to stopping barking is to distract the dog with a simple command, one that the dog both understands and knows can lead to a reward.

The woman, who appeared to be in her early fifties, was petite—my size—and had bleached blond hair but with dark eyebrows, currently set in a deep scowl. She looked a lot like someone I knew she couldn't possibly be.

"Are you Allida Babcock?"

"Yes, I am. Did . . . we have an appointment?"

She narrowed her beady eyes. "No, though we'll be seeing a lot of each other unless you give me my dog back."

"*Your* dog?"

She gestured in Maggie's direction without looking at her. "Maggie is my dog, yes. I'm Mary Culberson. Ken Culberson's ex-wife."

Chapter 8

I stared at the woman. Her wealthy ex-husband had died today, and now, a few hours later, she'd emerged from the dead. Could she have faked her own death in order to get away with his murder? Beside me, Maggie assumed an aggressive posture as she barked relentlessly. Her hackles were raised, her head lowered, and her paws spread wide. I understood the sentiment.

"Ken said that you were dead. That you died in a hit-and-run accident."

She nodded, averted her gaze, and gave what I read as a play-acted sigh intended to rouse my sympathies. "I was badly injured and was in a coma for a few days, but I recovered. I felt I had no choice but to mislead him, for my own protection." She gestured at the chair beside her. "Mind if I sit down?"

"Go ahead." I made a halfhearted effort at quieting Maggie, but was too anxious to hear whatever Mary had to say for herself. Mary ignored the noisy dog and took a seat. Her features betrayed the obvious tension of someone deliberately pretending to be not at all affected by something especially bothersome.

"What do you mean . . . 'for your own protection'?"

"Ken was a violent man, and I decided I'd be better off with him thinking that I was dead. Before he got the chance to make me that way himself." She shut her eyes and took a halting breath. "Now *he* is."

"Our impressions of your late ex-husband are

vastly different. Mine was that he was the gentle-giant sort."

"You weren't married to him. He physically abused me several times."

"Did you report this to the police?"

She shook her head. "He would've killed me."

Her delivery struck me as well-rehearsed; she'd anticipated my obvious questions and was giving me stock responses. It *was* true, however, that I'd spent only a few hours with Ken, and maybe what she was saying was possible. Ruby had said Ken was dangerous, but Yolanda had said the exact opposite. The tie-breaker here was Maggie, who was still barking her head off at Mary.

"You've had run-ins with Ken's dog, I see," I said over the noise level.

Mary gave Maggie only a darting glance, then answered in clipped tones, "She's my dog, now that Ken's dead. She'll get used to me."

"How did you find out about that? He died just this morning. And you two obviously haven't been in close contact. Understatement of the year, since he'd thought you were dead."

"I own a police scanner. I happened to be listening to it this morning."

Except for her annoyance at the dog's barking that was tightening her features, her demeanor was so casual that I said in unmasked sarcasm, "The news must have come as quite a shock."

"It did, actually."

"How did you trick Ken into believing that you were dead?"

"That wasn't by design. Someone at the hospital made a mistake, contacted him as next of kin and said that I'd passed away. When I found out about the error, I knew it was my ticket to freedom. I wouldn't have to live in fear any longer."

Her lines, delivered in a halting half whisper, struck me as overacting. "When did your accident occur?"

"A year ago last winter."

This matched what Ken and Ruby had said. "Ken told me you were in a coma for a year."

She shook her head. "It was only a few days. And, as you can see, I'm perfectly fine now."

"Okay, but if someone at the hospital accidentally reported your death during your coma of 'only a few days,' the time line is way off. Ken thought you died last spring."

She shrugged and let out a nervous laugh. "That Ken could never keep his facts straight. He always marched to his own drummer. And right into brick walls."

"Ken would have known the difference between your having died eighteen months ago or a couple of months ago." This was beginning to make sense now. "You were deliberately conning him, weren't you," I said, crossing my arms and leaning back in my chair. The woman repulsed me. "Let me guess. You found someone to pose as your nurse and tricked Ken into paying for full-time, in-home nursing care for more than a year. Then you faked being comatose whenever Ken came to visit you."

The guilty look on her face told me all I needed to know, although she cried, "That's not true! I *did* need a full-time nurse, because I was so badly hurt! And besides, *he* was a wife-beater! I felt in danger for my life. I let him think I was in a coma and then dead so he wouldn't kill me!"

"How did Ken get the impression that *he* was driving the car that hit you?"

She balled her fists and said nothing for a moment. "Look Allida, I'm not here to get the fifth degree. I just want my dog."

"That's another thing that's really puzzling. How did you know where to find Maggie?"

"After I heard about Ken's death, I drove out there . . . to see if the police needed my help. I saw you pick Maggie up from Yolanda's, and I followed you. So that I could get my dog back."

"Well, you wasted your time, because there's no way I'm letting you take Maggie."

She snorted. "There's no way you can stop me. She's my dog, not yours."

"Ken officially appointed me as her guardian in his will."

Her eyebrows shot up. She was momentarily nonplussed by my statement, her features tensing and splots of red forming on her cheeks. She made a fist and pounded her thigh. "He had no right to do that. He and I bought Maggie together while we were still married, and our divorce entitled me to half of everything we owned in common, *including* the dog. When Maggie was a puppy, Ken told me he was leaving her his money in a trust fund, so that *I* could take proper care of her. That's what he wanted. Only he thought I died first."

Disconcerted at the ramifications of her story, I glanced at the dog, who was still letting out the occasional *woof* from her stance beside me. Damn it all! Yesterday I'd made a crucial mistake during my standard procedures when taking on a new client. I'd neglected to have Ken fill out my customized form that would give Maggie's full background. Talk about something coming back to bite me! I needed to compare Maggie's purchase date with the date of Ken's divorce. Maggie seemed to be about two years old. It was possible that the divorce had been finalized less than two years ago, so her claim could be authentic.

I feigned indifference and countered, "According to my records, Ken bought Maggie after the two of you were already divorced. And even if what you're saying is true, I'm not releasing this dog to anyone until I have the chance to determine where Maggie will be best taken care of."

She let out a puff of indignation, then rose and stepped toward me. This also meant that she was nearing Maggie, who resumed barking. "Let me get this straight. You're basing your decision on who should inherit a couple of million dollars on a *dog's* best interests?" she asked, emphasizing the word "dog" as if she considered canines to be inanimate objects.

A couple of *million* dollars? For an instant, I weighed the notion of keeping Maggie myself—buying that large homestead where Maggie could be a happy member of my canine menagerie. But that hadn't been what Ken had stipulated; he'd wanted me to choose someone from his and Maggie's circle of friends and family. Besides, that's not how I wanted to earn my money. I answered firmly, "Yes. According to Ken's instructions in his will."

She shook her head and gestured as though she intended to grab me by the shoulders, but thought better of it when Maggie snarled at her. "That dog is half mine."

Maggie bared her teeth and growled at Mary. I decided not to correct the behavior.

"Unless you can prove that to me and get some court order to stop me, I'm proceeding as if Maggie had been strictly Ken's dog, which is certainly the way she's behaving."

She gestured at Maggie. "That's Ken's doing. He deliberately kept the two of us from bonding."

"That must have been very disappointing to you."

My sarcasm clearly not lost on her, she pursed her lips and visually sized me up. "Let me give you a friendly little warning. Don't mess with me. I have friends in high places."

"Since Boulder is more than a mile above sea level, most of us can make that claim."

Meanwhile, Maggie was again barking away, and out of frustration more than anything else, I murmured, "Maggie, sit."

To my surprise, she did; plus she quit barking. Just testing, really, I then said, "Maggie, lie down."

Again, to my happy surprise, she obeyed.

"Good dog, Maggie!" I was so delighted that I knelt and gave her a hug around the neck. She looked at me with those big brown eyes, full of devotion, and I knew I was hooked.

Mary, however, clicked her tongue and muttered, "So big deal. The dog can finally do what any idiot dog can do. Christ almighty! Watching you react, you'd think she just delivered the Gettysburg address."

I eyed her at length. "I've got to say that I can't really picture you and Ken together."

She snorted. "He had certain charms."

"Such as his money?"

She smirked at me, then whirled on a heel and marched out my door. Maggie promptly stopped barking and wagged her tail, giving me that eager expression that resembled a prideful smile.

"What a bitch," I murmured. "No offense, Maggie," I said, giving her a pat. She looked at me with her adorable eyes. "Don't worry. Bet you dollars to dog biscuits she would have said she'd be right back with proof of your date-of-purchase and her date-of-divorce if what she was claiming were true. In the meantime, I'm fighting back."

I fetched Officer Hobbes's business card and snatched up the phone, explaining to Maggie, "I have a feeling that the police will want to look into how Mary Martin Culberson was bilking your owner, don't you?"

Maggie sat down and looked up at me, the fur of her tail sweeping along a wide arc on my floor.

The next two hours were taken with client appointments at my office, so I let Maggie take over Russell's office. Afterward, my confidence about preventing Mary from getting Maggie was on the wane. She had to be familiar with the messy state of Ken's trailer. That would zap anyone's bravura to pronounce that she'd provide documentation momentarily—even if she did know it existed. Plus, I'd remembered that Joanne Palmer, Maggie's veterinarian, had said that she'd met Mary.

Joanne would surely have records indicating the birth date and ownership. I called her office and left a message with her receptionist asking that she call me back. Considering our contentious first meeting, it struck me as unlikely that she'd rush to do so.

After examining Maggie's claw marks in the wood, I put *Buy Russell a new door* on my list of things to do. Then I called Yolanda to see if she could shed any light on whether Ken and Mary had still been married when Ken purchased Maggie. If so, Mary and I might be in for a legal battle, because there was no way I would ever allow that woman to take custody of Maggie.

Yolanda answered on the first ring. I identified myself and asked whether or not the police were still investigating next door.

"Oh, you better believe it. Got the whole place dug up now."

"They're digging up Ken's lawn?"

"Mmm-hmmm. It's like they're digging for oil."

That was interesting. They must be looking for more bones, though the bigger issue would surely be how and why someone's stolen bones had wound up in some construction site in Ken's neighborhood. "I was wondering how well you knew Mary, Ken's ex-wife."

"Miss Hoity Toit? Oh, she'd never associate with the likes of me. No one could figure out why she'd associate with the likes of Ken either, for that matter."

"Were you in the neighborhood before they moved in?"

"Before she moved in, sure. Ken was here long before either of us, though."

"How about Maggie? Was she Ken's before or after their divorce? Do you know?"

"Can't say for sure. But Mary never lived here with Maggie. I do know that much."

"So she had moved out by the time Ken brought Maggie home?"

"Right. Weren't like her to take to something soft and cuddly. That kinda described Ken, too, now that I think about it." She sighed. "Poor guy. Wrecked his life when he met that . . . woman."

"Did you ever see Mary with Maggie?"

"Just enough to know she hated that dog."

I was curious about whether or not Yolanda had any suspicions about Mary's faked death, so I asked casually, "Did you go to her funeral services?"

"They didn't hold 'em in Colorado. 'Cording to Ken, the services were held back east or someplace, wherever her people are from. Not that I would've gone even if they were right next door, mind you."

There was no hint of deceit in her voice. She truly seemed to believe that Mary was dead, too. She also appeared to have had no idea that Ken Culberson had been wealthy. Testing, I asked, "Did you get the impression that Mary had married Ken for his money?"

"Did you say 'his money'?" She laughed heartily. "Oh, right. That must've been it. She just took one look at that luxurious trailer of his and was swept right off her feet." She had another laughing fit. "Matter of fact, ever since my Robert passed away, I gots to beat off suitors with a stick for that very reason."

Despite the seriousness of the situation, her words made me smile. Also, it was reassuring to know that there was at least one person in Ken's life who'd apparently cared for him for his own sake and not his money. "Thanks for speaking with me, Yolanda. I'd better let you go now."

"If'n you're having trouble finding someone to take his dog, I'd be happy to. Unless you want to see the dog stay in the family, that is."

"Did he *have* family?"

"Mmm-hmm. His brother Arlen lives in the area. He and Ken had a falling out, but he still came over to visit Ken once a month or so."

"Do you happen to have Arlen's address or phone number?"

"No, sorry."

"That's okay. I'm sure there's only one Arlen Culberson in town. Thanks again."

"No problem. But like I said, watch your backside," Yolanda said and then hung up.

The phone rang. I glanced at my watch, prepared to be surprised if this was Joanne Palmer calling me back so soon. It had been a long, hard day, and I found myself hoping that this would be my last appointment, calling to reschedule. I picked up the phone and said, "Hello, this is—"

"Allida," my mother interrupted. "I just heard on the news that the police are investigating the death of a man in a trailer park. And that his body was discovered by his dog's trainer. Please tell me that wasn't you."

"I wish I could," I murmured.

"Oh, my God. Was that Maggie's owner?"

"Yes, and that's not the half of it. Ken left all his money to her and appointed me her temporary guardian, and now his ex-wife, who Ken thought was dead, has shown up and says that she and Ken were joint owners of Maggie before their divorce."

"So she wants Maggie."

"Right. And she's this . . . horrid gold digger. She's getting this dog over my—" I stopped myself from saying "dead body," realizing the possibility, somewhere, of a killer who would be willing to turn that phrase into more than a figure of speech. "I don't know what to do. I don't even have an approximate purchase date for Maggie, and I don't know when they divorced."

"That might not matter, if he was smart. He could have put a clause in his divorce settlement about his having sole custody of Maggie."

I scoffed. "You never met Ken. He was something of an idiot savant . . . totally naive and incapable in some respects."

"Call my friend, Carol Ann Wilson. She's a financial advisor for divorces. Maybe she can give you some insights."

I glanced again at my watch and decided I had time to make the call and got the number from my mother. Then she said, "I take it Maggie will be living with us for a while."

" 'Fraid so. I hope you don't mind."

"Of course not. Living with dogs is easy. For one

thing, you know not to expect your *dogs* to keep you informed."

I winced. I'd started to think I was going to get off scot-free for failing to call my mother at the first opportunity and tell her about the mess I was in. Before I could apologize, Mom said, "My student's here. I'll see you at home."

"Have a good—"

She hung up. Her next student could be in for a rough flight. Mom's a pilot and gives flying lessons part-time.

I called Carol Ann and introduced myself as "Allida Babcock, Marilyn's daughter."

"Hi, Allida. How are you?" she asked pleasantly.

"Fine. But something's come up at work that I'm hoping you can help me with. A client of mine died recently, and I need to know how to find out about some of the terms of his divorce settlement."

"Did the divorce take place in Boulder?"

"Yes, about two years ago."

"That's all a matter of public record. You could go to the Clerk of Court's office at the courthouse."

"Great. Thanks."

"In fact, I'm going to be there with a client this afternoon anyway. If you'd like, I can look the information up for you myself."

"Could you? That'd be great. The couple's name was Culberson. Ken and Mary."

There was a pause, and I assumed Carol Ann was simply writing down the names, but she said, "That's a coincidence. Mary Culberson was a former client of mine."

"She was?"

"Briefly. She hired me and then refused to take my advice. If memory serves, twice a year, her ex received large payments for some television circuit he'd invented. He wanted to give her half of those payments semiannually, as well. Against my advice, she insisted on demanding a one-time cash settlement. She was impossible to work with—always insistent that she knew everyone's job better than they did. Eventually she fired both me and her lawyer. Even so, she called me afterwards, absolutely livid, to tell me how she'd made a paltry settlement, something on the order of two or three hundred thousand."

"Did she ever claim to you that Ken had physically abused her?"

"No, and it was quite the other way around. One time, Ken came in with a black eye. He wouldn't tell me how he got it. Then she got so irate during a meeting that she punched him, right in front of me and both lawyers."

"Do you remember if they had a dog? Or if they ever discussed the dog's custody?"

"No . . . I'm pretty sure the subject of a dog never came up, but I can't say for certain. Want me to check the records for that?"

"Could you please? I need any information on the dog, including the date of purchase, as well as the date the Culbersons' divorce was finalized." I could see my next client approaching—a woman carrying her puppy. Maggie, too, spotted them and started barking. Uh, oh. Wrong client for such a harsh greeting. I said hurriedly, "Carol Ann, thank you so much. I've got to go. I'll call you from my mom's." I hung up and rushed to the door.

Sally—my new client—had arrived early. I held up my palm to indicate for her to wait a moment. Sally had called to complain that the dog was afraid of nearly everything that moved. Having a large golden clawing at the other side of a door was not going to be conducive to overcoming those fears.

The woman, paling at the sight of Maggie, looked ready to flee. I shouted through the glass to her, "I'm going to put this dog in the other office. I'll be right back."

I grabbed a rawhide bone from a cabinet drawer, then dragged Maggie into Russell's office with me. Moving his couch back a few inches, I then dropped the bone back there. This way she would occupy herself with trying to figure out how to retrieve the bone. Sending up a small prayer that she wouldn't shred the upholstery in the process, I left, noting that so far, my strategy seemed to be working. Maggie was indeed transfixed by the hidden treasure and was trying to wedge herself between the wall and the back of the couch.

I returned to my office, where Sally was seated along with her mixed-breed puppy, Sebastian, though my current view of him was of his rear end as he burrowed behind her cardigan. I apologized profusely and explained that, no, their having been greeted by a large barking dog was not part of my desensitizing training, but rather an unfortunate complication. I gave her the option of rescheduling, but she declined.

Not repeating my mistake with Ken and Maggie, we began our session by filling out a full background report on Sebastian. My first impression was that Sally herself was actually much more timid and jumpy than her puppy. Fearfulness in dogs is one of the hardest problems to overcome and can be very serious, because a fearful dog is often a biter. In this case, it was clear that I would have to start by assuring the owner that her dog was picking up on her own nervousness.

Not fifteen minutes into our session, Mary barged through the door. Sally gasped and shrank back into her chair. The puppy jumped and started yipping, while cowering behind his owner's chair.

"God! More damned barking dogs," Mary snarled. She pointed at me. "I have to speak to you for a minute."

"Not now. I'm with a client."

"Suit yourself, but I'm here as a courtesy. Just wanted to tell you that you'd better get yourself a lawyer."

I sighed in exasperation and turned to Sally. "I'm sorry. This will just take a minute."

"That's okay. Take your time." She smiled nervously. It was quite obvious that, between Maggie's greeting and Mary's interruption, I was not making the best of impressions on my client.

I held the now-scratched-up door to Russell's office.

Maggie started barking, but at least didn't barge through the door—yet. Mary started to follow me, then turned to Sally and said, "If I were you, I wouldn't waste my time waiting on her. Unless you want to find yourself in my shoes, having to hire a lawyer to get your dog back."

Incensed, I thrust my finger in Mary's face. "You'd better ask your lawyer for a definition of the word 'slander.' " I turned back to Sally, whose jaw was agape as she pressed back into her chair in horror. "Again, I'm sorry. I'll explain everything just as soon as I handle this."

For the sake of Maggie and my clients, I gently closed the door behind me instead of slamming it. "What?" I asked through a tight jaw.

She glanced at the fervently barking Maggie, but then returned her focus to me. "My lawyer tells me that we can get punitive damages from you for trying to keep Maggie yourself, in spite of my husband's wishes."

"Your *ex*-husband, you mean, and I am doing no such thing."

"My lawyer also told me that since Ken believed his dog was channeling me, he obviously meant to leave his money to me, had he not believed that I'd already died."

"A thought pattern which would, in turn, make you the prime suspect."

She grinned at me. "Maybe so, but fortunately, I have an alibi."

"Good for you."

Mary gave me a haughty smirk. "I'm innocent of my late husband's murder. But I want what is rightfully mine. Besides, anyone with half a brain could figure out that Ken's last-minute change to his will wasn't legal. You're holding onto this dog when you have no legal rights whatsoever to do so."

"Look, lady. Yesterday I was hired by a sweet but eccentric man to work with his sweet but badly behaved golden. I want nothing more than to see to it that Maggie is placed in a good home and to never have to hear about Ken's inheritance again."

"Good for you," she fired back at me with relish. "As for me, I want what is rightfully mine. And my lawyer is going to see to it that I get every penny that's coming to me."

"Perhaps it's time you let this lawyer of yours speak for himself. Up until I hear from him and the courts tell me otherwise, I'm going to do what I think is right."

Her voice and mannerisms suddenly softened. "Maybe I can help you figure that out. See, if you give this dog to anyone but me, you're not getting a dime of my late husband's money, Allie; however, just to hurry this along, I'll cut you in on a percentage or two of the inheritance. We're talking thousands of dollars, just for you to do what the courts will eventually decide anyway. It'll be way more money than you make in a whole month of dog duty."

I gritted my teeth and put my hand on the doorknob. "Ms. Culberson, or whatever you wish to be called, I will see to it that you don't get this dog if it's the last thing I do." I swung the door open and held it for her.

She pursed her lips and, again, narrowed her eyes at me. "Watch what you wish for."

She marched past me, then stopped and chuckled. Sporting a big grin, she turned back to me, gesturing at her surroundings with a sweep of both arms. "By the way. Seems that your client took my advice and left."

The phone rang, helping me to keep a caustic reply to myself. I answered. In a smoldering voice, the caller immediately said, "This is Dr. Thames. I've just completed a rather lengthy interview with the Boulder police."

"Yes, I gave them your name."

"We're even, then. I've known all along that he was leaving his money to his dog. So when they asked me if I knew of anyone who might have a motive to kill Ken Culberson, your name was the first one that came to mind."

He hung up before I could reply.

Chapter 9

Maggie fell asleep in the back seat as I drove home without needing her harness. To me, however, it felt as though a belt were tightly cinched across my rib cage. Through no fault of my own, I was making enemies of the small circle of people in Ken Culberson's life, one of whom might very well have murdered him. I ran bits and pieces of past conversations through my head—with Ken's therapist, Maggie's vet, T-Rex's owner, and his now-no-longer-late ex-wife.

Ruby had warned me about Ken, yet he had been nothing but friendly toward her. In retrospect, it seemed to me that she'd deliberately lied to me, driven by some ulterior motive to suit her own agenda. Maybe she knew about Ken's wealth, had designs on him, and wanted to keep away the competition. Or perhaps her reasons weren't as sinister as all that. Maybe she had been the major complainant against Maggie to Animal Control and had simply convinced herself that her actions against Ken had been justified.

Regardless, here I was having taken temporary ownership of an orphan dog who had been overly attached to her owner. Without him, she was going to be horribly insecure, which can drive dogs to such awful behaviors as self-mutilation and defecating inside the home. I shuddered at the thought of how *that* would go over with my mother.

"So," I muttered to myself. "I'm ticking off a murderer while I try to decide who gets a millionaire dog that might

mother's carpeting. My life's a multicolored
ll right."

to find a good home for Maggie soon. Maybe
brother would be the answer. I tried to cheer myself
that possibility while quieting the nagging voice in
head: if Ken had thought his brother should own
ggie, he'd have stated so in his will.

Maggie awoke as I pulled into the garage. I left her in
car until I could properly greet my dogs in their right-
order—from top dog down. This meant my German
shepherd, Pavlov, followed by Sage—a male collie who was
top dog when my mother entered the house but yielded
authority and lagged back when I entered—and last, by
my buff-and-white-colored cocker spaniel, Doppler. My
mother wasn't home yet so the totem pole consisted exclusively of four-leggers. Then I brought in Maggie.

Properly prepared, the dogs got along fine. I headed
straight to the TV. Ken's death—reported only as having
been under "suspicious circumstances"—was on the
evening news.

I made dinner when my mother got home, and while we
ate, she expressed concern for the ordeal I'd suffered regarding Ken's death. She'd obviously forgiven me for not calling
to tell her about that "ordeal" myself. After dinner, I found
Ken's brother's name listed in the Longmont directory and
called him. The man who answered said, "Yeah?" instead of
hello. His voice was eerily similar to his brother's.

"My name is Allida Babcock. Is this Arlen Culberson?"

"Yeah."

"Your brother hired me yesterday to work with his
dog. Though I'd only just met him, I liked Ken a great
deal. I'm terribly sorry for your loss."

"Yeah. Me, too. I mean, thanks. What can I do for
you?" His voice betrayed no discernible emotion but, after all, why *would* he express his feelings to a total stranger
on the phone?

"Ken put me in the position of trying t[o] custodianship of his dog. I was hoping that the could arrange to meet in the near future so that discuss the matter."

There was a pause. "He asked *you* to do that? Last t[i] Ken spoke to me about his will, he told me he was planning on leaving all his money to Maggie. Did he go through with that?"

Bone weary, I rubbed my forehead. This again—Ken's money first and foremost on everyone's minds. "Yes, though I don't know anything about the legalities of such a thing. For all I know, the courts might say the will isn't legal and your brother's assets are to be divided among his survivors. I'm just following through on what he asked of me. Which was to find his dog a good home." In the corner of my vision, Mom looked up from the book she was reading and gave me a reassuring smile.

"Oh. Right. Of course. And I def'nitely want the dog. In any case. Even if the dog's got no money. I didn't even know Ken had kept his will that way. That was almost two years ago when we talked about it. Back when he first got the puppy and him and Mary was divorcing."

"Do you happen to know if the divorce was finalized before or after Ken bought Maggie?"

"Before. They was already divorced, *then* he got Maggie. I seen to that myself. Tol' Ken he'd best be careful so's Mary wouldn't be able to use his pup in a tug-of-war to weasel more money outta him."

"Good advice," I said, though I was thinking that Arlen's recollections could be tainted by his knowledge of the dog's inheritance. "Does Maggie know you at all?"

"Oh, sure. The dog's a good buddy of mine."

"Good," I murmured, though we would have to see about that. At least Arlen was a possible candidate for adopting Maggie.

"Ken 'n' me used to talk all the time. Course, it made it harder that he didn't drive and RTD don't get all that

determine two of us we could

close. Nearest stop's ten blocks away. But I'd come over to his trailer every couple of weeks."

Then why the "falling out" that Yolanda had mentioned? Why had Ken cut his own brother out of the will? I would probably have to learn the answers, but this was not the time to ask. "Are you free tomorrow morning?"

"Yeah, sure. Name the time and place."

I wanted to see for myself how suitable the home itself would be, so we agreed to meet at nine A.M. at his home, and he gave me directions.

After I'd hung up the phone, Mom asked, "How did—" She was interrupted when Maggie galloped into the room and leapt onto her lap. "Off!" she cried, giving Maggie a good shove. Maggie landed on all fours with a little whine. Mom said to her, "Well, sorry, but you've got to learn some basic manners!" She looked at me. "You're planning on taking tomorrow off to work with Maggie. Right?"

That was more an instruction than a question, and I normally did take midweek days off and worked weekends, but business had been too demanding lately. "I've got some time off in the morning, but I'm too busy in the afternoon to take time off." I looked at Maggie, who was panting and looking very insecure. I very much doubted that my mother knew how prone this made Maggie to lose basic-housebreaking skills, nor did I wish to share this particular insight. "You might want to keep her in the backyard as much as possible."

The phone rang and I answered. It was Carol Ann Wilson. She gave me the date of the divorce decree and said, "There was no mention of a dog at all in the divorce settlement for the Culbersons." I thanked her, thinking to myself that this, at least, was looking good. Their divorce had been finalized in early June, slightly more than two full years ago. Mary was not going to be able to claim joint ownership of Maggie.

Exhausted from the events of the last twenty-four hours, I went to bed early and fell right to sleep. During bleary, half-stages of slumber, I dreamt that someone was trying to knock down my door.

My mom called, "Wake up, Allie," and an instant later, my door flew open and a seventy-pound golden retriever burst into the room and launched herself onto me and my bed.

While struggling to push her off me, I cried, "What's happening?"

"The thunder," Mom said. "She's going nuts. Didn't you hear it?"

"No. I . . ."

Maggie's whole body was trembling. She'd moved to the side of me on my bed and was desperately trying to dig her way down and under it.

"I'm sorry," Mom said. "I just haven't been able to do anything with her, and she's got all the other dogs worked up, too."

There was another crack of thunder outside, and Maggie resumed clawing at the sheets and blankets with a feverish intensity. Before I could get up and get my wits together, she'd leapt onto the floor and was now squeezing herself underneath the bed.

"What do we do?" Mom asked.

"Phosphorus pills. I've got some in my glove box. We should also get her down into the basement where it'll be as quiet as possible."

Mom grabbed Maggie's collar. "You get the pills. I'll get the dog downstairs."

Happy to let my mother take the more physical part, I rushed out to the garage and found the small bottle of medication. The key was to get the dog to swallow an initial dose before he or she got into the kind of frenzy that Maggie was now fraught with, though.

To my pleasant surprise, once we were in the basement and I was seated on Mom's old couch, Maggie hopped onto my lap and settled down. Though she trembled terribly when the thunder hit, she stayed on my lap. I talked to her soothingly, and eventually we both fell asleep.

By morning, if I'd had a tail, it would have been dragging. Mom had already left for an early-morning flight instruction by the time I painfully made my way up the stairs from our basement. I'd slept in a semi-upright position and was pretty sure that the circulation had been permanently cut off from my feet and ankles from holding such a heavy dog on my lap for so long.

Maggie, on the other hand, looked fresh and ready to take on the day. She attached herself to my hip, at least to the extent that the other dogs allowed. "Time to meet your uncle," I told her.

I got her into the car, but didn't have the energy to get her into the seatbelt harness. She'd slept in my back seat yesterday, so she was starting to mellow a little. I gave her a rawhide bone, and she gnawed on that peacefully.

In his straw hat, plaid shirt, baggy jeans, and leather boots, Arlen Culberson was dressed like a rancher, but lived in a modest two-story home in one of the residential neighborhoods that had sprung up to surround the golf courses between Boulder and Longmont. He was a thinner, older version of his brother, and I got the perverse image of him as Ken, after having been left out in the sun to dry like a raisin. His open garage was full of television sets in various states of disrepair. He was tinkering at a workbench in the back when I pulled into his driveway. He tried to give Maggie a pat through the car window, but he quickly withdrew his hand when she barked at him. In and of itself, the barking meant nothing. Many dogs get territorial when confined in such a small enclosure as a car. For the time being I left her in the back seat and got out to talk with Arlen.

"Do you live here alone?" I asked.

"Yeah. Divorced, and the wife got the kids." He gave a

casual shrug, but his features revealed some resentment there. "Typical story."

"Do you have a dog?"

"No, but that don't mean I don't like 'em. I do. I just don't happen to own one."

"Have you ever?"

"Oh, sure."

"What kind?"

"A mutt." His face had taken on a reddish hue, and I suspected he was lying.

"I love dogs, of course. Do you happen to have any pictures of yours?"

"No. My ex-wife got the photo albums, too."

"What was your dog's name?"

"Umm, Fido."

I nodded, but was now convinced he was lying. Unfortunate, really, but this wasn't in itself going to make me rule out Arlen as Maggie's permanent guardian. "Fido is a common name, but I have to say it's one I've never understood. It's always sounded to me like an acronym an engineer might come up with—First In, Dud Out."

I grinned, mentally patting myself on the back. Here was a man tinkering with electronic parts, and I'd managed to forge a conversational bridge between his life's work and mine. That was as close to charming as I ever came. Arlen, however, just scratched his nose and muttered, "He was a stray. Followed my kids home from school, and that was the dog's name on his collar."

I nodded again, thinking I could press the issue and point out that most "strays" didn't have collars, but decided to let it pass.

He glanced over at the car, where Maggie was watching us intently. "So if you pick me as her new owner, does that mean I inherit the money?"

"I'm honestly not sure, Mr. Culberson."

"Arlen. Please."

"Is inheriting your brother's money important to you?"

It was a stupid question, I knew, but I wanted to see his reaction. He furrowed his brow and looked at me. "Of course. I surely wouldn't turn it down. But no more so than it would be to most folks. Wouldn't buy a yuppie estate and move up the top of the hill, either. And I got enough of a yard to let Maggie roam around a bit. Yard's as big as Kenny's was at the trailer, and my house is a lot nicer."

"That's good," I murmured. "What's much more important to me, though, is how good of a caretaker you're going to be for Maggie."

"So you're going to give her to me, then?" Arlen asked, brightening at the prospect.

"Not necessarily. I haven't made up my mind yet. But let's get Maggie out of the car."

Arlen stiffened. "She's . . . never been here before. She's not going to be comfortable. I can guarantee it. But that don't mean she won't ever feel at home here."

"Right. I'm going to take all of that into consideration."

"Oh, sure. Course. It'll be good to have Maggie. She's a good dog."

Truth be told, I couldn't bring myself to believe that anyone who didn't like dogs enough to own one would call Maggie a "good dog." Maggie leapt out the car. I kept a leash on her. She was content to sniff the floors as Arlen gave us a tour. They ignored each other almost completely.

When our tour was complete, Arlen escorted us back into the garage. "As you can see, she'll have a lot more room in my house than she had in Ken's. I even got a fenced yard for her."

"Do you want to see if she'll walk on leash with you?"

"Oh, er, you want I should take her leash?"

"You don't have to."

"I'd rather not, then. How 'bout we schedule another visit another time, and I'll show you how good we get along then. I'd like a chance to . . . I got an appointment to keep. Have to leave in a few minutes."

Arlen was looking decidedly uncomfortable now. He had taken off his hat a moment earlier and was now turning it in a slow circle with his hands.

"It must have been very disappointing to you when you found out that your brother was leaving all of his money to his dog."

Arlen put his hat back on and gave me a sheepish smile. "That was just Kenny, for you. He loved that . . . he loved Maggie so much, and he never did think twice about his money. It wasn't important to him, and so he couldn't imagine why it was important to other people."

I nodded in agreement with Arlen's assessment.

He gave me another smile, which could only be described as nervous, at best. "There wasn't anything in his will that specifically excluded me from being able to get Maggie, was there?"

"I don't think so, no. Was there a reason you expected there to be one?"

"No. No." He shook his head. "We've had our share of disagreements, is all. Ken and me. Just like in any family. I'm sure you know what I mean."

"Yes, I do. I've got a brother myself." We both stared at Maggie, who seemed content to sit between us. This was decidedly un-Maggie-like behavior, but I doubted it would last, unfortunately. "It was nice meeting you, Arlen."

He shook my hand enthusiastically. "Nice meeting you, too. So . . . you'll call me, right? Or just drop by?" He reached into his jean back pocket and gave me his card. "About when you want Maggie to come back?"

I gave the card a quick glance and replied, "Yes. Unless you'd rather set up a time now."

"No, I'd just as soon . . . wait a bit. Get things fixed up for her a bit."

" 'Fixed up'?"

"Maybe build a doghouse, that sort of thing."

"Don't go out of your way, Arlen. As I said before, I haven't made a decision yet and may need at least a couple of days."

"Okay. Be hearing from you then." He watched as Maggie eagerly hopped back into the back seat. I read his card. He was self-employed as a television repairman. His company name was Culberson TV Repairs. I wondered if, before Ken had struck it rich with his invention, that title had once been Culberson Brothers. He lifted a palm as we drove away. I needed to drop Maggie off at Mom's house. I just couldn't have her with me, tearing up Russell's office or sitting in my car for hours on end.

We drove home. Maggie barreled past me and through the door, toward my mother. I managed to press the button on my noisemaker just before the exuberant dog could jump on my mother. The noise, which had emanated from my pocket, did its trick and she pulled up short and looked around.

Her attempt to rush toward my mother was a massive breach of dog etiquette, and Pavlov let her know this by barking at her and snapping in the direction of Maggie's muzzle. This could have deteriorated into a fight, because Maggie was unaccustomed to being in another dog's domain. Fortunately, Maggie did the right thing and backed off, while I played my part and greeted Pavlov first, then the other two dogs.

Meanwhile, Mom went back to searching for something in the junk drawer. She said over her shoulder, "I listened to an interesting little piece about your furry friend here on my drive home from the airport this morning."

"You heard something about Maggie on the radio?" I asked in alarm.

"From our favorite talk-show host."

"Oh, no." A friend of mine, whose softball team I played on—and we had a game tonight, in fact—was forever blabbing things on the air about existing police investigations. Where she got her information was a mystery to me.

"Yes, Tracy broadcast the fact that Maggie, here, was the recipient of a substantial inheritance, and that you, local dog psychologist, were in the process of determining who Maggie's caretaker should be."

"That's great," I muttered. Though she was a fun person to be around and I enjoyed playing on her softball team, Tracy Truett was not one to hesitate to blab someone's secret on the air, without considering the possible consequences.

"Now everyone listening to today's show knows that we've got a millionaire dog in our yard."

Chapter 10

Though perturbed at my deejay friend, I didn't have time to stew about it. I wanted to pay a visit to Ruby before my first appointment to see how T-Rex was doing. I said good-bye to my mother, then had to go through considerable effort to get out the door without Maggie following. She was so good at getting her muzzle into the doorway, in fact, that I finally had to partially close the door on her face while pushing on her nose with one hand. Maggie was making me feel like a complete novice dog handler.

Ruby was home. I knew she'd blow up at me if I admitted I was there to check on her dog, so I said I was "in the neighborhood and thought I'd say hello."

She smirked and said, "Seein' as we're such close friends you mean?"

Okay, not one of my better excuses. "How's T-Rex feeling today?"

She gave me a hateful glare but, to my surprise, swung the door open and gestured for me to enter. "See for yourself. He's his old self again. I should've trusted myself. I knew there was nothing wrong with him." As I stepped around her to look at her dog, she grumbled, "Now I s'pose you're gonna try to convince me to hire you. And I wouldn't pay you to squeeze his butt."

"Good thing butt-squeezing isn't on my list of specialties, then." As devastating as that was to my self-image, I added to myself. Indeed, T-Rex seemed to be doing well.

He wagged his tail and sniffed my breath as I got down on one knee to pet him.

"So where's Maggie at?" Ruby asked. "Did she finally get herself taken to the pound?"

"No, she's got a temporary home and is doing fine."

"That won't last. Dog's a nuisance. Wait till this 'temporary' owner starts hearing from his neighbors."

"Had you told Ken about how annoying you found his dog to be?"

"Sure. Didn't do me no good, though."

Someone tapped on the screen door immediately behind me, and I quickly stood up. It was a tall, pretty, fortyish blonde, attractively dressed in black slacks and a beige silk blouse. She gave me a winning smile. "Hello. My name is Rachel Taylor. Is Ruby Benjamin here?"

"I'm here," Ruby answered, leaning around me to look at her visitor. "Come on in."

"I brought the job application you asked for," Rachel said, pulling a sheet of paper out of a folder as she entered the trailer.

"Application?"

"As I told you over the phone, for you to live in a person's home and provide care, we'll need references and work history."

She glanced at both sides of the form as if overwhelmed at the notion of filling it out, which was understandable for an illiterate person.

I said to her, "I'm glad T-Rex is doing better."

Ruby winced as though I'd let the cat out of the bag, which was true, but there was no way she was capable of being a health-care provider when she could misread the labels on her dog's medicine bottles.

"T-Rex?" Rachel repeated. "Was your dog ill?"

Ruby merely glared at me as if waiting for me to leave, but I felt it was important that Rachel Taylor know about Ruby's limitations for providing health care. "No, he was overmedicated the other day."

"Was not!" Ruby snarled. She screwed up her features and mumbled, "I gave him a double dosage by mistake. It was just an accident and it won't happen again." She shot me an accusatory glare, as if my spoiling her job opportunity was an unpardonable offense. It would have been a worse offense to allow someone like this to perhaps "double" dose a human being under her care.

Rachel Taylor's expression was inscrutable, yet I immediately sensed that she'd picked up on the intent of my statements. "Mail the application back to me once it's completed, Ruby. Or give me another call, and I'll come pick it up next time I'm in the area." Rachel gave her a warm smile, which was not returned.

Ruby grimaced and crossed her arms.

"I'd better be going," I said. "Take care, Ruby."

"Let me walk you to your car," Rachel said to me, then shifted her focus to Ruby. "You know, Ruby, having a friend and neighbor die unexpectedly like this is difficult. Sometimes we find ourselves grieving when we least expect to. Don't hesitate to call me if you want to talk."

"I won't," Ruby said evenly.

Rachel held the door for me, and we left together.

We walked a few steps away from Ruby's home so that we would be out of earshot. "What happened with the dog? Did she misread the directions on the medicine bottle?"

"I got the impression she couldn't read the prescription."

She sighed. "She won't be working for me anytime in the near future, then." Her face looked grim. "Too bad. An adult-care provider is a really difficult position to fill."

"Terry Thames gave me your card the other day." I turned and looked at Ken's trailer. "He said he'd referred Ken to you."

"Yes. Poor Ken was just so sweet and guileless. I had my hands full, trying to protect him from certain individuals who were intent on taking advantage of him. He spoke very highly of you, however."

"He did?" We'd only just met, though, the day before he died. "When?"

She gave me a small smile. "Actually, I'd asked around town about you before Ken ever came to see you. He needed someone excellent to work with Maggie, and you came highly recommended."

"Thank you." Considering the rancid opinions that Ken's psychologist and veterinarian had of me, this was music to my ears.

Her expression grew somber. "Ken and I spoke again, right before he was . . . before he died. He called me in a panic, because you had his dog and he was alone. Naturally, he told me about his decision to appoint you temporary guardian of Maggie. I told him he'd done the right thing. That you were the right person for the job."

"I'm not so sure of that," I muttered.

"Perhaps I can help you in deciding who gets his dog. Ken always expected his dog to outlive him. He had a weak heart and was overweight and . . ." She paused as if struggling with the sadness. "Anyway, he told me he didn't want Maggie to go to a stranger, and I'm fairly familiar with the people in Ken's life."

"Thanks. Bearing that in mind, what do you think of his brother, Arlen?"

She frowned a little and said, "He wouldn't be my top choice. For one thing, he pretty much hated Maggie. Terry Thames would be a good choice, however. He's good with dogs, and I know Ken trusted him implicitly."

I stifled a grimace at the thought of my rewarding Dr. Thames with Maggie and her money. "I'll keep that in mind, but Dr. Thames and I didn't hit it off."

"No? He *can* be rather full of himself sometimes. Typical doctor-as-god syndrome." She rolled her eyes, and I couldn't help but chuckle. She added thoughtfully, "Both he and his wife work and aren't home a lot." She paused and shook her head. "Come to think of it, I'm not sure who I *would* recommend. Too bad you can't just violate the conditions of the will and put the dog in a good home . . . let the courts resolve who should inherit the money."

"My thoughts exactly," I muttered.

"It's all so sad. I spoke to the police at length. Apparently he was murdered, though they didn't say how."

"They didn't tell me that either." He had to have been suffocated, I thought; if he'd ODed on the ACP, the police would probably still be considering his death a possible suicide.

"It's so hard to believe," Rachel continued. "The man couldn't possibly have brought himself to hurt anyone, regardless of the circumstances. If only the burglar had realized that."

" 'Burglar'?"

She nervously fluffed her short, blond hair as she spoke. "That's an assumption on my part, but the papers this morning said that he'd been asphyxiated during a struggle. Asphyxiation seems to be a code-word these days for strangulation. All I could think was that he could have battled with a burglar and lost. He was so careless with his cash. He'd told me he'd been at the police station that night, and the way he always bellowed when speaking, some punk probably overheard him talk about how he kept cash in a shoe box, then followed him home."

Ken couldn't have been killed in a burglary—at least not because he had interrupted one in progress. The man had died on his bed. I didn't want to share this information, however, and instead feigned ignorance and asked, "He kept his money in a shoe box?"

She nodded. "He had two. One for the hundreds, the other for the smaller denominations."

Someone cleared her throat harshly and we both looked over. Yolanda was standing with her arms crossed, glaring at us from her side of the fence. In a strangely loud and carefully enunciated voice, Rachel said, "Hello. How are you doing today?"

"I *do* just fine, missy. I can *hear* just fine, too, so you don't have to shout. And I un'erstand English just fine, too."

"I didn't mean to imply—"

"Course you didn't mean to imply nothin'. You jus' don't know any better. Always making assumptions about people."

The color rose in Rachel's cheeks. "We were just chatting about your neighbor's untimely death. It's such a tragedy."

"Tragedy?" she repeated and let out a puff of indignation.

"Yes. It was."

"The likes of you have no right to call Ken's death a tragedy."

"I'm sure I don't know what you mean."

She let out the deep, rumbling laugh of hers but the smile never reached her eyes. "That's funny, missy. 'Cuz I'm pretty sure you *do*. I seen you the night Ken died."

Rachel's expression grew hard. Through gritted teeth, she said, "I have no idea what you're talking about. Nor do I care for the implication."

"I seen you drive past our trailers around three A.M. On the night Ken died."

Rachel spread her hands. "There was nothing sinister about that, Yolanda. You're Ruby Benjamin's good friend, right?"

Yolanda, rejecting Rachel's attempts to establish camaraderie, maintained her stone-cold front. Her lips were set in a frown and her brown eyes, magnified by her thick glasses, were unwavering and hateful as she stared into Rachel's.

Undaunted, Rachel continued, "Ken called me, distraught because he wasn't used to being home alone without his dog. I reassured him, but couldn't get back to sleep. I decided to drive by just to see if his lights were out and his home quiet. Everything looked peaceful, so I drove home without stopping."

Yolanda let out another puff of air and tossed her

head, her short gray hair maintaining its brittle-stiff appearance. "A likely story."

"I reported it to the police already," Rachel said evenly.

"Course you did. Like you had any choice, since I already tol' them about you myself." Yolanda spat out the words, and I had to admit that she was making me nervous. This was not a woman I would want to cross. I was reevaluating her as my top candidate for guardianship of Maggie; perhaps she lacked the patience and warmth to be a dog owner.

"What can I say, Yolanda?" Rachel asked. "I was worried about my client and drove past his home. That's all there was to it."

"So you was just *innocently* spying on Ken at three A.M.," Yolanda said. "Sure am glad I ain't one of your so-called clients." She pivoted on a heel and marched off in the opposite direction of her home.

Rachel sighed and glanced at me. "That's a very angry woman. I run into her kind too often in this job."

"I'm sure you do," I murmured, feeling awkward at having been a silent witness to Yolanda's hostility. I suppose I should have been grateful that, for once, someone else was playing the part of the fall guy.

I glanced at my watch. I had an appointment to keep with a burrowing basenji—which wouldn't have been so bad, if he'd confined his digging to outside, but the dog had dug through two couches and an ottoman. "I'd better get going, Rachel."

She searched my eyes. "Don't take this the wrong way, but as I tried to tell Ruby Benjamin, I'm a trained counselor in helping people handle their grief. Don't hesitate to call me if you should feel the need yourself."

"Thanks." I hesitated as I started to get into my car and watched her getting into hers. "Do you own a dog, Rachel?"

She smiled. "Yes. I love dogs. I have a schnauzer-mix named Cinnamon." She stared at Ken's trailer behind us for a moment. Her expression grew somber. "Though, if you're in any way considering giving me Maggie, perish the thought. I put in too many hours away from home to take on an untrained golden. And Cinnamon doesn't get along with other dogs."

"Okay, then. Bye," I said and left. Ruby was standing outside as I drove off. I smiled and waved, but she merely glared at me.

About twenty minutes later, I arrived across town at the home of the basenji, who was, in my opinion, the victim of an unscrupulous or ignorant pet store salesperson. Basenjis, as is widely known, are the "barkless" dog. They are not mute, but make a yodeling sound that resembles a many-pitched howl. Active, headstrong, and willful, basenjis are great pets for attentive dog lovers; not so great for a leave-the-dog-home-alone-for-ten-hours-during-workdays owner.

The black-and-brown short-haired puppy needed some outlets for his intelligence and energy that didn't include damaging property. One suggestion I not only made but also sold to them was a toy that challenges the dog to figure out how to feed himself. It is a hollow ball that they would fill with his breakfast kibble. The opening to the ball was small enough to release only one kibble at a time, and this changes meal times from five minutes of gobbling from a bowl into an hour to two hours of the dog kicking the food ball around.

We discussed diet and exercise routines at length, as well as a plan to have them simulate leaving the house for work on weekends as well, and varying the lengths of time that they stayed away, so that Benji didn't take every time his owner departed as indicating a ten-hour separation.

I had another appointment with the Akita mix and her woeful owner, still in need of my "magic wand," then grabbed a late lunch and headed back to the office. To my surprise and immediate concern, my mother's pickup was parked outside. I pulled into my space and raced to the stairwell, to find Mom and Maggie sitting on the bottom step. Mom was reading a paperback, with the loop of

Maggie's leash fastened over her forearm. Maggie's tail started wagging at the sight of me and she tried to run toward me, but Mom quickly reined her in.

"Mom, what are you doing here?" I asked as I unlocked my office.

She stared at me with a blank expression on her face and said, "Maggie wanted to go for a drive."

I ushered her and Maggie inside. "Did you use the dog seatbelt?"

"No, that wasn't necessary."

"You didn't have her stay in the bed of your pickup, did you?" I asked in alarm.

"Of course not," Mom snapped. "She stayed in the back seat of the king cab."

"She's making some progress, then. That's good."

Mom raised an eyebrow at Maggie, who was intent at sniffing the immediate surroundings. "She still has a long way to go, though. And Sage isn't handling this well." She shook her head. "I hope we don't find dog-staging battles when we get home."

"She's driving you nuts, isn't she, Mom?"

She rolled her eyes. "My patience isn't what it once was when you kids were young."

I grinned, but chose not to point out that, if anything, her patience had improved greatly since my older brother and I were growing up. Much of my childhood had been difficult; we'd had to deal with the death of my father in a car accident when I was only six.

My brief reverie was broken by the sound of Maggie coughing as she gasped for air while pulling on her leash. She was not wearing her Gentle Leader but some other collar Mom must have found in a drawer. Mom let go of her end of the leash, and Maggie rushed off to sniff at Russell's closed office door.

Mom said, "She's a beautiful dog, and you know how much I love goldens. But she's so untrained. I left the dogs alone in the backyard while I grocery shopped after you left for work. You should see how many complaints we have on the machine from the neighbors. Apparently she just howls incessantly when she's away from human companionship."

I winced but made no comment.

"Then I let her in for a while and went out to the mailbox, forgetting how exuberant Maggie is about breaking free into the great outdoors. She nearly knocked me over, then she just kept going." Mom made a gesture with her hand representing an airplane's takeoff. "She outran me, so I had to drive after her. Fortunately, she leapt right into the truck once I caught up with her." Mom clicked her tongue. "It's pretty bizarre, when you think about it. When she's outside, she gouges the back door and upsets the neighborhood with her despair over not having human companionship, then she runs away the first chance she gets."

That wasn't at all surprising behavior to me. "She thinks of herself as pack leader, and so she's allowed to leave the house but protests when the rest of us overstep our bounds and leave the pack leader behind."

"I guess I can appreciate her wanting to be in control of her location. Especially considering she's been wrenched from her home and her owner." She gave my arm a gentle squeeze. "But Allie, I can't take a leave from work to stay home with her, and I can't tick off all of our neighbors or let her claw her way through the walls to get back inside the house."

I glanced around. "Maybe I can keep her here at the office."

"What about Russell?" she asked, perking up a bit at the mention of him. Mom was so fond of Russell that I sometimes got the feeling she pictured him in a tuxedo and me in white whenever she saw us together.

"He's out of town for a week or two."

"Oh. Maybe that would work, then," Mom said, casting a gaze at Russell's closed office door. "If you could keep an eye on her during the day and just bring her home with you in the evenings."

I nodded, but had visions of my office landlord hearing about it if I left Maggie alone in the office for days on end while I went to work with a client. What was I going to do? Give her to Arlen despite my doubts about him?

"I'm sorry it didn't work out having her at the house alone."

"That's okay. You really don't owe me an apology. Maggie is my responsibility, not yours. I'm glad you brought her to me now rather than letting your whole day get ruined."

She gave me a hug and then left. I dropped into my desk chair, still pondering what I could do about this. Maggie followed my mother to the door, then trotted over to me and put her head on my lap. "So, Maggie. It's you 'n' me again." I sighed. It simply wasn't fair to my clients to have Maggie constantly barking just next door in Russ's office.

Much as it rankled me to do so, only one solution struck me as viable. I needed to contact Maggie's vet again, Joanne Palmer, and have her put Maggie on the proper dosage of Clomicalm to get this separation anxiety under control.

As I dialed, a memory hit me that had been lost in the excitement of the past couple of days. Dr. Palmer had said Maggie was already on a prescription of Clomicalm. But why would Ken have had a prescription for Maggie when the two of them were never apart? And why had he never mentioned that prescription to me?

I called and managed to make an appointment immediately, which the receptionist said was due to a cancellation. This is sometimes the truth, but having been in the position of starting a new business myself, I knew that a "cancellation" was also a euphemism that struggling practices employed to explain why they were so wide open for appointments.

With Maggie in tow, we drove to Joanne's office. The receptionist appeared to be eighteen at the very most, probably a C.U. student working here part time. "Hi, I'm Allida Babcock. I called earlier."

"Yes. Dr. Palmer had something come up, but should be back shortly, if you can wait."

I glanced at my watch. My next client appointment was in less than an hour. "I'll wait as long as I can. Thank you."

I sat down and started paging through a copy of *Dog Fancy*. There was an article titled "When Your Lover's Not a Dog Lover" that immediately caught my eye. I had gotten through the first couple of paragraphs, which were anecdotal examples, when Joanne Palmer rushed into the room, looking more than a little flustered. "Made it back," she said to the girl behind the counter as she grabbed a folder that undoubtedly contained Maggie's records. I returned the magazine to the table. The article was probably only going to give obvious advice anyway. Still, if I could just learn how to retrain *Russell*, I'd be happy.

Joanne's face fell slightly at the sight of me. Then she held out her hand. I rose and shook her hand, saying, "Sorry we got off to such a poor start the other night. That was a stressful situation."

"Yes, it was," she said pleasantly. "Come on back and we'll take a look at your . . . at Maggie."

Maggie trotted beside me happily on her leash, showing none of the fear of the veterinarian that Doppler, my cocker, for one, showed. Whenever I brought him to my vet's office, he couldn't stop trembling. We reached the examining room, and Maggie hopped onto the metal table as if she were expecting a dog biscuit for the feat, which is exactly what Joanne gave her.

"It's the separation anxiety," I explained, taking on the corner bench while Joanne Palmer lavished attention on Maggie in the process of giving her a cursory examination. "I've got to be able to leave her alone in my office for a couple of hours at a time at least."

Joanne examined the dog's ears. "You're in the process of determining her new guardian, isn't that right?"

"Yes." I had to fight back a sigh. "You heard about the inheritance, I take it?"

"It's the talk of the town. Do you have any idea how much longer she'll be temporarily under your care?"

I shook my head. "No. Which reminds me, I called yesterday trying to find out what you know about Maggie's date-of-purchase and ownership history."

"Oh? I mustn't have gotten the message."

"Do you know for certain if Ken was the sole owner, or was he once a joint owner with his ex-wife?"

She glanced through her folder for Maggie. "Maggie was born in April and purchased in June, two years ago, by Ken."

That all but cemented things. "The divorce was finalized June third. Do you know the exact date she was purchased, by any chance?"

She scoffed. "Of course not. But I can't see why that's a concern. His ex-wife is dead, after all."

Maggie rose to all fours and started to jump down. Once again, Joanne gave her a dog biscuit, and she stayed put while she crunched through that. She busied herself by licking up the crumbs off the metal surface.

"You said you'd met Mary. Right?"

"Once. When Maggie was about six months old. She came in with Ken, insisting I give Maggie something to calm her down, that she was destroying things and howling whenever Ken went anyplace without her."

They had to have already been divorced for four months or so by then. Odd that Mary would make the dog's behavior her business, but maybe she'd kept Ken wrapped around her finger even after the divorce. In any case, that only helped to refute her ludicrous claim that she'd been afraid of Ken. "That's when you prescribed Clomicalm?"

"Yes," she said, already bristling as if in anticipation of another debate on the topic.

I didn't wish to get into another disagreement and decided to offer up an olive branch. "Do you have any suggestions regarding who you think Ken would have wanted me to select?"

Maggie again rose to jump down toward me. This time Joanne let her as she turned her attention to making some notations in Maggie's records. "You mean, other than myself?"

"You?"

"I'm half joking, of course, but Maggie would be happy here with me. And heaven knows I could use the money." She didn't wait for a response—and wouldn't have gotten one if she did. She handed me Maggie's records. Maggie was already set to leave, standing with her nose an inch from the door. "Give that to the front desk. I've noted the refill prescription. I know I don't need to go into details with you regarding how to administer the medicine."

"Thank you." With the tension easing between us, I told myself I should leave it that way, but like a child picking at a scab, I heard myself ask, "Did you ever follow up on Maggie's medication? See how she was doing with Clomicalm?"

"Is that an accusation?" she asked through her teeth.

"No, just a question. I'm still puzzled about why Ken would put his dog on medication for separation anxiety, when he had such separation anxiety himself that he made sure they were always together."

"Like I said, it was upon his wife's insistence."

"They were already divorced by then."

"I had no way of knowing that at the time."

"Of course you hadn't." Short of asking Mary whether *she* was home with the dog herself before prescribing an antidepressant to a puppy, that is. But I kept the thought to myself. I was, however, grinding my teeth—but then by all appearances, so was she. Back to hating me again, it seemed. "Thanks for the prescription."

"Don't mention it, Allie," she said pointedly.

While waiting for Maggie's prescription to be filled, I got a chance to return to the article about non-dog-loving lovers. The advice was too generic to be of much use in Russell's case. I wrote out a check for the visit, loaded

Maggie back into the car, and returned to my office. The Clomicalm was of no use until I needed to leave Maggie alone, and I hoped to delay that as much as possible. I got Maggie inside and talked her into lying down by my desk.

I had to do some schedule-shuffling again, now that Maggie was with me. I had less than half an hour till my next client was scheduled to arrive, so I ignored the flashing message light and called that client and then my next one. After lengthy discussions, I managed to reschedule them as home visits tomorrow. With luck and a good reaction to Clomicalm, I'd be able to keep Maggie at the office tomorrow while I made those visits.

With a course of action in hand—or at least in mind—I pressed the play button on my message machine, hoping whatever this was wouldn't pose a serious setback to those plans. I heard a long pause. Just as I was about to give up and press the stop button, a woman's voice, sounding horribly drunk and slurring her words, said, "That you, Dr. Babcock? I don't know what's wrong. I feel so sick. I can barely . . ."

My heart started thumping as I listened through another long pause. I didn't recognize the voice. Who would call me "Dr. Babcock"?

"I gotta tell you somethin'. Right away. It's a emergency. It's 'bout your, uh, dog person thingee. The dog. Dead."

Now I was thoroughly alarmed, but there was still more on the recorder. What was she talking about? Was this woman, whoever she was, saying one of my dogs was dead? One of my clients?

"Oh, hey!" the voice continued but slightly quieter now as though she was no longer speaking directly into the phone. "Whatcha doin' here? This is my home! You get out! T-Rex?"

There was a click as someone hung up the phone.

T-Rex. Ruby Benjamin. My heart racing, I flipped through the phone book, got her number and dialed with shaking hands. No answer. Had she overmedicated *herself* with ACP?

Without waiting to consider any of the ramifications of what I was doing, I squeezed out the door, leaving Maggie staring at me through the glass. Then I got into my car and drove north up Broadway and toward the trailer park.

Leaving my car engine running, I raced out of my car, gave a loud, quick pair of knocks, then barged into Ruby's trailer.

She was lying in the middle of the living room floor. T-Rex was whining beside her and started to growl at me as I neared.

"Please, God. Not again," I murmured.

Chapter 11

My stomach was in knots as I fought back a scream of horror. Ruby's face was blue and her wide-open eyes bulged. Though it was probably pointless, I needed to check for vital signs but couldn't with her dog protecting her.

With my eyes on T-Rex, I turned so that we were sideways to each other and facing the same direction. A shoulder-to-shoulder approach was the least threatening to a canine's point of view.

"T-Rex, that's a good dog." I used my most soothing voice and stepped sideways toward him.

He continued to growl, his hackles raised. This was no time for the nice-doggie-I'm-not-going-to-hurt-you routine. I was too on edge, and T-Rex, sensing that, had become all the more agitated.

With a confidence I didn't feel, I demanded, "T-Rex, sit."

I had a few chunks of a dog biscuit in my pocket, leftovers from my previous client. I held the biscuit in my fist over T-Rex's nose and repeated, "Sit." As he looked up to sniff the treat, the dog's haunches touched down, and I gave him the biscuit.

With T-Rex having relaxed his guard, I put my palm on Ruby's neck and checked her carotid artery. No pulse. Her skin was warm. I put my ear to her chest and could hear no heartbeat or breathing.

I reached toward the phone, which was in its cradle on the floor near her body, then stopped, recalling the abrupt ending to my phone message from Ruby. Her phone could have been touched last by the killer. Deserting T-Rex for the time being, I ran next door to Yolanda's trailer and pounded on the door.

Yolanda swung the door open a couple of inches and said, "What?"

"I need to use your phone. It's . . . Ruby."

She maintained her post in the doorway, but her face paled slightly. "What's wrong?"

"She's dead."

"Oh, my God!" She sucked in a breath of air and in rapid succession, her expression changed from shock to sadness to anger. "It's that Rachel! I should've warned Ruby to stay away from that woman. I did in fact. Jus' after you left, I says to Ruby, 'Stay away from Rachel. She killed Ken.' "

"I need your phone," I repeated.

She stepped aside, but continued to talk. "Nobody listens to me. Everyone thinks 'cause I'm overweight and old and got no money that I got no sense. They think 'cause I'm not educated like you all that I got no brains. But I sees what I sees. And I'm telling you, it's that so-called social worker. She's crazy. She's killing off her clients, one by one."

While she spoke I scanned first the living room and then the kitchen. Her home, though much neater and better furnished than Ken's or Ruby's had been, had no phone in plain sight. "Yolanda, where's your phone?"

"Don't remember." She gestured at the empty cradle beside the refrigerator. "Press that pager button there and it'll ring from wherever it's at."

I did as she'd instructed and heard a series of three faint beeps from further in the trailer. While attempting to follow the sound, I muttered in frustration, "I can't just leave T-Rex over there. He's too upset. I've got to get him out before the police and the paramedics arrive."

More muffled beeps resounded, but I couldn't tell from which direction.

Yolanda began lifting her couch cushions. "Bring 'im over here. I love dogs. Used to own two, till they both passed away a couple years back." She handed me the phone, which had apparently fallen between the couch cushions.

"You don't seem very upset by Ruby's death."

"Of course I'm upset. We were friends and neighbors. Wouldn't *you* be upset?"

"Yes. I'd probably be in tears the moment I heard a friend of mine had died."

"You done seen all the things *I* seen in my life, you tend to mourn only when the time's right. You get a sense of when the crap's done hittin' the fan. It ain't nearly over yet, and I ain't letting the tears come till I'm all done ducking."

The police dispatcher instructed me to keep watch over Ruby's trailer until the police arrived. She hadn't specifically told me not to go inside again. I simply could not cope with the thought of poor T-Rex trying to defend his lifeless owner when the paramedics and police arrived.

Feeling trapped in my own nightmare, I returned to Ruby's trailer. T-Rex was lying beside her. Though he pricked up his ears and looked at me, he didn't rise or growl this time.

I spotted his leash, which was lying atop a couple of magazines on the coffee table near Ruby's feet. I then knelt and called him to me. T-Rex allowed me to snap his leash onto his collar and put up surprisingly little resistance as I led him next door, where Yolanda stood waiting outside. The dog's resignation struck me as horribly sad, and I had to battle tears as I handed over the leash to Yolanda.

The sirens were already resounding in the distance. I gestured behind me to indicate Ruby's trailer and murmured, "I've got to wait for the police," before excusing myself.

Yolanda nodded and stroked the dog's fur. "Guess you got yourself another dog to rehome, hey?"

That hadn't occurred to me till now. "I guess so. I'll probably have to let Animal Control take the dog to the Humane Society for adoption."

"If it's all right with you, I'll keep T-Rex." Yolanda straightened and met my eyes. "I used to have him over here every time Ruby went off to visit someone. Won't be much of a change for either of us. Hey, T-boy?"

The dog wagged his tail and looked up at her with loving eyes.

"Fine. Let's leave it this way, at least for now."

The paramedics' chartreuse van pulled into Ruby's parking area. Yolanda ushered the dog inside her house and, casting an angry glance over her shoulder as she disappeared inside, said, "It's that damned Rachel doin' this evil. I feel it in my bones."

In a routine that was becoming all too familiar, I went with the police to their station house to give them my full report. In testament to how shaken I was by Ruby's death, I had been there for some time and was in the middle of being questioned when I remembered Maggie. I leapt to my feet.

"I've got to do this later. I just remembered that I've got a very distraught dog left all alone."

"You're worried about a dog?" the police officer said in tones of barely suppressed disgust at my sense of priorities.

Through gritted teeth, I retorted, "It's Ken Culberson's dog. Everyone in this city seems to know that that particular golden is now worth a couple million dollars." A horrid realization hit me then, and I groaned and pressed against my forehead. "I'm not even sure I locked my office door."

I rose, trying to stay calm. At least anyone after the inheritance would realize that snatching the dog would be pointless; the money had to come through Maggie's trust fund, and her legal guardian had to be formally assigned by me.

The officer walked me to the lobby, saying, "We'll send someone over to pick up the tape from your answering machine. There might be something important we can get from it."

"I don't have a tape-style recorder. It's digital. You'll have to take the whole machine."

"That's fine."

"It's not 'fine' with me, though," I grumbled, my emotions still too on edge to be able to get a grip on myself. "I don't have a spare answering machine."

"You can get one of those answering services that do everything automatically."

"Thanks. I'll take that under advisement." In actuality, I'd already tried that service but hated having to dial another number just to hear my own messages.

"We know where to reach you," the officer said as he opened the front door for me.

"Good. We're even." I ran to my car and drove off. En route, I chastised myself for being so short-tempered with a police officer. In their eyes, I was undoubtedly a suspect yet again. This was hardly the time to make enemies of them.

Fortunately, much of the police force must have still been at the trailer park, for I broke the speed limits on my way to my office with no ramifications. Unfortunately, whatever time I'd saved by breaking traffic laws was spent in parking woes. Someone had ignored the "private parking" signs. Not only had Russell's clearly marked private parking space been taken, but so had my own.

Cursing the audacity of the parking scofflaws, I found a space on the street around the corner and made my way down the steep hill to my office. I trotted down the steps, then froze at the sight in front of me through the glass door. Mary, Ken's ex-wife, was sitting in the classic yoga position, while some purple-clad woman with straight black hair down to her waist stood over her, administering what looked to be a long-distance massage. Maggie, meanwhile, was lying on her side in the middle of the room.

I threw the door open and snarled, "What the hell is going on?"

My outcry immediately awoke Maggie, who had merely been asleep. The cloying smell of overly sweet incense reached my nostrils.

The purple-clad woman said, "Shush."

"Hey!" I marched up to her and jabbed a finger in her

direction. "You don't get to shush me! This is my office! You people are trespassing!"

"Shush," Mary said, eyes still closed, "We're almost finished."

"*You can't . . . shush me!* Trespassers are *not allowed* to shush people!"

"I'm doing astral manipulations, Allie."

Her voice was low and soothing, but in my current mood, infuriating. This purple woman I'd never seen before in my life was now calling me by my nickname.

"I've successfully moved Mary's astral emissions back to her and away from the retriever." She put her hands on her hips and studied me. "By the way, Allie, your astral projection is nearly a solid black. You could use my services yourself."

"Lady, it would be impossible for me to state just how unlikely the chances are of my hiring you to do anything with my 'emissions.' "

She sighed and shook her head, as if having to tolerate my lower level of awareness. "If you can see through all that blackness, you will notice that Maggie has been cured. She is finally back to being a dog."

Through my clenched jaw, I said, "I don't know who you are or what your game is, but I can assure you, Maggie is now and always has been *a dog*!"

She held my gaze for a long moment, then said, "There are books by greater minds than ours that I could recommend you read to show you otherwise, but I can see that I would be wasting my time."

Still seated cross-legged on the floor nearby, Mary was listening to our argument without comment, a bemused expression on her face. When Purple Person whirled on a heel and headed for the door with her nose in the air, Mary gathered up her purse as if she intended to leave as well.

"Mary, could I speak to you for a moment?" I asked with as little hostility as possible.

She looked surprised by the request, then said, "Oh. I suppose you want an explanation."

Purple Person was now battling to squeeze out the door while keeping Maggie inside. No way would I assist her with anything, which I think she realized, for she glanced at Mary and said, "Could you grab hold of the dog's collar, do you suppose?"

"Certainly, Theodora. And thank you again for all of your help."

"My pleasure."

Maggie was so focused upon squeezing out the door herself that she barely noticed that it was Mary, whom the dog despised, who had dared to grab her collar. No doubt it was the dog's surliness around Mary that forced her to bring Theodora to the dog, instead of vice versa. After giving Mary a pleasant wave through the glass, Theodora left. Mary released her grip on the collar, and Maggie then started barking at her. The dog then rushed forward and clunked her head against the glass door. Maybe I should get some fully padded cat-shaped decals after all.

Mary crossed her arms tightly against her chest and glared at me. "Theodora is one of the most respected psychics in the world. You treated her like a vagabond gypsy who'd intruded into your living room."

"Because she *did* intrude into my space, thanks to you, no doubt."

She chuckled and shoved her strawberry blond bangs from her eyes. "Hey, you're the one who left *my* dog here all alone. When I came looking for you and found that Maggie had been deserted, I took it upon myself to seek some help for the poor dog. A lesser person would have simply taken Maggie, since she *is* rightfully mine."

"She is not 'rightfully' yours, and we both know it."

Mary replied, "Theodora detected right away that Maggie did indeed possess part of my aura. She thinks that happened when I was in my coma after the car accident."

"Oh, please, Mary. You don't really believe that, now do you?"

"I most certainly do believe it, and I can get Theodora to testify to that effect and about what happened here today. The fact is that my late husband left his money to a dog who possessed *my* soul. Which makes a good case for the inheritance going to me."

"And just whom were you hoping to get to preside over the court? Shirley MacLaine?" I was just too angry at the world in general and Mary in particular to hold my tongue. "I know this is Boulder and that we tolerate all kinds of tutti-frutti philosophies here, but I grew up in this area, and it's been my experience that that stops short of the courthouse steps. Your daffy friend, Theodora, is not going to hold much weight with the judges. Furthermore, if you pursue this matter, you'll simply be demonstrating to the authorities what a prime suspect you really are."

She glared at me and thrust her finger into my face. "For the last time, I didn't kill Ken. I had nothing to do with his death, and I don't know who did."

"And you had nothing to do with Ruby, either, right?" I said in a taunting voice.

All traces of anger disappeared. She asked quietly and fearfully, "Ruby? You mean that drunk who lives next to Ken?"

My anger dissipated as well at witnessing her reaction to the news. "Somebody killed her, too. Sometime today. That's why I wasn't here. I was talking to the police."

"My God. That's . . . terrible. But, again, I had nothing to do with it. I didn't even know she was dead, till you told me." Her shoulders sagged and she shook her head. "That woman was such a loser. Of course, so was Ken. But if someone killed Ken for his money, they had to have a different reason to kill Ruby. Any money that woman ever got her paws on, she drank up."

Weary and shell-shocked, I dropped into my chair. "Hasn't it occurred to you, Mary, that if this is all about getting Ken's money, Maggie's new owner could be the next target? Until this killer is in jail, no one should *want* guardianship of the dog."

Her face fell as though she realized the truth in my statement. "They'll catch the killer, though. He won't get away with it."

"You're assuming that the police are going to solve this? Do you ever read the newspapers? Or watch the news on TV?"

She pursed her lips and repeated solemnly, "Whoever did this is not going to get away with two murders."

"I hope not." This wouldn't attract national media attention, at least. Two deaths in a trailer park were not likely to raise eyebrows around the country, where only residents knew that we even had trailer parks in Boulder, Colorado.

Without another word, Mary left.

Why would someone murder Ruby? She must have seen something or known something that put Ken's killer at risk of exposure. He or she had taken an enormous chance by walking into Ruby's trailer in the middle of the day, right under Yolanda's nose, and while Ruby was on the phone, no less.

Furthermore, I couldn't tell from the recording how much of the conversation the killer had overheard. The killer could think that Ruby had immediately divulged his or her identity, and, after hanging up the phone, Ruby might well have said that she'd been speaking to my recorder.

My heart pounding, I rose from my chair and stared at my phone. My phone recorder was missing! "Shit!" The killer had to have taken it, had to have known Ruby's final words had been intended for me.

I charged out the door and managed to stop Mary, who was just starting to pull out of my space. I waited impatiently as she rolled down the window.

"Mary, what time was it when you first got to my office?"

"I don't know. It was sometime after one, for sure. Or maybe after two."

"Nobody was here?"

"Just Maggie."

"And then, did you stay in my office until Theodora arrived?"

"No, I went to see her in person."

"So can you tell me what time it was when you came back?" She was already shaking her head, so I asked, "Or how long it was till I . . . interrupted you?"

"I don't know. I guess we'd been there for twenty minutes or so. What's all of this about? I told you already, we weren't trespassing. Your door was unlocked, and I assumed if you minded others being there this much, you'd have locked it up before you left."

"Somebody stole my recorder."

"Huh?"

"My answering machine. It was on my desk. Right next to my phone. A little white thing that plugs into the wall and into the phone line. Did you see it the first time you were there?"

"No, but come on! Who cares about some silly little answering machine? You're lucky they didn't steal something more valuable."

I wasn't about to explain the significance of the recorder to her. She drove off.

The killer had broken into my office. I hugged myself against a chill that ran up my spine despite the warm weather.

Chapter 12

As I watched Mary drive away, I continued to shiver despite the heat. This was a "dog-day afternoon" if there ever was one. I wanted to be with my own dogs, who loved me unconditionally and considered a whine or a grunt articulate, which was all I felt I could muster at this point; however, a police officer drove up while I was still standing outside my office.

It was the sharp-nosed, efficient officer who'd arrived to take charge of the scene at Ken Culberson's trailer when I'd first called. That seemed like weeks ago now, but I realized with a start that it had only been two days ago. The officer parked his black-and-white car and sauntered toward me. "Allida Babcock, isn't it?"

"Yes. If you're here for my answering machine, it's been stolen."

" 'Scuse me?"

"My recorder was stolen. I'd left my office unlocked when I went to see if Ruby was all right. By the time I finished giving my report . . . or whatever you call it . . . at the police station, my answering machine had been stolen."

"Why don't you show me where it used to be?"

Though he'd phrased his reply as if this were a request, his tone of voice—stern with a hint of skepticism—made it clear that I did not have the option of saying, "No, thanks." Yet this was pointless; it was not as though I had simply overlooked my answering machine or hallucinated about the fact that my phone jack was now minus the cord from said machine.

Maggie was whining as we came down the stairs, and she cowered a bit from the officer. Her bark was fearful.

"It's okay, Maggie." She backed farther away. I'd never seen her act this skittish. For the first time, I noticed that there was a welt on her muzzle. "Oh, my God! Someone hit the dog!"

I rushed over to examine her. I knelt and grabbed her head, taking care not to touch her too close to her injury. She shook her head as she struggled to keep her focus on the intruding officer and not on me, but I managed to get a good look. The welt was not large or bad, but the very thought of someone striking a dog—especially on the face, which is such a sensitive area—infuriated me.

"I don't see any wounds on her," the officer said, looking over my shoulder.

"Right across her muzzle. It looks as though someone whipped her with a strap of some kind." I glanced around the room to see if a likely weapon had been available and muttered to myself, "Maybe a leather leash." Though I struggled to keep my voice even, my inner turmoil was barely in control. I scratched her ear and stroked her back, then rose.

It could have been Mary, when she was here alone, that is; she would not have struck this dog in front of a witness. More likely this was done at the same time as when the recorder was taken. "The killer must have hit Maggie to make her quit barking and to let him get to my answering machine."

"Is this the phone jack?" the officer asked as he looked at the wall behind my phone.

"Yes."

"What kind of recorder was it?"

"I don't know the brand name. It was just a little digital recorder, about the size of a hand." I looked at my own hand. "Maybe five or six inches square, an inch or so thick. Small enough to be stashed in a pocket."

"I'll send someone out to dust the phone jack for prints. Maybe that'll tell us something."

"Why bother?"

" 'Scuse me?"

Impatient at what seemed obvious to me, I flicked a wrist in the direction of the phone. "Whoever did this was careful enough to take the entire recorder instead of simply erasing the message . . . and risking that a technician could recover the message. It's not like the person's *then* going to turn around and leave fingerprints on the phone jack."

"You've got a point there, I guess." His tone of voice was innocuous, but he eyed me in a way that made me nervous. For all the world, I wanted to cry: I'm telling the truth! I've found two bodies in two days, and I just want to go home and cuddle my dogs!

The officer took a step toward the door, and I said, "My biggest concern is that if Ruby's message posed enough of a threat for the killer to steal my machine, I'm afraid he'll think my having listened to it made me a threat, as well."

"You think the killer's a man?"

I clicked my tongue. "He or she. All I know is that he *or she* seems to kill with abandon."

"There's a big difference between waltzing into someone's unoccupied office and taking a machine and murdering someone."

"True," I replied, eyeing Maggie and thinking that the killer had to have gotten past her at one point to reach my desk and the phone. "But it would seem that this particular person is willing to both steal a machine *and* murder two people."

The officer headed for the door. "We'll put an extra patrol car in this area. And you might want to keep a low profile."

"Thanks," I murmured as he left, knowing full well

that he, too, knew how futile an extra patrol car was. And, how exactly did one go about keeping a low profile while in charge of a dog whose inheritance was by far the most likely reason two people had died?

Come what may, I was not going to award guardianship of Maggie to anyone until it was safe to do so—until the police had the killer behind bars. Maggie nuzzled my hand, lobbying for me to pet her. I obliged, murmuring, "You are just the sweetest doggie, underneath your mass of insecurities. I am going to find you a loving owner if it's the last thing I . . . no matter what."

I plugged the phone into the jack and jumped a little when it instantly rang. I managed a tentative "Hello?" in place of my usual professional greeting.

"Hi, Allie. It's me."

I breathed a sigh of relief as I dropped into my chair. "Russell. It's so good to hear your voice."

"You, too. Did you know that there's something wrong with your answering machine? Your phone must have rung ten times just now. I was about to hang up."

It wouldn't have been fair of me to dump my troubles on him when he was a thousand miles away and unable to help. So I merely said, "It's not hooked up at the moment."

There was a pause, but when I didn't elaborate, Russell said, "I realized that I forgot to ask you for a favor before I left. Would you mind watering my plants and giving my goldfish a weekend pellet of fish food? That is, if you can fit it in to your schedule today or tomorrow."

His voice sounded a little lifeless now. I said, "Sure. I'd be happy to."

"Thanks."

Neither of us spoke, and I finally broke the awkward silence and asked, "How are things going for you?"

He sighed. "I don't know, Allie." His voice had lowered even more than at the start of our conversation. "I'm out here in California and everything's different. New faces. New scenery. I feel disconnected. I try to focus completely on my job and try not to think about you. I'm having a lousy time, wishing I were back there with you. You couldn't know what it's like to have to wonder . . ." He paused for a long moment. "Have you missed me?"

"Yes, of course I have, Russell," I answered. If only I could tell him how much, but if I did, I'd start blathering about Ken's and Ruby's murders and my involvement. Then Russell would insist on dropping everything and running right home, his own business be damned. I couldn't let him do that, while I myself was so up in the air about our relationship. But . . . how was I going to get through this? How was I going to chat with him now as if hell wasn't breaking loose all around me? "You *do* know that I care about you, Russell, don't you?"

"I know you care. I just don't know how much. Except to know that it's less intense than my feelings are for you."

I rubbed my forehead in frustration mingled with despair. Maybe I was never going to be the kind of soulmate that Russell needed and deserved. "I'm not sure that there's a measuring device for that. But if it's any consolation, I'm quite certain that I'm having a much more miserable time than you are."

"Why? What's wrong?"

I hesitated. Maybe I should tell him. A shadow outside caught my eye, and I turned to look out the window. Just a pedestrian passing by; I was getting paranoid.

"I've got . . . some complicated problems with a client."

"Are you okay? When you say 'some problems,' you usually mean something pretty serious."

I glanced at Maggie, who was looking at me with plaintive eyes. She clearly could not handle not being the center of my universe. Unfair of me or not, at the moment I couldn't handle Russell's veiled hints that he, too, wanted that same stature. "Yes, and it's nothing that I feel like getting into over the phone. I'm sorry."

"Okay. I'll call you again later," he said, his voice glum. "It'll be a couple of days, probably."

I wanted to say something to reassure him, and I knew exactly what he wanted that to be. Instead of those three magic words, I blurted, "Okay. Take care."

He said, "You, too," and hung up.

I rested my face in my hands for a moment. "I'm lousing things up with him," I muttered to myself.

Maggie let out a little look-at-me yip. That served as a reminder—my skills were needed to train Maggie so that she would be suitable for adoption, which Ken had entrusted me to do. I stood no better chance at resolving my feelings for Russell under these circumstances than he did at riding in like some White Knight to rescue me. Aware that there was no way I could handle seeing clients after what I'd been through today, I rescheduled a problem-barker mixed-breed and a territorial terrier. A third appointment, unfortunately, canceled.

I needed to spend the afternoon helping Maggie learn that she could feel safe alone. Ironic that I needed to do so on the same day that she'd had someone smack her in the nose while I was gone. This was not going to be an easy fix in any case.

A seventy-pound dog, Maggie needed two pills for her initial dose. I checked my watch. Clomicalm takes up to half an hour to take effect and is best given a quarter hour before the owner leaves. She eagerly downed the soft doggie treats where I'd hidden two pills.

Next, I had to leave and return several times, for various durations, to inure Maggie to the terror of watching her owner—in this case her pseudo-owner—leave, and finding herself alone. The first time I went out, she tried battering through the door after me three times; I could hear her clonk her head against the door even from my post around the corner from the windows. After three five-minute sessions of my being outside and listening to her whine, the fourth time she assumed I would come right back.

The danger at this stage was that the dog can conclude that he or she was successful in bringing the owner back, such as by howling in the owner's absence. It is important to dispel this connection by returning *before* the dog howls or after he's quieted. This can make for a whole lot of trips and takes more patience than most owners—and most neighbors of the noisy dog—are willing to allocate.

By now we'd already built up to my getting my car from its space and driving around the block to get my space back, now that Mary and Theodora had relinquished our spaces. After partaking in a full hour of this counter-conditioning with Maggie, it was time for me to leave for a lengthier period. This would be a good opportunity to get some groceries and a new recorder for my phone.

Just as I pulled into a parking space at the grocery store, I noticed a familiar-looking pickup truck. I got out to investigate, and sure enough, it was either Arlen Culberson's truck or its exact double. Why would he be in Boulder in the middle of the day? Both his business and his home addresses were in Lafayette. Also, he was parked closer to PetsMart than he was to Albertson's, yet he didn't own a pet.

Out of curiosity—tainted with a bit of suspicion—I headed through the doors of PetsMart to make a quick check, grabbing a cart to make myself appear to be shopping there, and almost immediately spotted Arlen Culberson. He was browsing in the dog-book section.

"Arlen. Hello."

He looked startled to see me. "Oh. Hey there," he mumbled.

"This is a coincidence. What brings you out to a pet store?"

He shut the book and tried to hide its front cover from me, but I could see from the information on the back that it was on golden retrievers. He gave me a sheepish smile. "Just looking."

"I see you're reading up on goldens." I glanced at his cart, which had a half dozen varieties of dog treats, rang-ing from pig ears to multicolored dog biscuits. "And getting dog treats."

"Figured I should be seeing what I might be getting into before I go and volunteer to adopt Maggie."

"That's a little premature, I'm afraid. I have to tell you that the only decision I've made regarding Maggie is to wait until things settle before appointing a permanent guardian."

He followed my gaze to his cart. "The, uh, dog treats? They're for my neighbor's dog. I mentioned I was heading over here, and she asked if I'd pick these up for her."

"Your neighbor with the bichon frise, you mean?"

"Yeah. I guess that's what those things are called. I'm . . . surprised you noticed."

"I always notice dogs." And therefore, I silently added, had also noticed that the rawhide chews that Arlen had picked out were for a large dog, not at all suitable for a little bichon frise.

He rocked on his heels a bit, clearly nervous. Reasoning that I could always use more dog food and wanting to continue our conversation, I asked, "If you're not in a hurry, could you help me grab a sack of dog chow? It's a bit heavy for me."

"Be happy to, ma'am," Arlen said with, I thought, relief.

Arlen gave me a surreptitious glance from under the wide brim of his cowboy hat. "Er, Allida, you probably heard there was another death in that trailer park this morning. It's all over the news."

Already? I thought. "I did hear that, yes. Ken's next-door neighbor." It hit me that, during her phone message to me, Ruby had sounded as if she knew the person who entered her trailer . . . the killer, no doubt. Had Arlen been a familiar face? "Did you get to know your brother's neighbors at all?"

"Not really. Knew 'em well enough to say hey to, that's all. Once Ken and I ended our work partnership, we didn't used to socialize that much."

This was a different story from the one he'd first given

me, when he'd claimed that he went to his brother's place "all the time." I asked, "Why is that?"

He shrugged. "Couldn't stand that damned wife of his, for one thing. Mary. What a gold digger."

I made a sympathetic noise, agreeing completely with his assessment of Mary.

"All she ever wanted was to get money from him. See, Ken hit on a big discovery about TV circuitry. Happened a year after he and I had dissolved our business partnership. He struck it rich."

"What unlucky timing for you, hey?"

He chuckled and shook his head. "Ah, hell. Some people are born lucky. Others aren't."

"You think Ken was born lucky?"

"Not by a longshot. Neither of us were. He had to fight for everything he got in this world. Just like me. But he'd've given me half of his profits on his invention anyway. I was too stubborn. Told him if he could make a fortune on some sweep-line TV part, I'd outdo him. It wasn't as easy as I thought."

Arlen helped me load the forty-pound bag of dog food into my cart. "What brings you to Boulder today?" I asked. "Visiting friends?"

"Uh, yeah. Exactly." Arlen looked at his watch and said unconvincingly, "Oh, Jeez. Look at the time. I'd better get going." He started for the front, deserting his cart.

"Aren't you going to buy the dog treats you picked out?"

He turned to look back at me, but as he did so, I noticed the leather leash poking out of his pants pocket. It was curled up, the leather much too supple to be brand new. Why would he have an old leash with him?

"I'm . . . running too late now. I'd better just leave them. Nice seein' you, though, Allida."

"You, too." Perhaps his sense of urgency to purchase dog treats had been driven by the need to bribe his way into Maggie's heart, perhaps after having struck her today.

His eyes widened slightly, and he stashed the leash deeper in his pocket. "I, uh, look forward to seein' you and the dog . . . Maggie, I mean, soon."

"Yes. So do I."

Though I intentionally made it seem as though I wasn't looking, from the corner of my vision I saw him give me a slight double take as he left the store, his hand protectively jammed into the pocket that held the leather leash.

Chapter 13

As Russell had requested, I went to his condominium after work to water his plants, leaving Maggie in my car with the windows halfway down. It was a strange feeling—unlocking his door for the first time, walking into his home alone. Even to my inferior human nostrils, my first sensation was the pleasing scent of the place, a combination of too many fragrances at once to identify. Suddenly, I was filled with such a longing to be with Russell that my body ached. I wouldn't feel quite so helpless in the face of these murders if he were here.

Perhaps Russell had even guessed that I'd feel drawn to him in his living quarters; surely he had a neighbor who could have easily fed the fish and watered the plants for him. After all, he must have made similar arrangements whenever he'd left town before we met.

The goldfish was in the kitchen. I dropped in a pellet of "weekend food," and we locked eyes for a moment, the fish seeming every bit as unimpressed with me as I was with him. Or her. Good thing that goldfish never—to my knowledge—required therapy, as I was definitely unsuited for the job.

Russell hadn't told me specifically where to look for plants, but I filled the small, yellow-plastic watering pot by the kitchen sink and went in search of all things green and leafy. Upstairs, I threw open the first door and saw that this was the spare bedroom, which was the only messy room in the house. Russell used it as a junk room, tossing his various rock-climbing gear and odd pieces of furniture and doodads without regard to any logical placement. If there was a plant in there someplace, it had better be a cactus or a self-waterer.

I went into the master bedroom. I'd never been in his bedroom before and felt a bit of a voyeur to be there now. He had a king-sized waterbed, with a multicolored striped down comforter and matching pillow shams.

There was a fern on the nightstand, which I watered. A photograph on the opposite nightstand caught my eye. It was an eight-by-ten, which I had to pick up and study before I could verify that it truly was a photograph of me . . . a head shot from just my shoulders up. I couldn't place the picture, and only by noticing the unselfconsciousness of my smile could I remember the occasion. Russell had taken the picture at my house, just last month. He'd come to take me to some festival at Boulder Creek, and had asked me to pose with my dogs. I'd knelt between Doppler and Pavlov, but he'd cropped them out of the shot entirely.

Filled with sadness now, I set the picture back down and said quietly, "Oh, but Russell, I was smiling so freely because of my dogs. You can't cut them out and still have me."

I watered his other plants, stopped into Target for a new phone recorder, and drove home. Perhaps Maggie had picked up on my mood, for she was quiet the entire drive.

The dogs greeted one another and paid little attention to me. Mom gave me a big smile as she came from the kitchen to see me. Knowing Mom, she was probably feeling pretty guilty at having dropped Maggie off at my office.

She studied my features and said, "You look like you might have had a rough day."

"Yeah, I did," I muttered, not knowing where to start on my story of finding Ruby's body.

"I'm so glad you brought Maggie home. I was afraid you'd overreact and not bring her."

"She did fine. More or less." Not counting her having

been exorcised by a stranger in purple and smacked in the nose by a burglar-and-probable-two-time-killer.

"There was an article in today's paper about the horrid mess you're caught up in."

"Already?" I stupidly asked in alarm, thinking she meant about the second murder.

"It was about those bones that Maggie dug up," she went on. "They were from a grave in northeast Boulder. The police are thinking that it might have been some prank or initiation rites for a fraternity of some sort." An instant later my first reaction must have registered, for she asked me pointedly, "What do you mean, 'already'?"

Ignoring the question, I said, "I doubt the police really believe that the bones were just a prank. In any case, *I'm* sure the bones were a setup for Maggie to bring home, to push Ken over the edge."

Mom furrowed her brow, pondering this, then said, "I don't know, Allida. It seems reasonable to me that it could have been somebody's immature prank. Maggie's finding those bones might have been a coincidence."

"Unless that's what Ruby saw," I murmured, thinking out loud. "Someone working with Maggie on fetching those bones. And Ruby never realized how important that was."

"Who's Ruby? I can't follow a single word you're saying."

"She was one of Ken's next-door neighbors. She left a bizarre message on my machine today. I went to check on her afterwards and . . . she was dead."

"Oh, my God!" Mom leapt to her feet. "You found another dead body today? Allie, what is going on here?"

At the sound of her raised voice, all four dogs left their other canine activities and padded into the kitchen to join us. Dogs hope that any human outpouring of emotion might lead to their getting a tidbit, especially when the outburst takes place at the dinner table.

"I wish I knew."

While gripping the top of her chair so tightly her knuckles were white, Mom studied my face. At length, she smoothed an errant lock from her braid and said gently, "We've got to get you out of here. Someplace where you'll be safe . . . with your brother, maybe."

"Mom, I'm not running halfway across the country. For one thing, the police will think that makes *me* look guilty."

"Who cares? You're not guilty. You're my baby, and I want to protect you!"

"Mom!" I held my hands out, hoping that would be enough to help her realize that I was not a baby anymore.

"I wish you had never gotten involved with Maggie," Mom muttered under her breath as she sat down again.

The next morning, I drove out once again to the trailer park. I was concerned about the fact that I'd taken it upon myself to put T-Rex in Yolanda's care.

Despite what she'd said earlier, Mom now insisted on having Maggie stay home with her. This was convenient for me, but kept me preoccupied. Would Maggie drive Mom bananas by the time I got back? I assured myself that this would be a short visit; I had yesterday afternoon's rescheduled appointments piled on top of today's.

I climbed up the steps of Yolanda's trailer. The front door was wide open, and I could see straight through this front-door screen and the glass back door into the yard. I spotted Yolanda out back and rounded the trailer. Yolanda knelt at the base of her small vegetable garden, with T-Rex lying on his tummy, his side pressed against the wire-mesh fence enclosing the garden.

"Good morning, Yolanda. I just wanted to drop by and check on T-Rex. How's he doing?"

"Fine," she answered over her shoulder, not looking up from her work of pulling out the tiniest of weeds from her soil. "You like cucumbers?"

"Not especially."

"Me, neither. They sure like to grow here, though." She rose and knocked the dirt clots from her knees. "Dog's fine, as you can see."

T-Rex rose and came over to me. He looked better than he had in a while. "You didn't give him any medicine this morning, I take it?"

"Nah. No need for that. I took him out for a long walk first thing instead."

"That's great." I knelt and gave T-Rex some strokes down his shoulders followed by an ear rub. "He's got a lot of Labrador in him," I murmured, more to myself than to her. "He was bred for hunting and swimming. He needs exercise, not to be drugged into complacency."

Yolanda nodded, crossing her sturdy arms across her chest. "I know. Tried telling Ruby that. You know how folks are, though. We all seem to hear only what we want to hear."

"Did you see anyone coming or going from her trailer yesterday afternoon?"

She shook her head. "Must've happened when I was watching my soaps. I'm pretty much lost to the world then."

"I wonder if the killer was familiar enough with your routine to realize that."

Yolanda shrugged. "Could be. That damned Rachel seems to know everyone's routine around here."

I must have raised an eyebrow, for she narrowed her eyes behind her bottle-cap lenses as if in disgust. "Nobody wants to listen to me, but I'm telling you, it's Rachel Taylor. She did it. She killed Ken, and she killed Ruby, too."

"Why do you think so? What motive would she have?"

Yolanda pursed her lips and shook her head, her eyes distant. "I don't know *why* she did it. Just know that she *did*. I can read people." She turned her magnified black eyes toward me. "Now, see, when I look at you, I can tell you got a whole mess of hurt you're covering up for. But you got a bigger heart than you realize."

Her words cut a bit close to the bone, and I snapped, "You could say that about almost anyone and it would seem insightful."

She chuckled and shook her head, then got up and rounded the gate. "I was talking to this woman the other day. Lives down the other side of the trailer park. She says to me, 'Yolanda, if'n you so wise, what you doin' living here?' "

"What was your answer?"

" 'I guess that goes to show I ain't so wise, then.' " She stroked T-Rex's head. "My husband died a few years back. Left me enough money to live simply without working some eight-to-five job only to see it all go to the government." She made a sweeping gesture. "I chose this."

I nodded. Unlike my experiences with nearly everyone else in Ken's life, I'd grown increasingly fond of Yolanda. She had a certain dignity and self-appreciation that I admired. Although it had been only a couple of days since we'd first met, it was already hard to fathom that I'd first thought of her as homely. Her pockmarked skin, thick glasses, and short bristly hair now just struck me as giving her features character. I wished I could trust her, could know for certain that she hadn't killed her neighbors. But she might be running an elaborate act for me. She was intelligent and "read people," yet she claimed not to know about Ken's money, though he'd appeared to me to have blabbed about that to anyone and everyone. What if she knew all along about Maggie's inheritance? She could be playing dog lover to win me over, all the while pointing a finger at Rachel Taylor to keep me from rewarding Maggie to the competition.

I realized suddenly that I'd been lost in silent reverie for quite some time. I asked, "What would you like me to do about T-Rex? Should I go ahead and call the Humane Society?"

She shook her head. "I'll keep him. For good. Or at least, for as long as I live." She let out a sad chuckle. "The last couple days around this place don't give a person a whole lotta confidence in their life expectancy."

I didn't know how to respond and said only, "I'm sorry."

"Not half as sorry as I am." She shook her head. "C'mon T-boy." With the dog in perfect heel position, she headed for her door, saying over her shoulder, " 'Scuse me. I gotta find me a pickle recipe for all these cucumbers."

Wanting to subtly find out how she "read" Dr. Joanne Palmer, whom I personally considered as more capable of murder than Rachel Taylor, I called after her, "Ruby used to take T-Rex to Dr. Palmer, you know. Are you going to continue to use her as his veterinarian?"

"No way." She ushered T-Rex inside, then stood in the doorway.

"You don't like her?"

She blew out a puff of air. "She had some kind of scam goin' with Ruby and them damned pills. She'd give 'em to Ruby for free, and in exchange, Ruby'd talk up Palmer's service to everyone, to all her phone customers and everyone around here. You wouldn't know it to meet her, but you gave that Ruby a telephone, and she could talk pure honey. Best telemarketer I ever met."

"I can't imagine Joanne Palmer taking a chance like that . . . giving her patient's owner free medication, just to get some referrals."

She made a gesture as if pushing away my argument. "Well, whatever. I just know she was poppin' those pills herself, and that Palmer had to have known, too."

"You mean, *Ruby* was ingesting Clomicalm and ACP herself?"

"That's what I'm sayin'."

"How long has her practice been located just south of the trailer park?"

"Few years, is all. Of course, nobody in the trailer park used to be able to afford her, till Ruby gets into the pill business with her. Now a whole batch of my neighbors bring their dogs to her, claimin' their dogs are too excitable and need medication."

Yolanda went inside and shut the door without saying good-bye. I needed to go pay another visit to Dr. Palmer and ask about what Yolanda had just told me. If there was any truth to Yolanda's assertions, Joanne Palmer needed to find a new line of work.

I left my car where it was parked, opting to walk

through the neighborhood, down through the play-ground, and near the irrigation ditch where those bones had been found. As I walked, I tried to get a feel for how many dogs there were here. Would a veterinarian with a viable practice risk giving away canine medication just to drum up business? I'd heard that ACP was such a strong tranquilizer that people sometimes combined it with alcohol to get high . . . low? . . . but still. How big of a drug ring could *dog* medication possibly comprise?

Could my thinking about the murders be backward? Was Ken's inheritance the least of the killer's motive? Could Ruby and Ken have been killed because they found out about the veterinarian's unscrupulous practices? That seemed so illogical.

Ruby had come this way the other day, on her way back from Dr. Palmer's office, just after I'd found Ken's body. Maybe she had seen something that put her directly in the killer's path. There was nothing sinister in the view along the sidewalk now. It was a crystal clear blue sky, the air already getting hot. Ahead of me, the Flatirons stretched across the horizon, with only the traffic sounds from the nearby road marring the peacefulness. The long grass that flanked the irrigation ditch waved slightly in the faint warm breeze.

I paused, noticing a section in which the grass had been recently tramped down. This was in the same general area as the shortcut that Ruby could have taken from the vets, so I followed the makeshift path.

I'd not gotten far before I saw an offwhite piece of plastic on the ground. I knelt and picked it up, wondering if this discovery was just a coincidence. In any case, the plastic looked identical to the thickness, pattern, and color of the cover of my missing answering machine.

A few feet ahead of me, more plastic pieces lay, then an electric cord. I found myself staring at my stolen answering machine, smashed to pieces.

Chapter 14

Both the hard plastic shell and the electronic insides of my recorder had been smashed to small pieces, apparently between the two jagged rocks that were nearby. Not far from where I stood, I could see the construction site near the clubhouse that Ken had mentioned. This all but proved to me that the bones and the murders were related. Someone was using this particular stretch of public property as a private destruction pad.

I glanced back at the trailers, then across the street at Joanne Palmer's home and animal clinic. It was likely that the sound of the stone hammering had carried and could have been overheard at either location, but unlikely that there were any witnesses.

Why leave evidence to be found? Why destroy it out here in the open and not toss it into some dumpster? Other than me, there were few people who would recognize the significance of this particular piece of office equipment. Was the killer taunting me?

There was no sense in getting paranoid about this. Things were bad enough already. The killer had no way of knowing that I'd ever walk along this particular stretch of open space. Maybe the killer had finally made a mistake—had left the machine and telltale fingerprints here with the assumption that no one would see the significance in a smashed piece of electronic equipment near the side of a road. I had to tell the police about this and hope for the best.

In the meantime, there was virtually no chance of the

possible evidence disappearing. I decided to leave my
smashed answering machine where it was and go forth
with my original plan to see Joanne Palmer. According to
her posted office hours, this was before the time that she
would start seeing her patients.

Joanne was looking out the window with a coffee cup
in her hand when I reached her front porch. She opened
the screen door for me, its hinges squealing in protest.

"Hello, Allida," she said with a sigh. "More troubles
with Maggie?" Like her greeting, her expression held no
warmth at seeing me. She was wearing what looked like a
man's plaid shirt over a T-shirt and jeans.

"No, she seems to be adjusting reasonably well. The
medication does seem to be helping." Although, for all I
knew, Mom might be beside herself by now while Maggie
was tearing up the house.

"I'm glad to hear that." She stared out the window, the
morning light catching the lines on her face. In this lighting, she looked to be in her forties, older than I'd first assumed her to be. "I can't believe that a second of my . . .
that a second murder has taken place at the trailer park."

"It's more than a little disturbing," I muttered, still
studying her. Like Mary, she was a small-framed woman
who couldn't easily have physically overcome Ruby, let
alone Ken, without the aid of a sedative. She had such
easy access to ACP.

" 'Disturbing' is hardly the word for it. These are people
I know, whose homes I can practically see from my yard."
Joanne tore herself away from the window, which, I noted,
faced the irrigation ditch. "Can I get you a cup of coffee?"

"No, thanks." Wanting to test her reaction, I asked,
"Did you happen to notice anyone near the irrigation ditch
yesterday afternoon, or hear any hammering noises?"

"Not that I can recall. Why?"

"Just now I found a piece of electronic equipment left
there that looks as though someone deliberately smashed
it to bits."

"Huh," she murmured.

If the remains of my answering machine now suddenly disappeared, that was going to all but assure in my mind that Joanne was the killer. "Did you ever suspect that Ruby was taking T-Rex's medication herself?"

She chuckled. "You can't be serious. Why would she do that?"

"That's what one of her neighbors told me she was doing."

"Nobody in their right mind would do that, would take their pet's pills."

"Maybe she *wasn't* in her right mind, though."

Joanne set down her coffee cup and put her hands on her hips. "Let me guess where this is going. You're so obsessed with T-Rex and his medication that now you think I was Ruby's supplier, or something? That she was addicted to her dog's drugs, perhaps? What *is* it with you? You seem to think that I'm some sort of . . . veterinarian pill pusher!"

I spread my arms. "I'm just repeating what someone said to me." She was acting so defensive that perhaps she did indeed have something to cover up. I needed to report Yolanda's allegations to the police, bizarre as they were, and let the authorities sort them out.

Joanne's eyes flashed in anger. "Even if Ruby *was* taking T-Rex's medicine, how was—"

"Help!" cried a woman outside. "Help me!"

We raced to door. It was Yolanda, carrying T-Rex in her arms and trotting toward Joanne's clinic as fast as her large frame could bring her. We both charged toward her, Joanne a step ahead of me, and met Yolanda just as she was crossing the road.

T-Rex had been perfectly fine just minutes ago. Now he was deathly still in Yolanda's arms. "Something's wrong with T-Rex," she exclaimed between gasps of air. "He collapsed. I don't think he's breathing."

With my help, Joanne grabbed the dog from Yolanda and we both started rushing back inside her clinic. "Did he ingest something poisonous?" Joanne asked, again, a second before I was going to ask that myself.

Yolanda was panting so hard from exertion and panic that she was struggling to speak. "Don't think so."

The three of us made our way back over the uneven terrain toward Dr. Palmer's clinic. Joanne had taken the dog from Yolanda and was already straining under the effort. I was supporting the dog's weight as best I could.

Having just been there, I knew that the yellow crime scene tape was still blocking off Ruby's trailer, but I asked, "Did you go back over to Ruby's just now?"

"No. But earlier this morning I did. Used my own key. Just wanted to get some more dog food. And I brought T-Rex with me."

We made our way up the concrete steps to the porch. I said to Joanne, "There were pills all over the floor when I was there yesterday. He must have eaten some." Although it must have been a pill or two that had escaped the police's attention, since they undoubtedly cleared the scene of all such evidence. "You'd better pump the dog's stomach."

She glared at me. "Thank you, Allida. I know what I'm doing. Just get the damned door for me."

Chagrined by knowing she was right to snap at me, I did as instructed. She carried T-Rex herself the rest of the way and laid him on an examining table in her clinic. Yolanda, meanwhile, hung back in the doorway, watching.

Joanne examined T-Rex and said to me, "He's still breathing, but faintly. Know how to do mouth-to-mouth on a canine?"

"Of course," I replied, as Joanne angled the plastic resuscitator tube into his mouth.

"Have at it, then. We don't have much time."

Performing mouth-to-mouth on a dog was the same procedure as for a child of that size, with shallower, more frequent breaths than for an adult. Meanwhile, Joanne set up an EKG, attaching the clips to the knee joints of his front legs and rear right leg. She then had Yolanda hold T-Rex's front leg in place while she inserted an IV.

"Move back," she told me. I stepped out of her way. She explained, "His heartbeat is steady, and he's breathing on his own now, but I'm going to do a gastral lavage." She began to pass a plastic tube down his trachea. She started to pass another longer tube down T-Rex's mouth and into his stomach. "I've got to get this stuff out of his system."

I tried to cover my gagging at this sight by coughing. Though I hated to admit it to the likes of Joanne Palmer, I had to be careful now. I'd taken courses at the veterinarian school in Fort Collins, but had fainted during a couple of medical procedures, which helped seal my fate to stay at the behavioral side of canine treatment. I averted my eyes and started to count by threes to keep my mind occupied.

"Get me some towels out of the supply closet," Joanne demanded, indicating the direction with a jerk of her head.

I obeyed and used the opportunity to collect myself, already feeling a bit woozy, to my consternation. I found the towels finally and returned.

Joanne was clearly losing patience with me and must have seen the whiteness in my face, for she clicked her tongue and said, "Both of you. Go to the waiting room. I'll come get you when I'm finished here."

When I looked over at her, Yolanda was still hovering in the doorway and frowned at Dr. Palmer's remark, but said nothing and turned on a heel. I followed her into the waiting room and plopped down into a seat across the small room from her.

"You all right?" she asked.

"Fine, just disappointed in myself for getting dizzy. I can be a real wimp sometimes. My mom and my brother are pilots. I have fear of heights. I'm also a bit claustrophobic and, as you just witnessed, squeamish during some medical procedures."

We sat in silence for a couple of minutes.

"You got yourself a boyfriend, Allida?" Yolanda asked finally.

I let out a derisive laugh and rolled my eyes. "Now that you mention it, none of my phobias can hold a candle to my biggest fear . . . love. Toward a man, that is. Dogs are much safer. Not to mention more loyal."

Yolanda let out a deep, rumbling laugh. "I was married for nearly thirty years, 'fore my husband passed away. We said, 'I do,' and we never questioned out loud whether we *still* did, just put up with one another. Our stayin' together was probably more a matter of inertia than anything else." She grimaced, then said under her breath, "Love ain't so scary. 'Specially not when you look at the things *hate* can do."

We again sat in silence. At length, Joanne entered the room and said calmly, "His vital signs are stable now."

"Is he gonna make it?" Yolanda asked, rising.

"I can't say for certain, but I'm optimistic."

She frowned and shook her head. "Wish I knew how this happened."

Thinking of how the police had asked me about crushed tablets of ACP in Ken's house, I said, "Maybe, rather than forcing T-Rex to take his medication, Ruby just crushed up the pills and mixed it in with his food. She might have given him an incorrect dosage."

"Oh, Jeez," Yolanda cried. "I forgot all about that. There was almost a full can of dog food in Ruby's fridge, and since I didn't have her dry food, I gave him all of that for his breakfast this morning." She put her hands on her hips and glared at Joanne. "See what happens? You let my friend have all those pills for free, and it done near killed her *and* her dog!"

Joanne blushed and gave no reply. To my surprise, rather than deny Yolanda's charges, she looked directly in my eyes and said, "It appears as though I owe you an apology, Allida. It does seem as though Ruby *was* abusing T-Rex's prescriptions, perhaps in more than one way. To be on the safe side, I'm going to report this to the police. They can test his stomach contents."

"Can I see him now?" Yolanda asked in a snarl.

Joanne nodded and escorted both of us into a back room. He was now in a large pen, lying on a pad. He was sleeping soundly, but obviously breathing much better than he had when Yolanda first brought him.

"Can I take him home with me?" Yolanda asked, her anger at Dr. Palmer still evident in her voice.

"I'd rather keep him here today for observation," Joanne said.

"And I'd rather take him home with me for observation," Yolanda retorted.

"Fine. We'll compromise. Come back before I close tonight . . . six P.M. or so. He should be groggy, but able to walk on his own by then."

The mention of time made me snap to attention. I glanced at my watch. I had already missed my first appointment of the day, and unless my mood changed rapidly, I'd be a basket case for my second one.

"Can I borrow your phone?"

Joanne said, "Sure," and pointed me to a phone behind the counter in the lobby. I'd had it with subterfuge, so I told my clients that I was currently with a dog who'd swallowed some pills and nearly died. They were both so understanding that it renewed my spirits some. I decided I'd try my best to at least keep my third appointment that day.

Yolanda was still with T-Rex when I returned, but Joanne's first scheduled appointment had arrived, along with the receptionist. She let me wander back into the recovery room to get Yolanda. I found her sitting on the floor next to T-Rex's metal kennel, stroking him through the open gate. She stopped petting him and shut the kennel when she spotted me.

She frowned and shook her head. "I feel so bad about this. Should've known Ruby'd just mix up the meds with the canned dog food. Typical of how Ruby did things." She awkwardly repositioned herself and got to her feet.

"It was just . . . penny-pinching on my part. I wasn't willing to let a can of dog food go to waste."

We started back toward her place, my mind in a whirl. My destroyed answering machine was still there. Should I insist on our taking the long way to avoid our stumbling across it? I asked, "Do you have a car?"

"Never got my license, if you can believe it. RTD bus stop's just five blocks from my home, though. I can get anywhere I need to be."

She was automatically heading toward the path through the open space, and I opted not to try to detour her. It might be interesting to see her reaction. No matter what, there was little chance that she'd taken my recorder, if she didn't drive. She couldn't possibly have managed the logistics of taking the bus to my office and back yesterday during the hour or so that I was at the police station giving them my statement.

She was puffing with exertion on the uphill course back to the trailers. I was silent, deliberately staying behind her to allow her the opportunity to spot the recorder.

Just as we were all but literally on top of my phone equipment, she paused and pointed at it. "Lookee here. Looks like it might've been an answering machine or something. The thing must've broke after the warranty expired, and someone got so ticked off they smashed it to smithereens."

"It's mine, actually. Someone stole it from my office."

"You're pulling my leg!"

"No, I'm not."

"Why would they do that?"

There was no reason to lie about this. "It used to contain a phone message from Ruby, which may have also held an important clue as to who killed her."

"How would the killer know that? How would they know she was talking to your recorder? Or who you were?"

"The person must've overheard her end of the conversation. Or Ruby told whoever it was who she'd called."

Yolanda let out a slow breath. "Two people dead already. The killer thinks you might've heard something you shouldn't've heard." She shook her head. "You could be in a mess of trouble."

"Tell me about it." Pulling a tissue from my pocket to keep myself from overlaying key fingerprints with my own, I retrieved the larger pieces to give to the police.

"Sure wish somebody would lock that woman up before she kills again."

Meaning Rachel again, I thought. As much respect as I had for Yolanda's street smarts, I was still more than a little skeptical when it came to her deadset determination that the killer was Rachel Taylor. To my knowledge, Yolanda suspected Rachel because she'd heard her drive past Ken's house the night of the murder—which Rachel had explained—and a gut instinct.

Would Rachel have taken the inexplicable risk of returning to the open space next to the trailer park with my recorder and smashing it here? That seemed too unlikely. Maybe it was another trailer-park resident, whom I hadn't met. Yolanda was surely not a good enough actress to have feigned her concern for T-Rex just now. Ruby was dead; they'd been the only two residents I'd met.

I saw Yolanda to her home. She insisted upon giving me some zucchini for my trouble. I didn't bother to tell her that I'm equally as un-fond of zucchini as I am of cucumbers. This particular one was larger than a Scottish terrier.

I drove to the police station and the receptionist—if that's what they're called even in a police station—summoned the officer to whom I'd given my statement. I gave him the remains of the answering machine. He lectured me about "removing evidence." I told him the fragments were still there if he wanted proof of its original location. Then I tried to offer him a terrier-sized zucchini as compensation for my muffing his evidence, but he refused.

In attempt to redirect his suspicions away from me and, I hoped, *toward the killer*, I asked, "Did you ever find out whose bones those were in Ken Culberson's yard?" I already knew the answer was yes and figured that he would answer me, now that this had already been reported in the press.

Indeed, he nodded. "We matched dental records. 'Bout two months ago, somebody dug up a grave and stole some of the . . . remains."

"Someone did that to try to push Ken over the edge, I think. To convince him that he killed his ex-wife . . . maybe drive him crazy so that he'd be declared mentally incompetent."

"Who would do that?"

"His ex-wife, who wasn't dead in the first place. If she'd gotten him locked up, maybe she thought she'd get control of his fortune."

He eyed me, saying nothing.

"Look, I'm not trying to tell you how to do your job, but I feel like I'm the killer's target. I'm the one with the dog who inherited all of Ken's money."

"Mary Culberson has an airtight alibi the night of the murder."

"Airtight?" I repeated.

"She was at the police station in Longmont. For a DUI. Didn't get out till eight A.M. the next morning."

I muttered some exit line and left, driving back to my office. Back at my desk, I sat staring straight ahead for several minutes. The realization that the killer wasn't Mary after all had stunned me. Mary might well be the only person I'd ever met who struck me as heartless enough to kill. After all, she was the one who had been so ruthless in her pursuit of Ken's money. She'd faked her own coma and death. This was someone who, to my mind, *would* give a dog human bones simply to drive that dog's owner insane. Yet someone *else* had murdered Ken?

I jumped at the sound of my door being opened and whirled around, prepared to launch into fight-then-flight mode. It was Tracy Truett, my disc-jockey friend, who was not usually prone to dropping in unannounced. She was wearing her typical thick makeup and a brightly colored pants suit.

She put her hands on her ample hips, glared at me, and said, "Do the words 'softball game' mean anything to you?"

They did, and I cringed. Tracy was captain of a co-rec softball team that both Russell and I played for, which was sponsored by Tracy's radio station. "We had a game last night, didn't we? I forgot all about it. I'm sorry. And Russell's out of—"

"Town. I know. He called me from California two days ago to say he couldn't make it. I had a feeling you might forget without him around to remind you, so I tried calling you all yesterday afternoon. What's up with your recorder? It wasn't working."

"It . . . was unplugged yesterday. It's all hooked up again now." I glanced at my watch. "Aren't you supposed to be on the air right about now?"

"My show just ended. Seven A.M. to ten A.M. The hot hours for morning commuters."

My ignorance of her time slot probably made it all too obvious that I was not a regular listener, but if that bothered her she gave me no indication. She plopped down in a chair, ran her hand across her short, spiked hair, and said, "And speaking of my show, what do you know about this other murder? Some woman. Lived near that guy with the billionaire dog."

"She's not 'some woman,' " I snapped. "Her name's Ruby Benjamin. I didn't really know her, but other people did, and now she's dead. And the dog's a millionaire, not a billionaire."

Tracy held up her palms. "Mea culpa. Didn't mean to be an insensitive hard-ass."

I held Tracy's eyes for a moment and sighed. I'd snapped at Tracy because she was guilty of portraying the same indifference to a person's death that *I* was. "You're just doing your job, the same way I'm doing mine. Business as usual. With all due respect to John Donne, the bell doesn't toll very loudly 'for thee,' when it's someone you've never met, or only spoke to a couple of times." I sighed again. "Their dogs are orphaned now. Ken's and Ruby's. And I feel for them."

"Sure you do," she said softly. "That's how you are."

I clicked my tongue, not wanting to discuss my sympathies with Tracy. "To answer your question, I don't know anything about the woman's death. Even if I did, I wouldn't tell you, because you'd put it on the air."

She spread her hands. "Like you said yourself, that's my job. It's local talk radio." She leaned directly into my vision so that I couldn't help but meet her eyes. "Plus, you're lying. You couldn't fool a beagle with that acting job of yours. So what gives? Did this woman witness the first murder?"

"Tracy, I really don't know."

"Did you work with her dog?"

I hesitated for just a moment, which was enough of a reaction for Tracy to smile and snap her fingers in her small triumph.

"I *knew* you were involved. The moment a dog's a big story in this town, you're right in on it. So pardon the pun, but I've got to play newshound here. Tell me, Allie, is this a second dog that's going to inherit something?"

"I've got a large zucchini in my back seat. Would you settle for that instead of a story? Because that's all I'm going to give you, Tracy. That and my apology for missing last night's game."

She got to her feet. "Ah, don't sweat it. We won without you. But, if it'll make you feel better, I'll take the zucchini." She looked at me, her expression softening. "Just be careful, Allie. You could be in the killer's crosshairs."

Chapter 15

The rest of the day passed peacefully; my client sessions went well. When I arrived home, Maggie even allowed me to greet her last, accepting her bottom rung in the canine hierarchy.

The weekend, as well, passed without a hitch. These being the easiest days for working clients to schedule house visits, I had a heavy schedule. I went to Russell's condominium on Sunday and fed his fish, watered his plants, and left him a note in the top drawer of his dresser. I agonized over the wording so long that I went through half a note pad in the process, but finally was satisfied that I'd struck the right blend between chummy and romantic.

Monday was supposed to serve as my one day of rest for the week, but Ken's funeral was that afternoon. There were more media members than mourners in attendance. This was bad news for me, because I'd hoped to discover a grieving, dog-loving mourner, but none seemed to be in attendance—not counting Yolanda, who was there, her eyes red and puffy. She still came the closest to filling the bill. I couldn't help but notice that Rachel Taylor, who was also in attendance, was situated on the very opposite side of the funeral parlor as Yolanda.

There was a reception afterwards, with a table of cookies and sandwich fixings set up in the vestibule, though I had no appetite. I gave a quick word of sympathy to Arlen, whose eyes, like Yolanda's, were red-rimmed. He looked ill at ease in his black suit, which reeked of cigarette smoke.

Dr. Thames, also in a black suit but looking perfectly natural in his, almost bumped into me as I stepped away from Arlen's receiving line. He looked as displeased to see me as I did to see him, but he said, "Allida, I apologize for my bad manners when I called you at your office the other day. I was upset at Ken's death and lashed out at you. I'm sorry."

"Apology accepted," I replied. He nodded, turned on a heel, and walked over to where Rachel Taylor was standing. He and I were indeed colleagues of a sort now—both of us suspected and disliked the other in equal measure because of a former client's death.

I scanned the room, curious to see if Mary had been a late arrival at her ex-husband's funeral, but there was no sign of her. Theodora—her long-haired, purple-clad psychic—was there, however, which *did* surprise me. Our eyes met, and she pursed her lips and shook her head. I managed to resist calling out: See? I'm psychic, too; you're thinking that my aura is still a deep, funereal black.

While I was still glowering at Theodora, a voice behind me said, "Hello, Allida." I turned to see Rachel Taylor had made her way over to me. She was wearing a dark blue dress that was plain but flattering to her tall frame. Her short blond hair was neatly combed, giving her a distinctly professional appearance.

"Hello, Rachel."

"Depressingly small turnout for such a warm-hearted man," she said with a sigh.

"No kidding," I muttered. "I'd hoped to meet some nice, deserving relative of Ken's here, but no such luck. Preferably someone covered in dog hair, sporting an 'I heart-sign dogs' bumper sticker."

She frowned. "I don't envy you. I think if Ken had asked me to find a home for Maggie, I'd just keep her myself." She gave me a wink. "Maybe hire you to help my own dog learn to share her territory."

Surprised at her statement and, having heard Yolanda

Clay's frequent accusations regarding Rachel, I was a bit suspicious. "You'd originally said I shouldn't consider giving Maggie to you. Are you making yourself a candidate, after all?"

She widened her eyes a little and gave me a sheepish smile. "Well, actually, I haven't given the idea much thought. What I meant was that's what I'd do literally *if* I were in your shoes . . . that you should keep Maggie yourself. Ken had told me he was hoping you'd be—"

She broke off suddenly and looked past my shoulder where a straggler from the service had emerged from the main room behind us. It was Yolanda, her features stony in defiance of the dampness of her cheeks.

"Hello, Yolanda," Rachel said.

Yolanda continued walking without acknowledging Rachel's presence. She brushed past us and headed out of the building without a second glance.

Rachel stared after her and said quietly, "Poor woman. Both of her immediate neighbors murdered. Let's hope the police make an arrest. Soon."

When I awoke on Tuesday morning, I experienced the sinking feeling that this brief respite from turmoil had been the eye of the hurricane. For a little added security, I brought Pavlov, my beautiful—and exquisitely well-trained, if I do say so myself—German shepherd into work with me.

Before I'd had the opportunity to put away my keys, I got a phone call from Terry Thames, who said he needed to speak to me "right away." My first impulse was to decline—not being in the mood to serve as a target for his hostile superiority, but I was curious.

I glanced at my watch. "I can manage a brief meeting, as long as you can come here. I have a client arriving in half an hour."

"This shouldn't take place at either of our offices," he said. "For all we know, they could be bugged."

"Bugged?" For a mental health professional, he was sounding certifiably paranoid.

"We can't be too careful. Somebody has been leaking information to the media."

Uh, oh. Tracy Truett could be at it again—digging up stories like the newshound that she was. Or rather, the sensationalist that she was. "What kind of information?"

"That Ken Culberson had been receiving therapy from me, and that I'd been using HypnoReiki."

"What's that?" It sounded like some sort of exotic African beast.

"Reiki is an ancient Japanese deep-relaxation technique, which can be combined with other therapies, such as hypnosis. Few people are even familiar enough to know the word 'Reiki,' yet somehow my use of it during Ken's treatments has become fodder for a local radio talk show."

I winced at the description "local radio talk show." My friend Tracy was behind this, all right, and that made me immediately feel somewhat responsible for Terry's predicament. "Where do you want to meet?"

"How about the park at Canyon and Broadway? Near the old train."

"Okay."

"When will you be free?"

"After my session. Ten-fifteen."

"That will have to do." He hung up.

I put Pavlov in Russell's office, where she, unlike Maggie, waited so quietly that although my rambunctious little client was aware of her presence and sniffed at the door several times, his owner was not.

Afterward, Pavlov sat up the moment I opened Russell's door. She'd been lying in front of his couch and picked up her head to await command, her beautiful brown eyes meeting mine. She deserved a nice walk in the park.

Terry Thames was pacing in front of the antique train engine in the small park at the intersection of Canyon and Broadway when we arrived several minutes later. Although the morning sun was bright and the air warm, his arms were wrapped tightly across his chest. Once again, he wore chinos and a sports shirt—yellow this time—but his white hair was tousled. His dark glasses masked his eyes, but he gave me a quick smile, then turned his attention to Pavlov. "He doesn't bite, does he?"

I couldn't resist saying, "Not unless I tell her to."

He squared his shoulders. "Thanks for coming."

"No problem." I instructed Pavlov to sit, but Terry seemed too agitated to sit down himself, so we remained standing on the concrete walkway by the train. "What's going on?"

"I wish I knew. Someone's trying to make trouble for me. I didn't listen to the show myself, but an associate told me that some anonymous female caller to a radio show yesterday accused me of being the mastermind behind everything."

"Behind what? The murders?"

He nodded. "That and Ken's delusions. The caller knew more about my specific treatments with Ken than she should have. The worst part is, my associate said that the talk-show host asked *where* she got the information, and she said she got it straight from me, not from Ken. That's nonsense, of course. I never divulge information about a client's treatments. Never."

"It could have been a crank caller. Someone who just wanted to hear herself on the radio."

Terry was already shaking his head and said, "The caller had to know Ken well enough to know that he was somewhat delusional, *and* that he was getting treatment from me."

"This caller accused you of trying to get at Ken's fortune by driving Ken crazy?"

"Something like that."

The suggestion made enough sense to bother me. I'd suspected that Mary had been doing this. If the intention was to have Ken declared mentally incompetent, as a therapist,

Terry would know how to push his buttons. "What a bizarre accusation. I wonder who would have even thought of something like that." Other than me, I silently added.

"No kidding. And even though it's total bullshit, with all the competition for therapists in this town, I can kiss my practice good-bye. I listened to the show myself this morning, and several callers were talking about their own ignorant fears of therapy and hypnosis. My name came up more than once. I was going to call in myself, but I knew that would just make everything worse." He massaged his forehead. "I could lose my license. Who knows what people are willing to believe?" He whipped his glasses off, then stared into my eyes. "So, I need to know. Was it you? Were you the anonymous caller?"

"Of course not! Why would I do such a thing?"

He stared at me for a moment. "Then it must have been Mary. She denied it, too, but you can't believe anything that woman says. She's the only other person who knew about the content of my therapy sessions with Ken."

"Mary Culberson?"

"Yes." He put his sunglasses back on.

"You know that she's alive?"

He nodded, his expression grim. "Last week I found that out, yes. That's why I didn't want you to begin working with Maggie right away. Mary knew Ken was leaving his money to Maggie. I figured she'd come barging back into Ken's life the moment she heard about his having hired a dog trainer. See, her ace in the hole was that no one *wanted* Maggie, because she was so untrained. I'd hoped to have the chance to prepare Ken for the eventual shock of his ex-wife returning from the grave."

"I see." This made sense to me, and I now felt bad about having had such a low opinion of him.

"Obviously Mary's being alive wasn't news to *you*, either. I gather she came to you and demanded you give Maggie to her."

"The very same morning I discovered Ken's body."

"Mary stormed into my office, too, the day after that. Claimed that she was going to sue me for malpractice on her late *husband's* behalf. She said she was going to sue you, too."

I couldn't help but smile a little, despite the grim circumstances. "She's been threatening me with lawsuits, all right. But she'll have a hard time getting a golden retriever to testify in court against me."

He looked at me, his lips downturned. "I wouldn't take it lightly, if I were you. Mary will have no trouble finding a lawyer willing to pursue her case against you. Even if it's unwinnable, they'll make your life miserable."

"It's already no great shakes," I muttered. "The caller wasn't necessarily Mary, you know. It could have been any friend of Ken's whom he'd discussed his therapy with. Someone who wanted to show off on the air and got a big kick out of implying that you were violating doctor-patient privilege."

"Do you have any ideas about who that might be?"

His voice was so adamant that I decided there was no way I would share my thoughts about the woman's identity. Yolanda was a possibility. But she'd seemed so unaware of Ken's financial standing. For Ken to have told this mystery woman about that plus his therapy treatments, it had to have been someone who knew him fairly well: Mary—as he already suspected. Theodora. Even Joanne Palmer, perhaps.

"I'm afraid not." I gave him a reassuring smile. "I have to get back to my office, Terry. These . . . accusations against you will blow over, just as soon as Ken's killer is behind bars and all of this drops out of the news."

"Blow over. Sure." He sat down on the bench and made no move to rise.

"Don't you have any patients this morning?"

He shook his head and raked his fingers through his white hair. "They canceled. They offered reasonable excuses, but I'm sure the real reason is that now they're scared of undergoing HypnoReiki therapy with me."

"I'm sorry," I said, not knowing what else to say. Terry Thames was still not my favorite person, but he deserved better than this. I patted my thigh, and Pavlov rose and got into perfect heel position as we headed back up Broadway.

Upon reaching my office, the first thing I did was call Tracy at the radio station. Judging from her "hello," she was a bit harried. That made two of us. It was bad enough that I was involved in a murder investigation without having rumors broadcast on the radio by someone I considered a friend.

"Tracy, who was this anonymous caller on your show yesterday who supposedly knew about Ken's therapy treatments?"

"I don't know, Al."

I furrowed my brow at "Al," but decided I'd been called worse.

"It was some woman, calling from a pay phone," Tracy explained. "She really *was* anonymous."

"You're serious? You actually put some anonymous caller on the air without checking her credentials or anything?"

"Sure. Why the hell not? It's a talk show, not a witness stand."

She had a point there, but I rolled my eyes in annoyance. "Describe her voice to me."

"It was halfway between Minnie Mouse and Eleanor Roosevelt."

"I have no idea what that means."

"Well? Holy crow! It's a zoo here. The phone rings off the hook all the time I'm on the air. I haven't had a minute to myself, and I was trying to eat a bagel." Her next words were all garbled as she added, "Which is delicious, by the way."

"How was the woman's grammar? Did she say 'ain't' a lot and drop the G on I-N-G words?"

"Could be. And her diction probably weren't so hot neither."

I clicked my tongue, not sharing in Tracy's amusement.

"Can you replay it for me? If I come down to the station this afternoon?"

"Oh, hey. No problem. I'll just stay late and listen to my tapes of the entire show till I hear it. Shall I pick up a nice Chianti and some cucumber sandwiches for you while I'm at it?"

I gritted my teeth. "This could be important, Tracy. This caller of yours could be a major witness. Or it could be a total hoax. You've got to get a tape of the call over to the police, just in case."

"Wow! Would *that* ever make a big story, if a caller to my radio show breaks the case wide open. This could be the biggest break I've ever gotten! Thanks, Allida!" She hung up.

I stared at the receiver in surprise for a moment, then followed Tracy's reasoning and punched my thigh in frustration. I could already hear the publicity stunt that Tracy would put together: A source close to the double-murder investigation has just informed me that a major witness called my show yesterday.

I hit the redial, but got a busy signal. Shit! Ruby had apparently been killed simply for trying to leave a message on my machine about the killer's identity, and my answering machine had been stolen and then smashed. What if this caller *was* the killer, trying to deflect attention onto Ken's therapist?

After three more tries, I got her recording and said, "Tracy, if my friendship means anything to you, do not, repeat, do *not* say anything about yesterday's caller being a possible witness. Okay? Tracy? You could be riling up the killer. Call me back as soon as you get this message."

Tracy still had not called by my lunch break, so I called the station and was told that she'd "left for the day." It was all I could do to hang up the phone without relegating it to the same fate as my old recorder.

Maybe I could find out on my own who the caller was. I found an old directory that listed "M. Culberson" in a northeast Boulder address, but got no answer when I called. I decided to take Pavlov with me and drop in on Theodora, whose business address was listed in the yellow pages, to get a feel for what, if anything, she knew about a certain radio talk show. Yolanda and Mary were perhaps more likely candidates for the anonymous caller, but Theodora was the only one within walking distance, and I sorely needed a walk to calm myself.

Her business was squeezed between two stores on Fourteenth Street, just off of the Pearl Street Mall. It was upstairs and identified only by a wooden sign flush against the door. The sign—in the shape of a crystal ball on a stand, with lightning bolts emanating from the ball—looked more like one of those balls that collect static electricity than a sign for a soothsayer.

I climbed the first couple of steps. Pavlov hesitated, and I had to slap my thigh to get her to come with me. We walked up the narrow staircase, Pavlov a step behind me, and entered the open door at the top. I then ran into black velour floor-length drapes, which I had to push aside. Pavlov sat quietly beside me while I stood still, waiting for my eyes to adjust to the dim lighting.

A large fan rotated slowly from the ceiling, though the room was stuffy. The overwhelming aroma of incense was probably all but intolerable to Pavlov, which could explain her initial reluctance to come up here. Sitar music played from unseen speakers.

My eyes adjusted. We were in a small room, a couple of feet away from a sunken area filled with pillows that occupied most of the room. The pillows were perhaps intended to break the fall of those who boldly stepped into the center of the room before their eyes had grown accustomed to the dark.

"Hello?" I said tentatively.

"Be right with you, Allie," Theodora called from behind a closed door directly across from me and the pillowed pit that separated us.

The door opened and Theodora waltzed in. Once again, she was wearing purple. Her dress was in a thin Indian-style cotton print that might be see-through with better lighting. Her long black hair was fastened in a loose ponytail. She stepped down and lowered herself almost regally onto a pillow.

"Sit down, Allie. I was expecting you. A premonition, if you will."

"I'll stand. Was my dog part of your premonition, by any chance?"

"As a matter of fact, yes."

"Then I guess there's no need to introduce the two of you." Though I tried to be more mature about this, I found her too annoying and suggested, "Of course, if you could tell me my dog's name, I'd be much more inclined to take you at your word."

"That wasn't part of my vision, I'm afraid. He's welcome to join me on a pillow, too, where I'm sure you'd both be more comfortable."

"*Her* name is Pavlov. Apparently my dog's gender wasn't part of your 'vision' either."

She tented her fingers and rested her chin on her fingertips. "I sense hostility, Allie." She gazed at Pavlov and smiled serenely. "You'll be happy to know that, unlike Maggie, Pavlov has a very clear aura."

"That *is* a relief; however, I have more pressing matters on my mind. Such as why you anonymously called a talk show to cast aspersions on Ken's therapist."

I knew no such thing for a fact, of course, but my bluff hit its target, for she replied, "I need to stop that man. Letting it be known publicly that he's a sham was the very least I could do, in my duty as an aware woman." She met my eyes. "Terry Thames had been hypnotizing Ken into believing that he was his best friend. He was trying to get him to sign his money over to him."

"How do you know that?"

She raised an eyebrow. "Ken told me about the hypnosis,

though he needed my psychic abilities to learn what was happening during his episodes of hypnotic suggestion, since he, of course, couldn't remember."

So she'd lied on the air about where she'd gotten the information. "How did that subject even come up? Surely he didn't come to a psychic because he wanted to know what was going on during his therapeutic hypnosis."

"No, but I don't focus my psychic energies on just one aspect of my clients' lives. That would be tending to the tree for aphid infestation and missing the raging forest fire upwind. Originally, Ken came to me again because he missed his ex-wife and wanted to speak to her spirit. But I couldn't find her. Which, it turns out, is because she wasn't dead. I didn't know that at the time." She paused and gave me another of her too-placid-to-be-sincere smiles. "So he hired me to bring her soul into Maggie."

"Ken told me the exact opposite. That he'd hired you to get Mary's soul *out* of his dog."

"Ah, yes, but you see, that was later, once he found Maggie every bit as difficult to live with as he'd found Mary to be."

"Okay, I can follow that, I guess." Which was not to say that any of it made any sense to me or was even remotely believable. But then, Ken was a wealthy man living like a pauper who'd left his fortune to his golden retriever, and who'd put me, a virtual stranger, in charge of appointing the dog's caregiver. Within that context, hiring a psychic to put the spirit of a woman he thought was dead into his dog, only to change his mind later, was logical. "If Ken was your client, how did you come to know Mary?"

"They were both longtime clients of mine. From back when they were still a couple."

"This was several years ago, then? When they were married, you mean?"

"No, I only moved to Boulder four years ago. They started coming to see me every couple of months about three years ago. Two and a half, actually."

"Was it a shock when Ken told you about Mary's death, then?"

She chuckled. "My dear, I'm a psychic. Things rarely, if ever, come as a complete 'shock' to me. No, I'd have to say that I was more confused than surprised. I get a sense of when the spirit of someone I know has passed into the other realm. That wasn't the case with Mary. And, of course, in retrospect, it's quite obvious why that was so."

Also quite easy "in retrospect" to claim to have had those feelings.

Her features grew somber. "I experienced Ken's death, secondhand. It woke me from a solid slumber. I could barely breathe. I knew someone close to me had been murdered. His was such a forceful and reluctant passing to the other realm."

It was becoming awkward to continue to stand while she was seated so far below my vision, so I stepped into her conversation pit and sat down on the edge. Pavlov promptly lay down beside me. "You said 'someone close' to you. These . . . visions of yours. You don't know who they're concerning?"

She shook her head. "Sometimes they're quite specific. Other times just general sensations. The time I read about Ken's death in the papers is when I also realized quite clearly that Mary was still alive. I was expecting her when she came over the other day to summon me to your office and work with Maggie."

"Tell me something, Theodora. Am I the only person who sees how wrong what Mary did was? Did you point out to her how cruel her hoax was that she played on her ex-husband? Did you ask her how she could do something like that to him?"

She frowned and shook her head. "Mary is a deeply damaged woman. Believe me, if you, too, could see how her aura reveals her severe state of despair, you'd know to anticipate almost anything from that woman."

"Meaning that she's dangerous?"

She sighed, as if weighted down by my lack of empathy. "Meaning that she's frightened and lashes out when she feels cornered."

"With all due respect, she seems to lash whether she's cornered or not."

"She was moving to Texas at the time of her accident. Trying to get a fresh start for herself. She didn't tell Ken or anyone else that she was leaving. She got the idea of fooling him into thinking she was dead, and she spent a couple of months in Texas, then came back to settle her affairs just last week. She was going to tell him then that she was alive. He died before she got the chance to talk to him."

Having met Mary, I didn't believe a word of that, but it was possible that Mary had conned Theodora into believing she was a victim. "You know a lot about this. Did she explain all of this to you yesterday?"

She gave me a proud smile and said softly, "Yes, she did. Sometimes even in words."

I looked away, finding her attitude too annoying to put into my own words.

"But, really, you're here because you think I besmeared Terry Thames's reputation."

This was almost impressive, but I'd told her as much when I arrived.

"You're defending the wrong person, Allie. Mary thinks he killed Ken. I'm inclined to agree."

I didn't know Dr. Thames well enough myself to form an opinion, so maybe their suspicions were justified. I'd met with the man just today. A shiver ran up my spine.

Theodora rose. "You have a problem barker to attend to now, don't you?"

"Um . . ." I rose as well, slightly shaken, because she was exactly correct. Could that have been a lucky guess? "I do. I'd better go. Thank you."

I went straight home after work and vegged out in front of the TV. Mom had had another reasonably peaceful day with Maggie, who jumped on my lap only once—an improvement. I went to bed sometime after eleven.

The phone rang, jarring me from my sleep. Disoriented, I fumbled for the receiver on my nightstand, eventually found it, and murmured hello.

There was someone panting into the phone. My first thought was that this must be an obscene phone call, and I almost hung up.

"Allida?" a high-pitched female voice gasped. "Is that you?"

"Yes. Who's this?"

"Theodora. You have to listen to me. We're both in danger. The killer isn't through."

Chapter 16

This was the woman who, hours earlier, had told me she "rarely, if ever" was shocked? Now she sounded shaken to the core. I sat upright in my bed.

Theodora continued, "Allie, an hour or so ago, I had a vision. A clear one. I could see it was Mary. Somebody was trying to kill her, to stuff a pillow on her face."

"Who?"

"I don't know. I couldn't see that, the vision was . . . it was horrible! It's like I was seeing things from the killer's viewpoint. That's never happened to me before. Never! It scared me so badly I went to her house."

"Why? Why would you take a risk like that?"

"To see if I could help her, obviously! Only she wasn't there. Nobody's been there for days. There's, like, a batch of newspapers on the front lawn, and her mailbox is practically overflowing. I let myself into her house . . . it wasn't even locked. I went to her bedroom, and the closets are cleaned out. Then there was this . . . this note on her bed. All it says is: 'You're too late!' "

"Is the note in Mary's handwriting?" I asked, wide awake now but thoroughly confused.

"I don't know. It has her vibrations, so I think she wrote it, but I can't say for certain."

"When was the last time you saw her?"

"At your office, when I exorcised her spirit from Maggie's body."

"That's right when she found out that Ruby had been murdered. Maybe that scared her. She and Ruby could have been partners with a third person who then turned around and killed—" I stopped, realizing that Theodora could be playing me for a fool.

"Who?" she asked. "Terry Thames?"

"Maybe. The police need to look into this, Theodora. You need to report her missing."

"No way. You do it. I'm not talking to the police. Not if I can help it. I'm not exactly squeaky clean, and I don't want them checking into my past, you know?"

"Fine. I'll call the police in the morning, but I'm going to tell them everything you told me, so you're going to get pulled into this either way. It'd sound better coming from you, don't you think?"

"Can't you just make up some excuse and drive out here yourself tomorrow, then call them?"

"I could, but I won't. I'm telling the police the truth. It's easier and less incriminating that way."

She clicked her tongue. "You don't know what it's like, Allie. I never asked for these visions of mine. They've been here, all along, lousing up my life. I try to do some good with them now, but it's just made me a target for everyone's jokes and finger pointing."

"Be that as it may, Theodora, two people are dead, and you've just discovered that a third is missing. The police need to be notified."

There was a long pause. "Shit! You're right, damn it all!" She sighed, then added sadly, "They'll find out about my writing bad checks in Wisconsin. At least I'll have a permanent address for the next few months . . . the Boulder County jail."

"You don't know for certain that they'll put you in jail. Things generally don't turn out nearly as bad as we're afraid they will."

She hung up. So much for my platitudes. For the

countless time I reminded myself to limit my psychology to dogs. I dropped the phone into its cradle and sat down on the edge of my bed.

Mom tapped on my bedroom door and opened it a crack. "Allida? Is everything all right?" She'd probably been standing there for a while now, listening to my end of the conversation.

"Not really."

Maggie barged past my mother and through the door, leapt onto my bed—stepping on my lap in the process—and, tail wagging, lay down beside me, her head on my pillow.

"Who was that who called?" Mom asked, ignoring my new bed companion. Mom was wearing her robe, her braid undone so that her long hair hung below her shoulders.

"Theodora. Psychic healer of dogs and men. I'm sorry it woke you." I got up, turned my attention to Maggie, and pointed at the floor. "Maggie, off!" I grabbed her collar and gave a tug. She spread her paws. "Off!" I got a second hand on her collar and put one foot on the side of my bed for leverage. I managed to drag her to the floor, though I now would have to remake my bed. "This dog could make a *mule* weep in frustration!"

Mom grabbed Maggie's collar and, in one sure movement born from years of manhandling large dogs, guided her out the door, which she shut between them unceremoniously. "What's going on?"

Her question brought the harsh reality back to me. I sat back down on my messy bed. "Somebody involved with Ken is now missing. Mary Culberson. Probably left town, because she knows who the killer is and is scared."

I shivered involuntarily and pulled my So-Many-Dogs-So-Little-Time T-shirt down to cover my knees, which I hugged against my chest.

Just outside the door, Maggie was whining in canine woe, but Mom ignored the noise and dropped into a hard-back chair by the door. "Oh, Allie. Isn't there some way you can get yourself extricated from all of this?"

Tired and thoroughly discouraged, I rubbed my eyes. "I don't think so, Mom. I don't know how I could even begin to go about untangling myself at this point. Until this murderer gets arrested, I'm just . . . trapped into being a part of everything."

"You could stay with your brother for a couple of weeks, couldn't you? Leave Maggie with me and just—" I was already shaking my head and Mom added angrily, "You don't need to be a hero."

"I'm not trying to be one. Just to do what's right by my late client and his dog. Now, suddenly I feel like a duck in a shooting gallery."

"Then get out of the gallery, Allie! Do what this . . . Mary Culberson did. Go away for a few weeks!"

"And desert my business now that it's finally getting to be profitable?"

"If that's the price you have to pay to stay safe, yes!"

"But, Mom, what if the police don't ever catch the killer? Am I supposed to stay away forever?" I gestured at the closed door, where Maggie's whines had mutated into howls. "I've got to rehome Maggie eventually. I'm stuck with that responsibility, whether or not I . . . go into hiding first."

Mom set her lips in a straight line and rose. I knew she was angry at the situation and not at me, but that didn't make things any easier. "I don't understand any of this," she muttered as she let herself out, pulling Maggie with her.

"Neither do I." I got back into bed, though I knew sleep would now be out of the question.

At seven-thirty A.M., the doorbell rang. It was the detective who had interviewed me following Ruby's murder. He wanted to know what, if anything, I knew about Mary's disappearance. I told him everything that Theodora said during her phone call to me. I added that Theodora had known Mary—and Ken—a lot better than I had. In case it was relevant, I recounted yesterday's conversation with Terry Thames about the anonymous caller, and Mary's having threatened to sue him. He informed me that Theodora had, in his words, "turned herself in" last night.

If any of what I said was enlightening to the detective, he masked his interest well. After my being of no help to him, he left. Mom had some flying lessons scheduled, and she left soon after the detective did.

Today Maggie was either going to have to be left home alone or come with me on client calls. Either way, she needed to show better manners and obedience than she'd displayed last night. I worked with her in the backyard, going over sit-stay-lie-down routines, which she performed adequately.

It was a gorgeous morning, with a slight chill to the air that would soon warm from the bright sun. Pavlov, Sage, and Doppler would be happy to stay outside today, and I'd greatly prefer to let Maggie be with them. That meant, though, that Maggie would be in the backyard, potentially driving the neighbors crazy with her barking.

To test her behavior, I left her out back and drove around the block. When I returned, quietly letting myself in through the gate, she was tunneling under the fence as fast as her paws could go. The other dogs were watching her progress with interest.

Spotting me, she stopped digging and trotted up to me as if she hadn't a care in the world. This was not a dog whose past experience had taught her to make the usual canine association—property damage plus owner's return equals a scolding—which so many owners misinterpret to mean "my dog feels guilty because he knows he's been bad."

I looked at the tunnel, sighed, then looked at the dog. "Maggie, you know what? Don't tell my clients, but I don't have the time or energy for this." I haphazardly pushed the pile of dirt back in place with my foot, grabbed Maggie's collar to keep her from running away, and led her to my car.

As we drove, I scolded myself. Here I was, not practicing what I preached. My actions were the very anathema of the dog trainer—I was rewarding bad behavior by giving the dog what it wants. Ah, well. Nobody is as insightful with their own troubles as they are with others'.

At a stoplight, I glanced into the back seat. "You know, Maggie, I'm only doing this this one time because I got so little sleep last night. Then had to lose so much of the morning talking with the police. Fortunately, I know you understand every word I'm saying so I won't have to undo any setbacks my laziness has caused."

We went to my appointments. Although I had a full load for the next few hours, I was fortunate enough to have them with dog owners flexible enough to allow me to put Maggie in their backyards while we worked indoors. My busy schedule had also provided me with much-needed distraction. I managed to push from my mind all thoughts about the murders.

Those thoughts came crashing back when I pulled into my parking space at the office that afternoon and saw a horrible sight: Theodora engaged in conversation with my friendly loose-lipped media maven, Tracy Truett, on the sidewalk in front of my entranceway.

"Damn it!" I smacked the steering wheel with the heel of my hand. Knowing Tracy, tomorrow's radio broadcast was going to be all about the story of a psychic's exorcism of a certain golden retriever.

I fastened a leash on Maggie's collar, and we got out of the car. Tracy spotted me and called over her shoulder to Theodora, "So this is the actual dog right here, isn't it?"

"As a matter of fact, yes," Theodora answered proudly.

I looked at Tracy, taking in her typical flamboyant outfit—all the way from her brightly colored loose-fitting blouse and scarf down to the knees of her black lycra leggings. Her bleached-blond hair was in its spikes and her eyelashes thick with mascara. Under the circumstances, I was unable to muster any appreciation at seeing my friend again. "Let me guess. You heard about Ken's ex-wife's disappearance last night and came here hoping to get a scoop."

Tracy laughed and gave my arm a squeeze. "No, I'd never use the phrase 'get a scoop' from someone who works with dogs. Pooper Scoopers are the last thing I need."

Out of respect for our friendship, I resisted making a crack about the type of shovel I felt she needed for her show.

"Plus, I wanted to drop this off. The tape you wanted to borrow. I hope it proves helpful." Keeping up her guise, she turned to Theodora and said conspiratorially, "Relaxation tape," then slipped me the tape, which I pocketed. I hoped she'd made a copy of just the anonymous phone call so I wouldn't have to listen to her whole show; having to listen to a three-hour discussion about Ken's murder would be as far from relaxing as a recording could possibly get. Plus, Theodora had already admitted to making the call.

I shifted my attention to Theodora. "You're not in jail, I see. That's a good sign."

She beamed at me and tossed her long hair from her shoulders. She had bounced back well from last night's trauma, I thought sourly. She was wearing the same purple frock she'd worn yesterday. "I suddenly had this vision that I needed to drop in on you now. And, as a result, I'm going on your friend's show tomorrow."

I gritted my teeth and glared at Tracy.

"You're not pleased, I know," Tracy interjected, in an obvious attempt at cutting me off. "But we'll keep your name out of it. I promise."

"That's nice. Mind keeping everything having to do with Maggie out of it as well?"

She let her jaw drop as if at the absurdity of my request. "Then I wouldn't have a theme for the show. Sorry. No can do."

I deliberately held Maggie on a short leash, so that she couldn't try to make friends with Tracy or Theodora. "How about if I threaten to never speak to you again, quit the softball team, and ask Russell to quit as well? *Then* could you find a new theme?"

Tracy's face fell, again overdramatizing her reaction, but this time with more sincerity. "Hmm. Well, that does put me in a bit of a jam. You we could get around, but Russell's irreplaceable. We barely won without him."

She was kidding. I was one of the best players on the team, and we both knew it. Plus, we were friends, even though unorthodox issues kept cropping up and driving a wedge between us. Such as her theory that her right to free speech gave her a license to trample all over my right to privacy.

Tracy turned to Theodora. "Change in themes. We'll focus exclusively on how your psychic abilities led you to discover another potential victim last night." She turned back to me, studied my features, and said, "I get the feeling that this isn't a good time for me to visit. I'll talk to you soon. Such as at tomorrow night's softball game. Don't forget, or I'll have to bench you for two weeks."

"I won't forget."

She smiled, tossed her long scarf over her shoulder in a final dramatic gesture—I suspected she often wore scarves precisely because they allowed her to make that motion—then she turned and gave Theodora's hand a quick squeeze. "Theo, see you tomorrow at the station. We'll kick ass."

Tracy headed down Broadway toward downtown Boulder. I unlocked my office door and let Maggie in first. I asked Theodora, "Do the police have any idea what Mary's note meant?"

"No." Now that she was no longer in Tracy's presence, her cheer quickly fell away and she looked exhausted and sad. She combed her fingers through her long hair. "I was up all night talking to them. Nowadays I'm getting used to less sleep. It's getting so that I'm afraid to close my eyes at night."

"I know what you mean." I unfastened the leash, and Maggie trotted off to investigate the new scents in the room since her last visit.

Theodora dropped down into a chair near my desk

and indicated that I should do the same, which was nervy since this was *my* office. "Allida, something is very wrong."

"Even I, with my paltry five senses, realize that much."

Ignoring my mood, she seemed to deliberately put herself in a trancelike state. By the time I was seated at my desk, she was rocking slightly. With her eyes half closed, she said in hypnotic tones, "There is a dangerous energy shift in your aura, Allie. I can read it as plainly as if you were crying aloud for help."

"Somebody has murdered two people I've met in the last week. How placid do you expect my aura to be?"

Theodora stared into my eyes. "The dogs will go wild with this cosmic energy. They're very intuitive creatures, you know."

"Yes, I'm well aware of that."

She shut her eyes. After nearly a minute of silence, which seemed interminable, she said, "The worst is yet to come, Allie." Her face was a portrait of sorrow, and she shook her head as if to blot it out. "Another attempt will be made. We are both in jeopardy, you and I."

"From whom?"

She opened her eyes, lifted a shoulder, and looked to the heavens. "If only I could control my visions, I might know. But that's just not the way they work." She rose. She watched Maggie as she trotted toward me and lay down at my feet. "Watch the dogs, Allida. They're your only warning. Your only defense."

I studied her. She was being utterly sincere. If she was a mere scam artist, she had come to believe in her own scam. "I'll do that," I said. "I guess it's a good thing you've got your . . . visions to serve as your own personal watchdog, right?"

"Indeed." She gave me a long look, then said, "I've got to get back to my office. I've got a client coming in a few minutes. What I really need now is a lawyer, to clear up matters in Wisconsin. At least one good thing has happened lately. This Tracy Truett show will help me get new clients. Thank you."

"That was totally unintentional on my part, of course, since I wasn't even here, but you're welcome. I hope things work out for you."

She left and I found myself alone in my office, not counting Maggie. I immediately retrieved the tape of Tracy's show and looked at it. On the label, Tracy had written a number followed by the words: female caller. Maybe Theodora, if she was indeed the caller, had said something that would be a clue.

Russell sometimes used a tape recorder. He was such a cautious sort that he took oral notes when going over his designs. I let myself into his office and searched his desk, then his filing cabinet. Indeed, his bottom drawer contained a tape recorder, and I plugged it in and inserted the tape. Maggie let out a little whine, and I saw her looking at me from the doorway. She was worried that I was trying to trick her into feeling content to be in this room, then would leave her alone in here again. That reminded me that I had yet to replace his door. And that I hadn't fed his stupid goldfish since Sunday. Talk about pathetic girlfriends!

"You won't give me your name?" Tracy was saying, distracting me from further self-abasement.

"Just call me Jane." I couldn't tell for certain if this was Theodora; the caller was obviously deliberately disguising her voice, speaking in the breathy tones of someone with a bad case of laryngitis.

"All right, Jane. You say you know something about the recent murders in the trailer park?"

"I know that if I were the police, I'd be talkin' to Ken Culberson's therapist, Terry Thames. He'd been using HypnoReiki on him."

"You were a friend of Mr. Culberson's, and he told you about his therapy?"

"I'm acquainted with Dr. Thames. I figured exactly what he was up to. Ken Culberson was rich, with no kids or wife. Thames was using hypnotic suggestion to convince Ken to make him his inheritor. Thames was trying to drive Ken nuts . . . trying to make it so he could get himself appointed as his legal guardian."

"That's quite an accusation. Do you have any proof to back any of this up?"

"It's not like I got a signed confession or anything. But I can read auras accurately. They're like personal diaries of the soul."

"That's Theodora, all right," I said aloud, just as Tracy's taped voice was cutting to a commercial break. Theodora, I was certain, was just trying to get publicity. During tomorrow's broadcast, she would probably even reveal herself as the caller. I listened to the remainder of the taped conversation, which ended shortly after they returned from the commercial. Tracy had obviously begun to suspect that this aura-reading caller was a fruitcake, for Tracy cut Theodora off when she started talking about what an "innocent aura" Ken had possessed. I wondered how long it would take Tracy during tomorrow's show to figure out that the fruitcake and her guest were one and the same.

After putting everything away and locking Russell's office behind me, I checked my messages on my new answering machine and found that I had a couple of inquiries from potential new clients. That was good news for me, but I couldn't shake a prevailing sadness. Two people were dead. For what? Because Ken Culberson was an eccentric loner who didn't spend his money and, instead, left it to his beloved golden retriever?

Mary had had the most to gain by his death and might have orchestrated the whole thing. Had she worked with someone else and then grown afraid of her partner in crime? I still suspected that Ruby had witnessed the murder or some piece of it that endangered the killer.

The thoughts continued to "dog" me as I headed east to work with a dog in Longmont late that afternoon. This was a mixed breed, a recent acquisition from the Humane

Society in Boulder. The dog had not acclimated well to his new home and was terrorizing the children's rabbits, despite their being physically protected by their hutches. The dog's territorializing had increased such that he considered it his responsibility to keep everyone and every animal from entering his reign of control, which was two feet or so to the other side of the fence. My task was to shrink his boundaries to a more appropriate area, and his perceived status to a lower rung.

To my disappointment and the owners' discouragement, we had a bad day. The dog was obstinate and seemingly had unlearned all progress he'd made to date. I reassured the owners as best I could afterward that there were always peaks and valleys in anyone's "learning curve," including dogs'. We set up another appointment, and I hoped that they wouldn't fire me in the interim. Afterward, I had enough time to drop off Maggie at home. Mom had returned from work and was willing to assume responsibility for Maggie on my behalf. It felt as though Mom and I were teamed in a never-ending marathon, with Maggie functioning as the baton to pass.

It was a late night for me, working as I was on not just one but two separate cases of fearful dogs—always the greatest challenge. Fearful dogs can bite for no reason, plus it's easier to retrain a dog to overcome one specific behavioral problem than it is to change a personality characteristic. Afterward I kept a social engagement made weeks ago with some friends from high school. I deliberately evaded the subject matter of the murders in Boulder, which were on my friends' minds, just as they were on all Boulderites' minds.

It was dark as I drove home up Hover Road; dark *except* for the headlights of the person tailgating me, that is. I kept hoping that the car would turn off, but it was still tailing me by the time we reached a relatively deserted stretch of road. The bright lights reflecting off my rearview mirror were so annoying that I pulled onto the shoulder of the road to let the person pass, but the driver merely turned her high beams on and pulled in behind me.

My heart rate increased instantly. For a moment I assumed it was an unmarked police car, but the driver made no move to put official lights on the car roof. I certainly wasn't going to stay here or risk getting out of my vehicle, so I pulled a quick U-turn.

The other car did the same. Within moments, it was right on my bumper. Shit! I tried to see if I could identify the make of car or the driver, but the headlights were blinding.

What should I do? Common wisdom was to drive to the nearest police station, but a few years ago in Denver, a woman tried to do exactly that, only to be shot in the police parking lot.

I decided to keep going south on Hover until I reached the Twin Peaks shopping mall. The parking lot was well-lit. Maybe the driver wouldn't risk following me, for fear of being identified.

I made a sharp left turn into the parking lot of the mall, my tires screeching. The other car flew past the entrance. At that speed, it had to have turned west on the Diagonal back to Boulder. Meanwhile, I drove through the mall lot to head east on the Diagonal, to head toward Longmont. I ran the red light rather than risk giving the other driver enough time to turn around and pick up my car again at this intersection.

My heart was pounding, but I drove below the speed limit. There was enough traffic on the Diagonal heading toward downtown Longmont that I could perhaps blend in. Then I could head to Berthoud up Main Street instead of taking the chance that my stalker was sitting in wait on the side of the road.

Should I call the police before heading home? Truth be told, I was too scared to get out of my car. If only I had a cellular phone! And what could I tell the police? That someone had been following me for a few miles, but that I had no description of the driver or the vehicle. What could the police do with that information? Plus, after I'd left my car to reach a public phone, I would have to wait in hope that the patrol car arrived before my stalker. Was that safer than driving home? I was closer to my own house than I was to the police station.

High schoolers in Longmont were known for cruising at this hour, which could have been all this was—some kids who spotted a woman driving alone at night down a country road and decided to get their kicks from intimidating her. I knew better, really, but decided I would hang onto that possibility because it was less frightening than the alternative.

On edge, I watched through my rearview mirror every time a car approached me and slowed down a little. Each car sped past me in the left lane. I realized though, that if I was wrong, if this person was following me deliberately and knew that I was going to Berthoud, he or she could wait for me.

As I neared the outskirts of town, I let out a sigh of relief to discover that I was very much alone on the road. I made a rubberneck at what could have been a sedan behind some shrubs well off the side of the road. My pulse raced.

An instant later, a car turned on its beams and pulled out behind me. I cursed under my breath as the driver focused the high beams on me and ran up onto my bumper.

Chapter 17

My heart was pounding so hard that I could barely breathe. With the high beams from that vehicle right behind me, it felt as though I was under a spotlight when my only protection was to be hidden in darkness.

What could I do to escape? And why the hell was this happening to me?

Every instinct urged me to stomp down on the accelerator and try to lose this maniac. Yet we were near downtown Berthoud. There might be other cars in the intersections, or pedestrians or animals on the road.

Instead, I battled my instincts and slowed, but did not pull over. The Berthoud police station was only a mile or so past my turnoff for home. I would have to drive there. I certainly couldn't lead this person directly to my home.

I winced as the driver behind me leaned on the horn, then shut the lights out entirely. I braced myself, expecting the car to ram my bumper. Instead, the driver suddenly pulled a U-turn and drove away.

I hit the brakes and looked back, trying to get a view of the license plate or the silhouette of the driver, but the car vanished from view down the hill.

Why would someone behave this way? I decided to stop in at the police station and report what had happened, in case the driver intended to return. The officer I spoke to was very nice, despite my inability to give him useful information. Upon his insistence, he followed me home in his patrol car and walked me to the door. He would have accompanied me inside, but I insisted "that would only alarm my mother, not to mention my dogs."

Despite my brave words, my hands trembled as I turned the knob and entered. The four dogs were there to dutifully greet me, despite the hour. I finished petting them and went into the living room. Mom was asleep on the couch, a book tented over her chest. A floorboard creaked, waking her. "Allida?" she asked groggily.

"Yes. Hi, Mom."

She sat up a little, closing her book and setting it on the coffee table. "I must have dozed off for a minute. How did your day go?"

"Well, nobody I know died, which is an improvement." I took a seat in the upholstered wing chair in the corner of the room.

"That's . . . nice, dear." She yawned and stretched as she sat up. Then her eyes searched mine. "You look a little pale. Are you sure you're all right?"

"I'm fine. I just had to deal with an obnoxious tail-gater, that's all." Before she could ask me for more details, I asked, "How was Maggie's behavior this afternoon?"

"Well, she's not exactly ready for the Westminster Dog Show, but she is getting a little easier to control."

The phone rang and I rose to answer while Mom clicked her tongue and muttered, "It's well past eleven! That's too late to be calling somebody. If this is anything short of an emergency, tell whoever it is to call back at a reasonable hour tomorrow."

"I will, Mom," I replied automatically, having heard this from her for years now.

"Allie?" a tense voice replied the moment I'd said hello. "This is Joanne Palmer. What the hell do you think you're pulling?"

Caught off guard, it took me a moment to place the name and realize that this was Maggie's veterinarian. "Could you back up a bit? I don't even know what you're talking about."

"I was just taking inventory of my pharmacy, and my pills are gone! All of my sample packets of Clomicalm and acepromazine! You were the only person to have un-supervised access to my supply closet, when you were sup-posedly looking for towels."

"You're accusing me of stealing medication for dogs?" I asked incredulously.

"No one else had the opportunity or motive. You could take a couple of years' supply of drugs and pass yourself off as a vet with no license."

"I did no such thing, Joanne! I can't believe you're even serious!" Maybe she'd been taking doggie drugs herself and was hallucinating.

"I always lock the supply cabinet. No one else has a key. Not even my assistant. Then I thought back a little and realized they could have been missing since T-Rex was here."

Though I told myself to stay calm, that Joanne was just reacting out of the heat of the moment, I didn't care for her much to begin with, and her absurd accusation was hard to take. I replied testily, "The problem with your theory, Joanne, is that I didn't touch your drug supplies. And why would I jeopardize my future just to steal a batch of pills?"

There was a pause and then a sigh. "You're right. Maybe I should have thought this through better. I guess if you wanted to get your hands on Clomicalm or ACP, it wouldn't be that hard for you to convince a veterinarian friend to give you a prescription."

"Right. What do the police have to say about the theft?"

"I haven't spoken to them yet."

"Why not?"

She ignored the question and said, "If it wasn't you who raided my supply cabinet it had to have been Yolanda. She was back here visiting T-Rex while we were all up front in the waiting room."

"My advice to you is to contact the police and let them

handle this. You're probably every bit as off base with your accusation of Yolanda as you were with me." I spoke with a confidence I didn't feel.

"No, no. This time I'm positive. It's Yolanda all right, and she's not going to get away with this." Joanne abruptly hung up.

"Who was that?" Mom asked as I returned the handset to its cradle.

"A fringe-element veterinarian in Boulder."

" 'Fringe element'?" Mom repeated.

"I watched her save a dog's life from an overdose, so she does know what she's doing medically. But she's too quick on the draw to prescribe canine antidepressants and tranquilizers. Now she's upset because somebody apparently stole a batch of pills from her."

"Why would anyone steal dog medication?"

"Doggie downers have been used for years as a cheap high. And I suppose, in combination with alcohol, the same can probably be said for Clomicalm. Though it's medically very similar to Prozac."

"So you think that the thief could be selling them for human consumption?"

"Yes. Or just using them herself. Or himself." The dogs huddled around my feet, vying for placement and attention. I scratched Pavlov's ear. The more I thought about it, the more the possibility of Joanne's being right the second time—that Yolanda might have been the thief— seemed plausible. Yolanda did have the opportunity to steal those pills. T-Rex had overdosed while under her supervision, and she blamed Dr. Palmer's pills for her friend Ruby's death.

"Could that have been the motive for the murders, do you think?" Mom asked.

"I suppose it's possible. It would have to be one heck of a huge drug ring, though. I can't imagine even a couple of hundred pills of Clomicalm or ACP being worth someone committing murder over."

Then again, maybe I'd been wrong all along. Maybe Ken hadn't really gotten his fortune from a patent on some obscure television circuit, but rather from pushing drugs. Or Ruby or Mary had been pushing drugs, with Ken completely in the dark, which struck me as more likely. But . . . still. Murdering someone over canine anti-depressants? That was just so implausible.

Mom stood up. "As I've said before, I don't understand why you're suddenly up to your elbows in crazy people. On the other end of the scale, Russell called. About an hour ago. He said he'd call again tomorrow."

I couldn't think about Russell right now and responded only to Mom's earlier statement. "I know what you mean. It's like everyone in Ken's life had a few screws loose."

Mom pursed her lips and crossed her arms tightly against her chest. "Maybe I should postpone my lessons tomorrow. I don't think you should be alone."

"I won't be alone. I'll take Pavlov and Maggie with me tomorrow. I've got mostly office visits on my schedule, and I could put them in Russell's office when necessary." At my own mention of Russell, I was filled with a longing to see him. "Did Russell leave a number?"

"Yes. I think I wrote it down when I was in the kitchen. He sounded depressed, actually. He said he misses you."

Mom went to bed, and I dialed Russell's hotel room. It was an hour earlier in California and I reached him. We chatted for a while, and I tried to ignore my inexplicable nervousness that was leaving me somewhat breathless.

After a pause he said, "It was a bit late when I called. I hope I didn't wake your mom up."

"If so, she didn't complain to me about it."

Russell remained silent, and I realized then what he was really asking.

"I got together tonight with some girlfriends from high school."

"Oh, good. Did you have fun?" Russell asked, sounding greatly relieved.

"Yes."

"How's the softball team doing?"

"I forgot to show up for the game last week, but they won without me."

"Must have been a fluke," he replied pleasantly. He sighed. "I'd better get back to work."

"It's—" I glanced at my watch "—ten-forty at night there. You're still working?"

"The sooner I can complete this project, the sooner I can get home to you. Uh, home, I mean, where you're also located. I didn't mean to imply that we were . . . I know you don't want to be rushed."

I smiled, wondering if my appreciation for the sound of Russell's voice would last. Though I was sorely tempted to reveal my longing to see him, my more immediate worries won out and I merely said, "By the way, I ordered you a new door for your office the other day. Your current one's pretty gouged up. I told the landlord about it, and he's just sending me the bill."

"Ah. You forgot that I was gone and couldn't wait for me to open the door?"

I chuckled and said, "Since the damage has already been done, you don't mind if I give a couple of dogs run of your office tomorrow, do you?"

"No, that's fine. Have 'em take a look at those schematics in my top drawer of my desk while they're at it. They might have some suggestions."

We said our good-byes and hung up.

The next morning, I folded the back seat of my Subaru hatchback down for the "additional cargo space" that the car ads were always talking about, and let Pavlov settle herself down. Then I fastened Maggie's seatbelt harness on her and put her in the passenger seat.

While I made the drive back into Boulder, I wondered again whether or not Ken could have lied about the source of his wealth. I'd seen the yellowed patent on his wall, but I'd never seen an actual patent before then and would never be able to discern its authenticity. Arlen, however, had verified the story about how Ken had struck it rich. Maybe another chat with him would let me be able to stop worrying about any possibility of Ken's having gotten his money from illegitimate sources. In any case, I wanted to know Arlen better. As Ken's one remaining blood relative, my having put him low on the list of inheritors had to be with good cause.

Once again, Arlen was in his open garage as I pulled into his driveway. He was wearing a plaid shirt and grimy jeans again, topped off with his beat-up straw cowboy hat. He had been working on his truck engine. He held up a greasy palm in greeting, but continued to stare at Maggie with apparent apprehension.

Wiping his hands on a rag, he rounded the truck to speak to me, and I rolled down the window. Maggie began barking at him, which made Pavlov sit up and take notice as well, but she knew better than to join in.

Arlen gave me a nervous smile. "See you got yourself a shepherd there, too, hey?"

"Yes, she's one of my own dogs."

He focused again on the still-barking golden retriever. "How's Miss Maggie doing?"

"She seems to be settling down pretty well. Not counting her current noisiness. I had her in the car and brought her over for a quick visit. Is that all right with you?"

"Um, sure, but I was just about to leave." He gestured at his pickup, which currently had its hood raised. A carburetor and a few less-recognizable engine parts were spread on the concrete floor of the garage.

"Okay. Maybe we can set an appointment and do this another time."

"Or not at all?" he suggested, then followed it up with a sheepish smile. "I mean, I *am* Ken's next of kin. I'm obviously the one to get his dog."

The dog's barking right in my ear was getting to me. I

got out of the car, rolled the window up, and shut the door to blot the noise. Watching for his reaction, I asked, "Did you hear about Mary's being alive? Though I guess she's now missing."

He frowned and nodded. "Wouldn't necessarily bet on her *still* bein' alive. That gal was always mixing with the wrong people. I swear. She could go to a gathering where there was a hundred or two folks and one of 'em was a hardened criminal, and she'd not only find the one rotten apple out of the batch, but he'd fall head over heels for her."

"Is that what your brother was? A rotten apple?"

"Hell, no. But that's why it couldn't ever have lasted with the two of them. Ken was decent. She hated that. She walked over his face."

"I've gotten the impression that Ken allowed a lot of people to 'walk on his face.' "

"Yeah. He was too kindhearted. Had no real idea of what people was really like. That's part of why we hired Terry Thames—to help him get a grasp on the real world."

"Who is this *we* who hired Dr. Thames?"

"Uh, me and Mary."

I was caught off guard by his openly admitting that he'd once been teamed with his former sister-in-law. "The two of you were friends at one point?"

"I don't know if you'd call us friends, exactly. Though I . . . kind of introduced Ken to Mary in the first place." The muscles in his jaw were working. "Mary and I were dating for a while. Till I made the mistake of telling her about how rich my brother was."

That was interesting. "Did you and she get back together after the divorce at all?"

"Hell, no. I saw her true colors by then."

"Do you know if she was dating anyone else?"

He shook his head. "Don't ever talk to her, if I can avoid it."

"And yet the two of you hired Dr. Thames?"

Arlen shrugged. "Kind of. But I was on Ken's side

all along. Mary came to me one day, insisting that
Ken needed to be declared incompetent. She just wanted
to be named as his guardian so she could get her claws on
his money. So I wound up talking Ken into gettin'
examined by Dr. Thames, and he became a patient. Dr.
Thames told me right off the bat that Ken was perfectly capable of takin' care of himself. I kind of explained about how Mary was after me to see to it that my
brother was declared incompetent, nevertheless. Dr.
Thames said he'd see to it that some adult-care provider
could work with Ken, so's Mary couldn't get away
with it."

"The care provider was Rachel Taylor?"

"Yeah. Then, supposedly, a month or so after that,
Mary had her accident. You ask me, I think the whole
thing was a con. I don't think she ever got hit by a car in
the first place."

I nodded and glanced again at the car and his work
that I'd interrupted. "I'd better let you go. Would sometime next week be good for me to bring Maggie for a
scheduled visit? Monday morning, perhaps?"

He stared through the windshield at Maggie, who'd
kept up her steady barking at him. "Yeah, sure. I s'pose
that'd be all right."

"Okay. I'll call first and set up an exact time. See you
then."

He tipped his hat then returned his attention to his engine. I drove off, Maggie quieting the moment we were
out of sight. Arlen was not comfortable in the dog's
presence, and the feeling was clearly mutual. I remembered that Ken had once said that he trusted me because
Maggie had liked me. Perhaps the corollary was also
true—he hadn't trusted his brother with Maggie because
she shied away from him.

Something bugged me as I drove, and I realized it was
a suspicion about Rachel Taylor. Something somebody
had said about her didn't match up correctly. Could

Yolanda be right about her? Then again, what about Yolanda herself? Could she just be casting aspersions on Rachel to keep them from settling on herself?

I remembered then that I'd forgotten to ask Arlen about Ken's patent. I still had an hour or so before my first appointment, so I decided to see if I could perhaps go into Ken's trailer and get the number on the patent. I sorely wanted to dismiss forever my notion that Ken could have gotten money by selling the Clomicalm that had been prescribed to Maggie.

Remembering what a watchdog Yolanda was and her ability to identify specific car engines, I left the dogs in my car in the shade of the clubhouse at the trailer park's entrance. Much as I'd come to like Yolanda, I was too concerned about her own involvement in the missing drugs to make her aware of my suspicions.

I made my way unseen to Ken's front door and tried the doorknob. It was locked. I went around to the back and tried that door. Also locked.

I was not about to break in just to examine the patent. Frustrated, I gave up and rounded the trailer to return to my car. I gasped and froze in my tracks at the sight of Yolanda, training a rifle on me from her post at the foot of Ken's property.

"Oh. It's you," she said, lowering the gun. T-Rex was off-leash beside her and trotted toward me with his tail wagging.

"You've got a rifle?"

"Don't have any ammo, though. Jus' keep it for its effect. What you doing here?"

"I wanted to get a look at Ken's patent. The door was locked, though. You don't happen to have a key, or know of anyone who does, do you?"

"Nope. Ken wasn't much on lockin' the place."

"Do you think his brother might have a copy of Ken's keys?"

She shrugged. "Could be, though I doubt it. Two of them

weren't too close. He always treated Ken like the black sheep of the family. Not much of a brother, if you ask me."

"Did Ken ever show you his patent?" I asked, feigning a casual attitude. Yolanda had struck me as uneducated, but as shrewd and observant as anyone I'd met recently.

She nodded. "Oh, sure. Ken showed it to darn near everybody who set foot in his place. Course, he also had this fantasy that he'd made millions on the invention, but I never met no millionaire that lived like this. It's like saying you live in the Taj Mahal, when you're really holed up in its outhouse."

"So you didn't believe him?"

"Course not. But we're all entitled to our little fantasies." She paused, studied my features, then asked, "Did you?"

"Yes, actually."

She chuckled. "Wouldn't that've been something? If I was really living next door to a rich man all this time and never . . ." She let her voice fade and her eyes widened. "Course . . . that could explain Mary."

"That she married him for his money, you mean?"

She nodded. "She obviously didn't ever love the poor slob."

"Ken had a shoe box full of hundred dollar bills. I saw them when I was here the day before he died."

Yolanda put a hand up to shield her eyes from the bright sun as she studied my features. "You serious?"

"Yes. I saw the money myself, though apparently the police never found it."

She let out a low whistle and shook her head. "Just imagine. Ken having all that kind of money, living in a dump like this."

"He was quite the eccentric."

I kept an eye on T-Rex, who had happily trotted ahead of us, back toward Yolanda's trailer. Partway there, he started sniffing and pawing at something wedged in the corner of the steps and the trailer.

"But why would—" Her voice broke off as she caught a glimpse of what T-Rex had now occupied himself with. She froze and turned her back on the dog. "Say, Allie. Maybe it'd be best if you didn't come in just now. The place is in a bit of mess and I think you should . . ."

I stepped aside to get a better view of what it was that T-Rex was playing with that she obviously did not want me to see. Transfixed, I rushed over to T-Rex and picked it up. It was a small packet of Clomicalm.

Chapter 18

Yolanda's jaw dropped. "Well. I wonder how that got there." Her cheeks had colored, further giving herself away.

I lifted the packet of pills. "You took these from Joanne Palmer's office, didn't you," I said harshly.

"No."

I could tell she was lying. "Why did you take the pills? Are you selling them?"

"Not me. That was Ruby's scam, like I told you." She held up her palms. "I didn't have nothing to do with that. That was Ruby's hot idea, 'n' I stayed completely out of it. She talked Ken into taking Maggie to that idiot vet for a prescription."

"Ruby orchestrated all of that on her own?" Frankly, that was a bit surprising to me. Ruby had seemed to have so little on the ball that I doubted she could outwit Joanne Palmer so easily.

"Yeah. That poor Ken was so trusting, he gave Ruby all of Maggie's pills at no cost. And she got the pills from Palmer for nothin' too 'cuz Palmer knew Ruby was drummin' up business for her. Plus Ruby got some deal goin' with another couple of dog owners, too, to get their pills in trade for something or other. Between T-Rex and the other dogs, Ruby got herself quite a stash collected. Then she'd sell 'em for ten times what they were worth. Only once you showed up, I guess she must've panicked and figured you'd find out somehow that T-Rex wasn't on medication but should've been, so she must've overmedicated him on the spot. And then I went and accidentally did the same thing, gave him the same spiked dog food."

I considered her story. Her explanation was at least possible. "That was quite a roundabout way for Ruby to sell drugs on the street. Not to mention that, even if she sold the pills for ten times their legitimate price, they wouldn't bring in all that much money."

"Yeah, but she'd done time at least twice for drug dealing and tol' me she had to be real careful. She figured what she was doin' now wasn't illegal. That nobody could give her a hard time for selling drugs that was really meant for dogs."

I nodded.

"Thing is, though, Ruby started eatin' up her own profits, takin' the damned pills herself. She was stoned half the time. I wasn't thinking clearly when I was in that vet's office. Her supply cabinet doors was wide open. And I was so mad at Ruby's dying, and T-Rex nearly dying, and Ken dying, I started thinking maybe none of 'em would've died, 'cept for the pills. So I swiped them."

"What did you do with them then?"

She shrugged. "Kept 'em. Then I calmed down and was thinking of trying to return them." She met my eyes, her own gray eyes magnified by her lenses. "Allie, please don't turn me in. I'd've prob'ly returned the pills eventually."

"Does this look like the same container of drug samples that you took?"

She nodded. "One must've fell out and I didn't notice it." She grinned and pulled on the neckline of her blouse. "That's an advantage of having some cleavage. I just shoved the lot of 'em down my blouse and waltzed off with a near grocery bag full 'fore anyone would've noticed."

"Did you tell the police about what Ruby had been up to?"

She shook her head and averted her eyes. "I tried to

help her out. Tried to convince her there was better ways of making money, but she wouldn't listen to me. 'Sides, I didn't ever really figure out what was goin' on till she tol' me about it. After Ken died."

"So the police still don't know, then?"

Again, she shook her head. "I don't like talking to the police. Makes me nervous."

"We have to tell them now. It could be related to the murders."

"Don't see why the police need to hear it from me." She held up her palms. "I know I shouldn't've taken those pills. I'm just gonna take 'em back to Dr. Palmer's office and apologize."

"I'll drive you, but after that, we must go to the police station so you can tell them about Ruby. Not reporting a criminal activity is a crime itself. And two people have been murdered. It would be asinine of us not to notify the police." I glanced toward the clubhouse, remembering that I had both dogs waiting there.

"I hope they don't go arresting me just for borrowing from Palmer's supply closet," Yolanda grumbled under her breath. She opened her door.

"They won't. You're returning them. For all we know, Dr. Palmer still hasn't reported the pills as missing. I'm sure they can't arrest you for stealing something and then returning it when it hasn't even been reported missing. I'm not worried."

"Yeah, but you ain't me."

There was no arguing with that statement. She tucked her rifle under one arm and grabbed T-Rex's collar once again. I held the screen door open for her. She paused as she looked back at Ken's home.

"All this blood spilled because of one man's money," she muttered. "Kind've turns my stomach."

We went into her kitchen and she stashed the rifle underneath her sink. Then she pulled out a metal and plastic-over-foam-rubber-padding chair from the table and stepped up on it to reach into the cabinet over the refrigerator. It was a bit daunting watching such a large woman on such a precarious perch, but she seemed perfectly at ease.

"It's that damned phony social worker. Probably killed both of them," Yolanda said, as if to herself. "Maybe she even dropped that packet of pills outside my trailer last night hoping someone would find them and she could frame me."

This had to be close to the tenth time she'd accused Rachel Taylor of committing the murders.

"The thing is, though, Yolanda, there *is* no way Rachel could have 'figured it out,' as you said, that you'd taken the pills from Joanne Palmer's supply cabinet. So she couldn't have deliberately set you up like this."

She glanced down at me. "You been working with dogs too long. You got yourself a pair of blinders when it comes to reading people."

"That's not true."

"Oh, no? Answer me this." With fists full of pill packets she stepped down, spreading the containers over the kitchen counter. "Why do you s'pose somebody like me can't get you or nobody else to listen when I tell you I know full well Rachel's the killer?"

"Lack of evidence, for one thing."

"And you don't want to believe that the friendly social worker to us poor folk is a cold-blooded killer."

"Well—" I paused, mulling over her assertion "—that's true, I guess. Nobody wants to suspect the person who's supposedly there to help people in unfortunate circumstances. But that doesn't change the fact that—"

"The facts are that two friends of mine who lived right near me are dead inside of a week! The fact is that, while I can't prove it, I know who done it!"

I sighed and surveyed the pills spread out before us. "Do they all seem to be there?"

She shrugged. "No idea. I didn't count 'em. If I had to guess, I'd say this is all of 'em, though."

"Let's get them into a bag so you won't have to use your bra again." I said this with a smile, and Yolanda laughed.

Someone knocked on the door. "Just a minute," she called out.

I automatically rose and looked around the doorway to see who it was. Joanne Palmer was standing on Yolanda's front porch. She stared at me through the screen door. "What are you doing here?" she asked me.

"I was about to ask you the same thing."

"I came to get what Yolanda stole from me." She let herself in through the unlocked screen door. Yolanda was now standing beside me. "I want my stuff back, right now, or I'm going straight to the police."

"Yet another coincidence," I said. "That's just where we were about to head, after returning your pills."

"Sorry 'bout stealing your medicine, Dr. Palmer. I shouldn't've done it." Yolanda swept the pills into a bag and handed the bag to her. "They're all here, as far as I know."

"There's no reason to take this matter to the police. Now that you've given them back, we'll forget all about the unfortunate incident."

"It's not that easy," I interjected. "There's too much involved. Two people are dead, and one of the victims had been selling ACP and Clomicalm herself."

"What? That's absurd."

Yolanda said, "Ruby was getting many times the amount of pills T-Rex needed. And you were prescribing 'em like they was Tic Tacs."

"Shit! Yolanda, you don't know what you're talking about! You're going to get yourself arrested for stealing and abusing drugs, and I'm going to have some stuffed-shirt from vet licensing breathing down my neck! Don't go to the police. Let's just drop all this nonsense right now."

Yolanda looked at me, then back at Joanne. Gesturing toward me, she said, "I tend to trust what she says more'n what you say. I'll take my chances with the police."

"You're making the right choice," I assured her.

Joanne leaned on the table and stared directly into

Yolanda's eyes. "The hell you are! You're going to wind up in jail if you listen to her."

"You will not. She's trying to scare you because she doesn't want to lose her license."

Joanne frowned at me, then threw up her hands. "Fine. Yolanda, go ahead and go to the police with this. We'll both take our chances." She narrowed her eyes at me. "Thanks a lot."

"Pardon?"

"This is the last thing my business needed, Allida. I'm barely scraping by as it is. I only wanted to help sick animals, you know. I went through ten years of college and post-grad work to get to where I am now, and it's all falling to pieces."

"I'm sorry."

"You don't mean that, so why say it? I did what I needed to do for my patients. You think you know better than me? Wait till you run into a canine client with a brain tumor. Then you'll see how fast you want to go with medicine over your training methods."

Her bag of pills in hand, Joanne stormed outside, the screen door banging shut behind her. I looked at Yolanda. "Going to the police really is the right thing to do, you know."

She nodded. "Let's get it over with."

We walked to my car. I rearranged Maggie to be in the back with Pavlov and gave Yolanda the passenger seat. Yolanda flipped on my radio and tuned in the Tracy Truett show. "I love this gal's show," Yolanda said. "Haven't been able to hear it all month, 'cuz my radio's broke. You ever listen to her?"

"Sometimes."

Over the radio, Theodora was using her trancelike voice to speak about how hard it was for psychics to "gain respect from the mainstream."

"*Is* there a mainstream in Boulder? Other than Boulder Creek, I mean," Tracy asked. "Stream . . . Creek . . . Get it?"

"Oh, certainly there is," Theodora went on, ignoring

Tracy's silly joke. "We're a city of the self-obsessed, finding ourselves and our inner thoughts endlessly fascinating. Which leads to our preoccupation with therapists. Boulder citizens find it more acceptable to take their pets to a therapist than their souls to a spiritual counselor."

"Oh, give me a break!" I muttered, ready to turn off the radio in my annoyance.

"Is that how you see yourself?" Tracy asked. "Are you a spiritual counselor?"

"Yes, and yet those with a license to practice therapy use some of the same techniques that I do." Theodora sounded jealous and defensive.

Tracy asked, "They say that no one can make you do something under hypnosis that you wouldn't do if you were fully conscious of your actions. Isn't that right?"

"So I've heard, but then, there is a greater range of what people are willing to do than what they might admit to themselves. For example, if I were to suggest to you, Tracy, that you flap your arms and cluck like a chicken on the Pearl Street Mall, you would refuse, right? You'd be too embarrassed. But you would do so without hesitation under hypnosis."

"Cluck, cluck, cluck, we'll be right back," Tracy said, causing Yolanda to slap her knee and laugh merrily.

I tolerated a couple of commercials, then turned off the radio.

My trips to the police station had become almost daily sojourns. This one with Yolanda proved similar to my previous experiences. We sat in a small, unexceptional room, and Yolanda told two officers the same thing she'd told me about Ruby's activities with the Clomicalm and ACP and how she'd gotten it. Yolanda was quiet and subdued as I dropped her off at her home and then returned to my office with just the dogs as company.

Before I could get the dogs settled in for a while with

water bowls and food in Russell's office, I heard what sounded like someone trotting down the steps. Maggie barked in warning, touching off Pavlov's barking as well. I returned to my office to see who this was.

The outer door flew open, and Theodora rushed in. She was wearing a redder shade of purple than normal, and her long hair was done up in some sort of a rat's nest. "Oh, thank God. You're all right." She put a hand to her chest as she struggled to regain her breath.

"Yes, I'm fine. What's the matter?"

"I had a vision. About you. You're in terrible danger, Allida."

I was not in the mood for this, and my temper instantly flared. "I *realize* that I'm in danger. And unless this vision of yours can tell me something useful, such as who the killer is so I can stay the hell away from him or her, I don't want to hear it."

She started pacing, her arms wrapped around her midsection. "It's not by choice that I get these psychic visions, you know. I've always had them, ever since I was a little girl, growing up in New Jersey. I can't control them, can't predict how specific they'll be or how revealing."

She closed her eyes and grimaced. She stared at Maggie for a moment, then turned her gaze to me. "I saw an image of you. It looked like you tied in a chair, and someone was holding a gun to your head."

"Oh, great. Didn't you hear me ask you not to tell me unless it would be of some help to me? What am I supposed to do with that information, Theodora? Stay away from all chairs, for fear someone will pull a gun on me? Obviously I'm not going to voluntarily get myself taken hostage at gunpoint, so it's not as though I've got any ability to avoid that scenario."

She looked at me, her face pale with fright. "We're connected in this. I'm not sure how or why, but we are. Otherwise, I wouldn't have seen you so clearly. You've got to beware, for my sake, too." She searched my eyes. "Only be around people you trust. That's the only thing I can suggest."

"Easier said than done."

"I realize that," Theodora replied. She turned on a heel and walked out the door.

Chapter 19

My next appointment wasn't scheduled for over an hour, and I needed to clear my head. If Maggie were easier to control, we could walk along Boulder Creek. But with the large number of in-line skaters and bicyclists that frequented the creek's walkway, doing so was out of the question. I took her for a brief walk around the block instead, then got Pavlov. I took care to lock the door behind Maggie, who promptly bashed the top of her head into the glass in an attempt to follow us.

The walk did me a world of good. I felt my spirits lightening. The mountains were beautiful. The gardens around the library, too, were resplendent in their colors and scents.

As we made the return hike up Mapleton Hill to my office, I heard Maggie's barks and quickened my pace. I was inwardly kicking myself. I'd thought her barking was under control, but something had obviously set her off. If she'd been barking like this for long, my landlord was bound to complain.

Arlen Culberson was standing at the bottom of my steps when I arrived, leaning against my glass door, his back to Maggie, who barked ceaselessly. He straightened when he spotted me. "Oh, good. You're back," he said, giving me a smile and ignoring, completely, my German shepherd. He held a colorful bouquet in his arms.

I mustered a smile and said, "Hello, Arlen. You brought me flowers?"

"No, I was just here waitin' for you when someone from FTD dropped them off."

Russell, I thought. *What a sweet man!* The flowers were in an indigo vase. It bothered me immensely that I had Arlen Culberson to deal with now, instead of being able to steal a few moments to luxuriate in romantic thoughts about Russell.

As I descended the steps, the dogs slightly behind me, Arlen explained, "Turns out, I'm gonna be out of town Monday, so I thought I'd come to you 'n' Maggie for a change."

"Okay, but this time *I'm* going to be a bit pressed for time."

Arlen gave me an embarrassed chuckle, gesturing at the barking golden. "Didn't think Maggie'd be so on edge."

"Neither did I." I opened the door, stepped inside, and the dogs followed me. Arlen came in last, keeping a wary eye on Maggie. She stepped back and mingled some growls in with her barks at Arlen, her hackles raised.

Arlen set the vase on my desk and then bent down toward the snarling dog. "Come on, Maggie. I'm just here to visit you, girl." He gave me a sheepish grin. "She looks good, anyways."

"Her lungs are healthy," I muttered, perplexed at her behavior. Pavlov was on edge now as well, and I quickly let her into Russell's office.

Meanwhile, Arlen took a step toward Maggie, and she backed away, still maintaining her shrill barks. This was the first time I'd seen her shy away from someone as though she was afraid of being struck.

Arlen apparently picked up on the dog's body English as well, for he stopped trying to get near her and put his hands in his jean pockets. "So, anyway, Allida, have you decided about my getting the dog yet?"

"No, I haven't."

"You can see how nice my house would be for her. She'd have a lot of room to run around."

"Yes, but I wasn't too encouraged by how anxious Maggie seemed to be when she was there."

"It was just a new setting. She's never been to my place before, that's all. I'm sure if you gave us a chance, she'd take to me. She always did."

"If you ask me, Maggie seems to have taken a dislike to you, if anything."

"She doesn't dislike me, do you, girl?"

She growled and barked louder. This was unusual behavior for any golden, but especially for Maggie, who seemed to love all people. When Maggie flinched as Arlen removed his hat, that verified what I had previously suspected.

"You've hit her at some point," I said matter-of-factly.

"No, I haven't. She probably just doesn't like men or something, or is scared of my cowboy hat."

"Please, Arlen. Don't try to con me. I've been with Maggie every day for ten days straight. She's never shied away from anyone till just now."

He clicked his tongue. "That was a long time ago and she deserved it. Chewed up my favorite hat. She can't possibly remember and hold that against me."

"Dogs have a long memory. And so do I."

Arlen's jaw dropped. "You're going to blackball me just for smacking the dog one time? You've got to be kidding me! I'm Ken's only living relative! I deserve his inheritance!"

"Then why wouldn't he make his will out to leave it to you?"

"Like I said, we used to have problems."

"He rewrote his will the day he died. Maybe those problems weren't completely resolved. And in any case, my entire agenda remains getting a good new owner for Maggie. I guarantee it's not going to be someone who thinks a dog deserves to get hit for chewing up something that shouldn't have been in the dog's vicinity in the first place."

Arlen glared at me menacingly. I remained standing by

Russell's doorway, ready to bring Pavlov in here for physical protection, if need be. Pavlov would never allow me to be manhandled.

Over the sound of Maggie's barks, Arlen said, "I know what you're up to, Miss Babcock. You're trying to keep Maggie for yourself so that you can get my brother's money. You're not going to get away with it."

He left.

I called, "Maggie, come," and knelt to pet her as she did so. At least I wasn't so distracted by Arlen's visit to forget to give Maggie a command that she could follow before rewarding her with petting her. I looked in the direction that Arlen Culberson had just gone, and murmured soothingly to Maggie, "There goes yet another dog hater who is not going to inherit you."

I went over to the flowers and read the card:

> *Hope these flowers are at least one-tenth as beautiful as you are. Love, Russell.*

My heart raced, and I reread the words, wondering if this was what it meant to have one's heart be aflutter.

The phone rang. Before I could barely get my "hello" out, the caller said, "Allida, it's Yolanda. You've got to come over here right away. There's a problem with T-Rex. He's acting all crazy."

"What do you mean 'all crazy'?"

"He's got me trapped on the kitchen counter. Whenever I try to step down, he snaps at me."

Something medical had to be causing such a sudden, radical change in personalities. My immediate thought was that it could be a brain tumor, but I tried to argue otherwise with myself. "Has he ingested anything unusual again?"

"No."

"I'm going to need help subduing him. I'm going to call Animal Control and—"

"Oww!"

"What's wrong?"

"I . . . got bit already. On my leg. It hurts when I move."

"How bad is it? Are you bleeding?"

"Not that bad. I'll be fine. Just don't go callin' Animal Control. They'll want to immediately put him to sleep!"

Another thought occurred to me. Rabies. "Is T-Rex foaming at the mouth?"

"No. He's just acting wild suddenly. That's all. I just need you to help me grab him and I'm sure I can get him calmed down. If we need more help, we can figure it out once you get here. Just don't call Animal Control, all right?"

"Fine, Yolanda. I'll be right there. Is the back door to your kitchen unlocked?"

"No, but the front door's open."

"I'll be there in ten minutes," I said and hung up. I wasn't going to argue with her, but I immediately called Animal Control and apprised them of the situation. They said they'd meet me there as soon as possible and suggested that I not enter the house myself. Agreeing with the advice, I assured them that I wouldn't.

No dog lover wanted to see a dog "put down," but sometimes that was the only option. I could only hope that T-Rex's sudden change in personality was caused by something reversible. He might have swallowed a sharp object, for example, that was putting him in so much pain he was lashing out.

I opened Russell's door, then had to squeeze past the now dejected Maggie to get outside, hoping that Pavlov would be enough company for her that she wouldn't start barking again.

I sped along Broadway, realizing that I was going to miss yet another appointment with a client, but that couldn't be helped. I soon arrived at the trailer park, then pulled into the empty space on the graveled area near Yolanda's home. There was a sound coming from her place—a blaring TV broadcast, I realized as I neared. She probably couldn't reach it from her perch on the kitchen counter. It had been fortunate for her sake, though, that she'd had her portable phone with her.

I entered the gate, shutting it behind me. The curtains on the front windows were shut. She'd said that the front door was open but the back door in the kitchen was locked. I raced up the steps, but felt a hideous deja vu. I'd entered Ken's trailer this way.

Now I could hear T-Rex barking from inside. Maybe it was just Theodora's warning about the gun at my head, but I wasn't going to take any foolish risks in my attempt to be a good Samaritan and help Yolanda. I would wait out here for Animal Control, and if that meant that Yolanda would have to spend an extra half hour trapped on her kitchen counter, so be it.

I needed at least to call to her, though, so that I could make sure she was all right—perhaps keep T-Rex occupied at the other side of this door. I tried the doorknob, planning to open it a crack so she could hear me, but it was locked.

"Yolanda? Are you okay?"

No answer. Maybe I'd be able to see her through the sliding glass doors in the kitchen. I started to round the trailer, but heard a metallic click from the front door. I whirled around in surprise as the door opened.

Rachel Taylor stepped out, a small black gun in her hand aimed at my midsection. "Come in, Allida. You scream and I'll shoot you dead on the spot," she said, her face eerily calm.

Chapter 20

A slew of four-letter words ran through my brain. Yolanda had been right all along! Could Ruby's life somehow have been spared if we'd all listened to her? "Where's Yolanda?"

Rachel directed me toward the trailer with her gun. "Get inside. We've been waiting for you."

I hesitated. I should scream for help. Somebody might come or call the police. Staring at the gun in her hand, there was no way I could be so bold. I was one finger-twitch away from death.

She must have tied up Yolanda. If she was still alive. If I just meekly entered Yolanda's trailer, I'd be trapped and killed myself. Desperately, I tried to think of another option, but couldn't.

Keeping the gun aimed at me, Rachel stepped back, and I entered the dimly lit trailer. Yolanda was tightly bound to a straight-back chair in the living room. T-Rex was barking from a back room. His barks bore the shrill pitch that indicated he was distressed.

Yolanda murmured, "Sorry 'bout this. I didn't want to call you. Tried not to."

My eyes adjusted, and I gasped at the condition of her face. She'd been beaten. Her lip was split. One eye was swelling closed.

Rachel pushed me forward and shut the door. There were no signs of a struggle, save for Yolanda's glasses, the frames broken in two, on the floor. Rachel must have punched Yolanda after she'd already been bound to the chair.

Did she intend to murder everyone Ken had known? If she was the only one left alive, it was going to be pretty damned obvious that she was the killer! I turned my face toward her and asked through gritted teeth, "What's the point of this?"

"Simple, really. You're going to sign this piece of paper I wrote up for you, appointing the permanent guardian for that disgusting fleabag of Ken's."

Though trembling from both rage and fright, I said defiantly, "Why would I do that? You're obviously going to kill us both before the ink's even dry. Besides which, for God's sake, think about this, Rachel! It'll be totally obvious that you're the murderer. You'll have a signed piece of paper from me giving you ownership of the dog, the very day somebody shoots me to death. How's that going to look? This is . . . totally nuts."

She chuckled and leaned back against the door, the gun still trained on me. "The trouble with you, Allida, is you think you're smarter than everyone else. But I'm way ahead of you." She pointed with her chin to the coffee table. On top of it was a typed form on a legal-sized sheet of paper. "Look at the contract."

I bent down to read it on the table, knowing if I picked it up, my trembling hands would give away how frightened I was. The person named by this contract to receive custody of Maggie—and thereby Ken's inheritance—was not Rachel Taylor. "You're forcing me to give the money to Theodora?"

Rachel grinned. "Who is then going to take the rap for two murders. Soon to be four."

Yolanda and I met each others' eyes. The feistiness that I'd always seen there was absent. She appeared resigned to her fate. I wished I could tell her not to give up hope, that Animal Control was bound to arrive any moment now.

"And what good does a signed contract giving Maggie to Theodora do *you*?" I asked Rachel in spite of myself.

"I've got a copy of a will, signed by Ken, dating back a couple of months ago, which makes me the sole beneficiary. That copy will go into effect once Theodora gets convicted of the murders, since it'll look like she killed Ken to get his inheritance. You won't be around to determine guardianship of the damned dog, so that piece of garbage *Ken* signed won't matter."

I told myself to stay calm. I just needed to stall for another minute or two until help arrived. "Okay. You outsmarted me. But I'm still not signing it."

"Sure you are." She trained her gun on Yolanda, who squirmed in her chair and moved her head away a little. "Do you want to watch me kill Yolanda in front of your eyes, Allida? You sign that contract, or that's exactly what's going to happen."

Yolanda shut her eyes. Though she was clearly frightened out of her wits, she said, "Don't do it, Allie. She's gonna kill me anyway."

"True," Rachel retorted, "but I would bet that our little Allie here would rather not watch you be in excruciating pain, thanks to her refusing to sign the contract." She lowered the gun a little, but still had it pointed at Yolanda. "I can put one bullet through her kneecap first if you think I'm bluffing, Allida. The choice is yours."

I held up my hands and shouted, "Okay. You win." My heart was pounding, with T-Rex's constant barking behind me only adding to the stress. Where the hell was AC? My office was much closer to this trailer than their building was, but we still should have arrived almost simultaneously. "I'll sign the thing. I just need a pen."

She tossed me one from her pocket. I knelt in front of the coffee table and feigned reading the words, though I was far too frightened to do so.

"Just sign it. Now. No stalling." She cocked the trigger.

"Fine. I'll sign it." Hoping that she wouldn't know the correct spelling of my name, I signed it "Alita Babcock."

Rachel glanced at the signature. She smiled. "Thank you, Allie. Now, that wasn't so hard, was it?"

"No." At least there was some consolation in knowing that, if I was about to die, it would be for the sake of a bogus contract that she'd never get past a judge.

Still desperately hoping that I could stall, I rose and said, "I wish you'd explain some things to me. Since you've obviously been a couple of steps ahead of me, all along, I mean. Such as where Mary Culberson is now and how—"

"My former little partner? She at least had the right idea . . . to hightail it out of here. I've got so much evidence on her if she ever comes back and tries to turn me in, she'll be doing *twice* the time I am. Oh, and while we're just shooting the breeze and all here, you can forget Animal Control arriving. Five minutes after I hung the phone up for Yolanda, who—" she gave an evil grin at Yolanda "—was tied up at the time, I called the Humane Society, claiming I was you. I assured them that the whole thing had been a false alarm."

My stomach clenched. I glanced at Yolanda, who gave me a sad nod. "They're not coming."

Rachel laughed. "I knew you'd call them, even though you promised Yolanda you wouldn't."

Don't panic. They might send someone anyway, just to verify that everything was all right. Surely they would, in fact.

I looked again at Rachel, who wore such a smug smile that I wanted to gouge her eyes out. "You honestly think you're going to get away with this? That nobody's going to . . . to look out their window when they hear you firing off your gun and see you run away?"

"Which is why I never intended to shoot you in the first place. Like I said, Allie, you're not half as smart as you think you are." Her features mutated into a hateful glare, making her the ugliest person I'd ever seen. "I never wanted to kill anyone in the first place. Way too risky. But you left me no choice. If you'd've stayed out of it, I'd be *Ken's* guardian by now, and everybody would be happy. But, no, you get all chummy with Ken. It was all I could do not to run you off the road the other night, but that wouldn't have gotten this contract of mine signed. Then Ruby and Mary get greedy and think they can cut me out of my own plan. Meanwhile, your fat friend here keeps mouthing off about me." She looked scornfully at Yolanda. "Jesus! I've worked way harder than Ken ever did to earn the money in the first place!"

"So both Ruby and Mary were your partners?" I asked, relieved to see that Rachel had relaxed her vigil a little and let her arms drop to her sides, the gun pointing down.

"Not partners, no. Ruby saw me kill Ken. She had a view of his bedroom window. And she couldn't resist trying to blackmail me. Now, Mary was more my *pawn* than a—"

The doorbell rang. In the blink of an eye, Rachel had the gun trained on me, again. "Just a minute," she called pleasantly, then grabbed the remote control with her free hand and turned up the already blaring television set beside Yolanda. More background noise, I realized, to drown out the cries for help. The sound of the doorbell had renewed T-Rex's barking.

Under her breath, Rachel snarled, "Shit! Bet those damned people came out to check on the dog after all! It never fails. Nobody ever does a damned thing, till the one time you *want* 'em to do nothing!"

While speaking, she grabbed a roll of duct tape from the floor, tore off a piece without relinquishing the pistol, and slapped the tape over poor Yolanda's swollen and bloodied lips. She let out a muffled moan of pain.

Rachel said into her ear, "You make one sound, and I'll shoot you and Allida dead before you can take another breath."

She gestured at me to head toward the door. "You go

ahead of me and tell them that everything's fine. Just remember, I'll still be holding a gun. And I've already killed
two people, so I've got nothing to lose by putting you out
of your misery, too."

Rachel stepped toward the door but stayed back a couple of feet. She crossed her arms so that her pistol wasn't in
view, then gestured with her chin that I was to open the
door. I pulled it fully open and two men in brown uniforms
stood there. The first one, a young, tall man, smiled at me
through the screen door. "Allida Babcock, right?"

"Yes."

I grabbed the latch for the screen door, but Rachel
coughed loudly, then said, " 'Scuse me." I let my arm drop
to my side.

"Chad Bowman," the young man went on. "I've seen
you around at the Humane Society."

"That's right. I work with the dogs there, whenever I
can spare the time." I kept my voice flat and tried to indicate Rachel behind me with darting motions of my eyes.

"That's cool. I hear you had some sort of false alarm
with a dog here. Is that right?"

"Um—"

Rachel said, "That was my fault, I'm afraid. I'm
Yolanda Clay, the dog's owner." She raised her voice at the
end of the sentence as if asking a question, donning the attitude of a woefully contrite homeowner. "I'm the one who
called Allie, here, to help me." My skin crawled as she patted me on the shoulder. "See, my dog, T-Rex, and I were
playing a game of tug-of-war, and I guess he took it a little
too far. Grabbed my sleeve and wouldn't let go. I guess I
kind of panicked." She chuckled, as if embarrassed by her
foolishness. "He's fine now, and so are we, as you can tell."

The second man, standing a step below and behind
Chad on the cinderblock stairs said, "We'll still need to
see the dog. Just to make sure everything's fine."

Thank God! Rachel was in a bind now, and I could feel
her stiffen. Though the men couldn't see the *real* Yolanda

from where they stood, she was in this front room with us, bound and gagged, just a few feet away from the doorway. There was no way Rachel could hide her without first shutting the door in the men's faces and dragging her someplace.

"Bureaucratic red tape," Chad said, grinning affably. It was more than that, though. Animal Control responded to distress calls much the same way as a domestic abuse case. Sometimes people with serious dog bites would cover up for their dogs, or would cover for their own retaliation.

"Fine. I've got him in a bedroom in the back, as you can hear," Rachel said. "We'll go get him and bring him out. But please, I . . . kind of had an embarrassing accident when I . . . got so scared about T-Rex. I've got some unmentionables hanging up to dry in here, so respect my privacy and wait outside. Please."

"Oh. Sure thing, ma'am." Both men stepped back, making it clear that they had no desire to trespass.

God damn it! My life was hanging in the balance, and they were scared off at the prospect of seeing some woman's panties?

Rachel grabbed my arm and pulled me away from the door in front of her. Though I was deliberately walking slowly in the hopes that Chad out there would find our conjoined-twin act suspicious, we rounded the corner into the hallway. A short distance away was the bedroom where T-Rex was keeping up his frightened, rhythmic bark.

This was going to be my only chance. Rachel and I both knew it. I craned my neck and gave a quick glance at Yolanda. Her eyes were wide open and she was fully alert. I could tell that she knew this would be her one chance, too.

"Not one false move," Rachel whispered in my ear, poking me in the back with the barrel of the gun. "You get the dog out here, nice and quiet."

My mind racing to calculate my best chance for survival, I stayed put. Rachel put one hand on my shoulder and pushed the point of the gun into the small of my back. "Like I said, I've got nothing to lose at this point.

You get those clowns to go away. In return, I'll let the two of them and T-Rex live. Try to pull any tricks, and you'll die knowing you could have saved the mutt's life, along with that idiot Chad and his buddy."

"I feel sick," I mumbled. "Just let me . . . collect myself."

"No time! Hurry!" she whispered harshly in my ear. I got a whiff of her reeking breath and nearly vomited for real.

"T-Rex," she called gently. "That's a good doggie."

T-Rex stopped barking for a moment to listen. As I'd hoped, she removed her free hand from my shoulder as I opened the door. Though I hated to do this, knowing it would incite T-Rex further, in one sudden, sharp motion, I flung open the door so that it banged into him.

Predictably, T-Rex barged out the door past me. I pretended to reach for his collar and yelled, "Grab him!"

Rachel was distracted by T-Rex's charge for the split second I needed. Momentarily out of balance, she dropped her vision to the dog, and away from me. I grabbed the arm holding the gun and pulled her toward me in the bedroom doorway.

Even though my action had caught her fully off guard, she was surprisingly strong. She started to pull her arm back and aim the gun toward my head.

Using every ounce of my energy, I hooked the bottom of the door with my foot and managed to pull it into us.

Throwing my shoulder into the door, I caught her wrist with the loaded gun. It was now wedged between the door and the jamb. I heard her gasp so as to suppress a scream that would alert the men outside. I shouted, "Help! She's got a gun!"

"Stay back or I'll shoot you!" Rachel countered. She pulled the trigger. Though the blast was frightening, she could not aim at me from this angle. The bullet whizzed past me into the room.

The thumping and banging noises told me that the men had barged into the trailer toward us, even though they must have believed they were rushing toward a loaded gun. I pressed with all my might on the door. An instant later Rachel cried out again in pain as one of the men cried, "Drop the gun!"

She let out another cry and then, finally, let the gun drop from her hand. I kicked it across the room. It slid harmlessly under the bed.

I opened the door. Rachel again cried out in pain, and Chad, keeping her arm pinned against her back, slammed her against the wall. "My arm's broken!" she cried.

"Don't move!" he said.

I pushed past them and into the living room, where T-Rex was barking and snarling at the second man, who was gingerly trying to pull the duct tape from Yolanda's mouth.

"Let me do that," I said. "Could you call the police?"

Though it was grisly work, slowly pulling the tape off her tender, wounded skin amid Yolanda's streaming tears, I finally succeeded. Then, with T-Rex licking her face, I cut the tape that had secured her arms to the back of the chair.

Still sobbing, she held her face in her hands and said, "Sorry 'bout the tears. But it's like I tol' you. The crap's finally done hittin' the fan."

The police sirens in the distance were drawing closer. I cut the tape off Yolanda's ankles, and said, "Yes, it is."

She pulled me into a long hug, which T-Rex kept trying to join. Chuckling through her tears, she petted him and said, "Man alive, this dog could use some better manners. Wish I could afford to hire you, Allie."

"You can. You're about to come into a whole lot of money very soon. If you'd consider taking in a wealthy but rambunctious golden retriever, that is."

"What are you talking about?" she asked me, her eyebrows raised. "All Rachel's nonsense about Maggie's fortune can't really be . . ." She let her voice fade, then stared into my eyes. "You lost your mind?"

"Quite the contrary," I said with a smile. "I'm finally

seeing things clearly. Maggie living with you and T-Rex is exactly what Ken would have wanted."

"That'd be okay by me," she said slowly, scanning the room as if considering the upgrade in living quarters she'd be capable of making. She stared directly into my eyes. "If you're sure about it, that is."

"I'm positive."

I shuddered as I listened to the crunch of gravel as the police cars pulled to a stop just outside. A person's hold on life was so very tenuous. It was all I could do not to cry with joy knowing that I would live to see another day after all.

I watched Chad's partner from Animal Control open the door. He'd helped save my life, and I didn't even know his name. I made a silent vow: I was going to contact every friend and family member I had and tell them how much they meant to me. Starting with Russell Greene.